CRAVEN'S WAR
INTO THE FIRE

NICK S. THOMAS

PROLOGUE

The decisive British victory at Porto had rocked the French Army in Northern Portugal and scattered them to the mountains as they tried to escape into Spain. Yet whilst Wellesley's army pursued for several days, they were unable to trap Marshal Soult's vast force before they could reach Galicia in Northern Spain. Despite losing his guns and baggage train, much of the Marshal's forces would go on to fight another day. Yet Soult was not the only threat to Portugal; Napoleon had directed his second invasion of the country as the three prongs of the trident. Soult had descended from the North, whilst Lapisse advanced from the East with nine thousand troops and Victor from the South. Napoleon meant to strike at British and Portuguese troops on all sides, whilst Spanish rebels were brutally suppressed to wrestle the Peninsular region into submission.

Wellesley's situation still remains precarious as vast French armies threaten lay waiting to pounce and continuously probe at the allied defences. Meanwhile, Captain Craven does his best to avoid Wellesley's eye and so get on with an easy life. Yet fate had something else in store for the roguish former prizefighter, for Wellesley advances into Spain and is in need of an officer with his particular set of skills.

CHAPTER 1

12th June 1809.

"Are you sure about this?" Moxy asked.

Craven was surveying the scene from the cover of the dense bushes. They bordered a farmhouse nestled away in a sleepy Portuguese valley; only the moon lit up the sky, but a raging fire inside the house was enough to cast light into a barn beside the residence. The door was open, and he could see several horses were stabled within. An elaborate French cavalryman's sabretache hung from a saddle just inside the doorway. An excessively lavish and decadent storage pouch that allowed the cavalryman to carry despatches and other papers which their outlandishly fitted and fashionable uniforms would not. Craven smiled back in a mischievous manner. None of them wore their shakos, though Moxy and Charlie wore their soft forage caps, and they all had on their grey wool greatcoats with caped collar reaching down to their elbows. They were as much for warmth as to cover their redcoats.

"What do you think?" asked Charlie.

"I think there are some mighty fine horses to be had," Birback grinned at her wickedly. He'd not forgiven the French for the blood they had drawn from him, but more than anything, for the humiliation of being knocked unconscious whilst on guard duty.

"There's only four of us," questioned Charlie.

"With good reason. Do you think Matthys would have gone along with this? Or Mr Paget?"

"A couple of months ago, Moxy, you wouldn't take money to face the enemy, and now you seek them out?"

"I'm not doing this for the Army, but tell me you don't want to do them some harm?"

Charlie smiled back. "Damn right, I do."

"So, we kill them all?"

Craven looked in disgust at Birback.

"We are not savages. Anyway, we can do them far greater damage."

Birback looked confused.

"You know how humiliating it is for a cavalryman to have to crawl back to his General and admit his most prized possession was snatched from under him?"

"I like it," Moxy said.

Birback looked eager for more blood, and Charlie was just as keen to do them harm.

"All right, any sign of pickets?" Craven asked.

"None, the arrogant bastards think they're out of our reach," replied Moxy.

"The way the Bandidos are working in these parts they

probably have no idea the British Army is even passing by."

"They sure will know, Charlie, if we go and introduce ourselves," replied Moxy.

"Bandidos you say?" Craven asked as he mulled it over.

"What are you thinking?"

"British troops have been known to work with the Banditti, Moxy, so why not us?"

"How does that help?"

Craven shook his head. He realised he had to spell it out for Birback. The man wasn't half as sharp as the sword he carried.

"As you know there are four of us. There could be many more of them, but if they believe we are more, it could go a lot easier for us," explained Craven.

"You think they'd believe we have an army of Bandidos out here?"

"If we can get right up to their door without being noticed, Moxy, why not?" Craven smiled.

"Let's do this," bawled Birback, and he quickly got up to lead the way before Craven gave the order.

"Leave your rifles for Moxy. You're staying put."

Birback begrudgingly gave up his weapon before drawing his sabre. Moxy lay down prone with all four of their rifles laid out in a row.

"Crazy son of a bitch," muttered Moxy as they moved out.

Unknown to him, Craven had heard his faint voice and merely looked back with a wicked smile. He agreed with the sentiment as he drew his beloved Andrea Ferrara blade with his right hand and took a pistol from his belt with his left. Advancing at night with their uniforms concealed beneath flowing coats and cold steel in hand, they appeared more as highwaymen than soldiers of the British Army. They hunkered down low and advanced quickly but quietly. They could hear the roar of laughter and soldiers making merry within the house, and that only further concealed their movements as the French seemingly partied the night away without any concern for who might be looking on.

The inviting and fragrant smell of wood smoke filled the valley and became eminently stronger as they closed in on the farmhouse. Craven could feel his pulse rising for the excitement was getting the better of him. The house was laid out over two floors and was substantial enough that it must have belonged to a wealthy farmer. Smoke was billowing from two chimneys. Craven caught up with Birback and held him back, as he took a knee and brought the other man down with him.

"Listen, we have to play this smart. We don't know how many of them are in there. We take the element of surprise and avoid a fight altogether, you hear?"

"Why?"

"Because if that was us in there, being stripped of our treasure would be insult enough. Death need not follow it."

"And if it is what they deserve?" Charlie was angry, for she was always eager to spill French blood.

"You heard me," snapped Craven. He was unwilling to argue the point.

They crept onwards as if expecting to find trouble at any moment, but they reached the edge of the house without incident. Craven reached the door opposite the barn and took up watch. He nodded towards the other two, and they went for the barn. Charlie was at the door first; although Birback was so much taller he merely leaned in over her to see for himself. There was no sign of any soldiers, and so they both entered the barn, but stopped in amazement at seeing a cart with a sheet covering it.

"Is that really it?" Birback asked.

Charlie pulled the cover from it, revealing wine kegs stacked as high as could be.

"Just as Craven said," smiled Charlie.

"How the hell did he know they'd be here?" Birback pondered.

"Don't know, don't care." She ran her hands along the kegs, realising they'd just found a small fortune.

Craven looked back and forth suspiciously, holding both of his weapons at the ready. He expected trouble to find him at any moment.

"Come on, come on, what's taking so long?" he muttered, looking back to the barn. He fancied himself in a fight with any man, but he didn't much fancy facing an entire room worth of cavalrymen. For as much as he didn't like to admit it, the French were fine swordsmen. Not just their officers and cavalrymen, for unlike the British, they attached Sword Masters to their regiments to instruct the men.

"Come on," Charlie insisted as she finished harnessing the two horses to the wine cart. Birback saddled up two of the finest cavalrymen's horses with the elaborate equipment beside them, including the one which they'd seen hanging from inside the door with its beautifully inlaid sabretache. As Charlie reached him, she drew out a brace of pistols from one of the saddles and passed one to Birback.

Craven was getting anxious, knowing sooner or later

trouble would find them. Thankfully, his worries were put to rest as Charlie and Birback stepped out of the barn, pushed the door, slowly and quietly to ensure the horses could not bolt.

"Did you find it?"

The smile on their faces was the only confirmation he needed.

"Okay, let's do this." Craven cocked back the hammer of his pistol, and the other two did the same. He pried open the door just a touch to see inside where ten Frenchmen made merry over numerous glasses of wine. Their swords were propped against the walls. Craven smirked, realising he'd caught them with their breeches down. He booted the door open and rushed through, making space for the other two who took up position either side of him, all three equipped with pistol and sabre as if about to rob them.

"Evening, gentlemen," declared Craven delightfully as they pointed their pistols at the astonished Frenchmen. Most of them froze in surprise, whilst two lurched towards their weapons.

"Ah, Ah!" Craven roared as he took aim at them, and they backed away.

"What is the meaning of this?" demanded one officer who was clearly the most senior. He was balding, though no older than his early thirties. He was in fine shape and wore a well-fitted uniform that showed off his athletic physique. He was the look of a man wise beyond his years and also experienced, as well as well tanned, as if having been on campaign for many years, though his well-kept uniform did not show it.

"You have some things we mean to take," replied Craven.

"How dare you, Sir!" yelled the officer.

CRAVEN'S WAR – INTO THE FIRE

"How dare I?" Craven laughed, "We are at war, and you, Sir, are foolish enough to not post a guard. What was yours is now mine."

The Frenchman looked furious.

"Who are you?" he demanded.

Yet Craven was not so quick to give any information up and enjoyed toying with the officer.

"Fifty Bandidos watch this house. Crack shots, that is all you need know."

The Frenchman laughed, and his colleagues soon joined in before he went on.

"Monsieur, you expect us to believe that many could have gone unnoticed?"

"We did. We walked right on up to your little party without so much as a single sentry to worry about. You're not back in France anymore, Monsieur. This isn't your country, and the people don't want you here. Get used to it."

"What do you want?" demanded the weary and angry Frenchman.

"We've already got it thanks, but whilst we're here, your carbines." He pointed towards the stack of short cavalry muskets. Birback holstered his pistol and picked the weapons up in a bundle.

"Thank you, gentlemen, and goodnight." Craven took an insulting bow before them, and they backed out of the building. The French officer was fuming whilst the officers and cavalrymen around him looked on in disbelief. The man growled and strode over to his sabre. He ripped it from the scabbard and raced on after the interlopers as his companions raced to catch up. They burst out of the barn to find the barn door open, and

Birback loading their carbines onto the cart beside the saddled horses they intended to steal also. Craven and Charlie raised their pistols to bring the Frenchmen to a standstill, none wanting to be the first to die.

"You dog! Will you not stand and fight like a man, Monsieur!" roared the Frenchman who was nearly shaking with fury, despite clearly being a veteran of the wars.

Craven smiled as he looked over to Charlie.

"Don't do it. We got what we came for."

"Killing Frenchmen, isn't this what you came for?"

"Yes, but not when it brings a world of trouble down on our heads."

"We carry goods for the Marshal Jourdan!" roared the Frenchman. He got no response, and so went on more furiously, "Englishman, are you too afraid to fight a real battle?" he shouted as he pressed for single combat.

Craven had heard enough as he held out his pistol for Charlie, forcing her to sheath her sabre and take it. A duel outside of the watchful eye and punishing nature of Wellesley was too good of an opportunity to pass up. He took off his coat and threw it to Birback who was watching with joy. Craven took a quick glance at the Frenchman's sword. That brief study was all he needed to understand what he faced. It also gave him some insight into the man. The sabre was of the light cavalry or Hussar type, the guard being of three bar design, but cast in silver instead of the usual brass or bronze. The beautiful weapon was intricately detailed down to the langets, which reached into the grip and also up towards the blade. Yet there was no decoration on the blade. It was a sword meant for fashion in the scabbard but fighting when out of it. Double fullers ran the length of the blade, yet terminated in a clipped point, far better at thrusting than the hatchet tip found on many similar swords. It was also clearly more agile than the hefty troopers French light cavalry sabres that weighed as much as the heavy dragoon swords of the British Army. Studying the sword was like translating an ancient language to Craven, its secrets revealing so much about the one who purchased and wielded it.

The man was one of skill, experience, and knowhow, and that fascinated Craven, for an easy victory would not bring near as much fun as a hard fought and earned one. The Frenchman raised his sword to an inside guard position, the edge of the sabre facing to his left and the point lowered and directed to Craven's eye. Like any Frenchman familiar with swordsmanship, he would be well acquainted with the smallsword and foil, unlike many British officers who were still ignorant of the art. The knowledge of which made one a refined and skilled opponent with any sword, for it required such fine control and precision which was not always a requirement of the sabre, even though it was very much beneficial to that weapon. Craven at first sighed as he wished he could see such skill from all on his own side, but he soon smiled, realising that same fact would lead him to be underestimated.

It is a perfect night for a fight, Craven thought.

The air was crisp and fresh, mixed with the occasional puff of wood smoke. The moonlight cast through the windows of the house made for quite the dramatic sight as both sides watched on. He couldn't have planned a better setting for a dramatic confrontation, and he relished the moment, smiling as he came to guard. The Frenchman quickly came forward, eager to punish the Englishman for the insult he had made upon the

Major and his companions. Thrust followed thrust just as Craven would expect from a trained Frenchman, for they were told to do so over and over again. For the thrust kills and the cut merely wounds, that is what was drilled into them. Craven knew it was a half-truth and a simplification. He parried each of the thrusts with half parade rotations, easily setting aside the attacks.

The Frenchman soon rotated his hand into a moulinet and brought down a cut towards Craven's head. It was powerful, but mostly from the speed that had been generated. The Major clearly meant to force through Craven's guard as he lifted his blade to parry. He had clearly not taken notice of the blade affixed to Craven's regulation infantry hilt, for it was no ordinary blade, and stopped the sabre dead with ease. The two reset to guard, and the Frenchman looked surprised, clearly realising something with Craven or his sword was different.

Craven came forward now and launched half cuts and thrusts as feints, trying to find his opening. He tried to force his opponent's guard by applying pressure against the foible, or tip of the sabre. Yet the Major's guard was firm. Next Craven slid down the length of his opponent's blade with a glizade. A sneaky move that would enable a cut to the head, but once again the Frenchman parried it away. Now the Major came forward again as his companions cheered him on. He opened with the same set of thrusts he had when the fight had first begun, and Craven fell into the trap of defending in the same manner. He knew he'd fallen into a trap he'd so often lay, but it was too late. As his half parade parry displaced a thrust, the Major rotated his blade and drove it forward, delivering a push cut to the front of Craven's right thigh. His trousers split open as the well service sharpened curve blade slashed them open, opening a long but shallow cut into his flesh beneath them.

The French cheered at their Major's success. Craven grit his teeth and took the pain as he got back to a strong guard in readiness to continue. For this was no first blood duel, nor a duel with any kind of rules of conduct. He was kicking himself for falling for such a common setup, and yet eager to exact his revenge. The Major was clearly riding high on his success and came forward once again, but Craven was in no mood to take a defensive stance anymore. He interrupted the attack with a thrust directly to the face, forcing him to parry and encouraging a thrust in riposte. It was just what Craven was looking for. Once again, he did not parry, but hit his opponent's blade with a strong beat, causing the point to fly offline. Craven quickly followed it with a cut to the inside of the hand where the sabre guard had little protection. His Ferrara blade bit into the base of the thumb and drew across the palm of the Major, causing him to lose grip of his sword. But before the blade had touched the ground, Craven had dealt another cut across the Major's cheek, as long and shallow as the one on his own leg.

He looked furious, but he dared not protest, knowing this was no honourable duel, but a brawl he himself had instigated. Yet neither was he willing to give up all that was about to be taken from them as Craven sheathed his sword, put on his coat, and took back his pistol.

"You don't have men surrounding this place," spat the Frenchman, calling Craven's bluff, before signalling for his companions to go forward, knowing they outnumbered the small band of robbers. The first man got only a single step when a shot whistled through the air and struck him in the chest, putting him down dead. It clearly rocked the others, and yet the Major was not impressed.

"One sharpshooter? Is that all you have?" he seethed and picked up his sabre from the ground with his other hand. As he took a step forward to lead the rest, a second shot rang out and another was hit in the right arm, causing him to cry out, and then another was struck in the left leg, putting him down on the ground. A fourth shot struck the floor in front of the Major. The Frenchmen froze for fear of a fifth shot, yet only Craven and his companions knew there was no such shot coming.

"Good evening, gentlemen," said Craven with a smile. Charlie passed the reins of a horse to him before climbing onto the other.

"You just made a huge mistake, Monsieur."

"Really, Major…?" Craven was still smiling.

"Major Claveria!" He merely pointed off beyond the barn. Craven directed his horse several paces so he could see beyond, and his eyes lit up. A dozen more cavalrymen were galloping towards him, and there were lines of tents with troops mustering upon hearing the gunshots.

"Move, move, go!" he roared to the others.

Birback whipped the carthorses into action, and Charlie followed. Craven came up alongside the French Major.

"I'll be seeing you again," he smiled as he held his bloodied hand.

"I look forward to it," grinned Craven before kicking his heels into the horse and launching on after the others. The cart had slowed ahead as Moxy climbed on board, but they dared not stop.

"What have we got?"

"A dozen or more cavalry," replied Craven coolly.

"What? We can't outrun that," protested Moxy.

"No, we can't, but we can't stay put either. Get moving! Charlie, you're with me."

He turned his horse about and dug his heels in, racing North as the cart went Westward. Moxy hurried to reload the rifles as they bumped along the rough track. As he reached around for his cartridge pouch, he spotted the pile of cavalry carbines. He continued to load as he asked after them.

"Those loaded?"

"No idea."

Moxy finally finished loading the fourth rifle when a shot whizzed past them and struck a tree ahead. "Where the hell is Craven?"

The French cavalrymen were hot in pursuit, and his companions nowhere to be seen. Another shot rang out and struck one of the wine kegs, causing claret to spill out like someone had opened a tap.

"That won't do." Moxy picked up his rifle and took aim at the cavalrymen who were closing on them. He rested it down on the kegs for stability and to maintain as much cover as possible. He noticed one of them prime the hammer of a pistol and take aim, and knew that would be his first victim. He aimed quickly and took his shot, striking the cavalryman in the shoulder. He dropped his pistol before abandoning the chase to lick his wounds. Moxy laid down his rifle and picked up the next. He took aim at the party of horsemen hot in pursuit like a lynch mob. He squeezed the trigger, but the wheel of the cart hit a rut, and his shot went off target, striking another cavalryman further behind and knocking him from his horse. Moxy's look of anger at missing his shot soon turned to surprise and then a smile, as he shrugged in amazement. Yet another shot rang out and clipped Birback's left arm, splitting open his coat.

"Not again, do something!" he roared furiously.

Moxy threw down the rifle and picked up the third to take aim. As he cocked the hammer back, a pistol shot struck the frizzen and blew off the hammer whilst igniting the pan. Moxy dropped the weapon in pain, causing the shot to soar off over the heads of the cavalrymen as he nursed his bloody right hand.

"What are you doing!" Birback bellowed.

"My hand," he complained, looking at the bloody mess.

"Get shooting, or it'll be your head!" Birback cried.

Moxy clenched his fist as best he could and was relieved to at least have all of his fingers, even if they were in agony. He picked up the next rifle, fighting through the pain as he pulled back the hammer on the last loaded rifle. As he got it to the shoulder, he realised the cavalry had closed rapidly, with one now wielding a sabre just ten feet from his face. He lifted the muzzle and fired from the hip, striking the Frenchman in the head. He collapsed onto his horse's mane and veered off the track. Another was closing quickly, and Birback turned back and shot him in the chest, giving Moxy time to pick up one of the carbines. Cocking the first of them he fired, and it snapped, not even a flash in the pan.

"Piece of dross!" he complained as he threw the weapon at the enemy, yet his clumsy throw fell short. He picked up the next carbine and fired. This time the priming powder in the pan ignited, but the main charge did not. He cried out in fury as he threw that one, too, but this time struck one of them in the head, knocking the cavalryman from his horse. As he reached down for the third, cavalrymen came up alongside the cart on each side. Moxy picked up a carbine and lifted it just in time to parry the heavy sabre cut, but the blow smashed the lock, rendering it useless. Birback ripped his small sabre from his side and lifted it in time to parry a cut, and he leaned out from the cart, holding the reins in his left. He offered to cut the Frenchman's head, but as he brought up his sword to parry, he redirected his nimble little sabre straight down onto the cavalryman's bridle hand, severing it at the wrist. The man cried out as he quit the pursuit.

Moxy parried another two cuts with the carbine held in both hands, swinging it back like a bat and smashing his attacker from his mount, but losing the carbine in the process. He snatched up the last carbine but could count five more cavalrymen in pursuit and closing fast. Moxy grimaced as he cocked back the last of the loaded firearms, having little hope in it. It was not nearly enough even if it would fire. As he aimed, they reached a merge in the road.

Craven and Charlie came galloping down the other fork, coming up alongside the Frenchmen with complete surprise. Craven carried his sword by the forte in his bridle hand, and a pistol in the right that he fired point-blank at one of the men. He then took up his sword and soared past another, slashing across his sword arm as he lifted it to cut. Charlie followed suit, shooting another down. One more of the cavalrymen gave point to Charlie, but she was closing fast and dropped the pistol. She took up her sabre in time to get under the thrust and cut up into his wrist, causing the weapon to fall from his hand.

The putrid and yet alluring smell of powder smoke filled the night air as the cart raced on with the two riders behind them. The French gave up the pursuit, but Moxy kept a keen eye on them until they were well out of sight, and Birback dared not slow down.

"Woo!" Charlie roared excitedly as they came alongside the cart.

"That was close, way too close," said Moxy. He drew out some cloth to bandage his bloodied hand.

"You're alive, aren't you, and a damn sight richer!" Craven roared.

"Did we really just do that?" Charlie asked in amazement, as though questioning if it were a wild dream. Craven spotted the leaking wine keg. He popped open his canteen and held it below the streaming claret before taking a taste.

"Yes, we did," replied Craven assuredly as he put on the stopper and tossed it to Moxy.

Charlie began to laugh at their dalliance with danger. The rest soon joined in as they rushed on through the night with a wagon full of a French Marshal's treasure.

CHAPTER 2

Major Spring strutted through camp in the early morning. Soldiers' tents stretched out as far as the eye could see. Some troops had arisen to begin their chores, or at least get some food and drink in their bellies. He passed two men attempting to dig into their ship's biscuit, the most common substitute for bread as it was so easily stored and kept for long periods. Yet for all the biscuits made up in convenience they lost in appeal, as one soldier pulled maggots from one and another used his shot to break another, for they were as hard as a rock. Yet few of the rankers complained, as to get a full ration was to be treasured no matter its condition. Nobody in camp was in a hurry to move. They knew they had a long march ahead of them, but there was no need to rush into it. They could hardly march all day, for foraging took time, and the Commissariat could barely keep up with the nutritional demands of the army as they moved cross country. Major 'Thorny' Thornhill soon stepped up by his side as they walked together with determination.

"You think he's the man for the job?"

"Absolutely," replied Thorny.

"He is a rogue, though, perhaps even a villain."

"And yet you backed him against Timmerman."

"Because Timmerman is even worse than him," admitted Spring.

They reached the edge of the camp and went on past several pickets. They came to a small cottage with a picturesque view of the valley beyond. It was just a few hundred feet from the bustle of the camp, and yet a pocket of tranquillity and luxury far beyond anything a captain could hope for when marching with an army. There at the entrance sat one of Craven's companions, Sergeant Matthys Keck. He was propped on top of a wine keg and leaning against the open front door. He looked a little worse for wear, but better off than those inside, as they were about to find out. Thorny took note of the cart and horses next to the building. The kegs were long gone, but the French saddles lay beside the horses with their elegant and unmistakeable sabretaches lying in the dirt.

"Craven?" Spring asked.

Matthys lifted a hand to his brow to cover his eyes before looking up into the morning light.

"He's inside, Sir," replied the Sergeant as he staggered to his feet.

Spring stepped into the cottage to find it stank of wine, sweat, and cooked beef, the remains of which still covered a table in the centre of the room. Leftover meat was such a rare sight amongst common soldiers, who would eat every last morsel of their rations each day, even when ordered not to.

22

Birback and Charlie were collapsed asleep over the table with the meat, whilst Moxy, Ellis, and Caffy were passed out on blankets at the sides of the room.

"Marching with Wellesley and yet drunk as could be, a shambles."

Spring made no attempt to hide his feelings as he said it openly and firmly, although his strong voice did not cause any of them to stir. He went on through to the next room and noticed an open doorway. Inside lay Craven on a bed with the Lady Lovelace draped over him, a sheet barely covering her. Both were as gone to the world as the drunken soldiers they'd just passed.

"Captain!" Spring shouted.

Craven roused slowly and didn't look at all surprised or bothered to see the two Majors towering over him.

"You," he croaked in an accusatory tone with a dry throat as he looked to Thorny.

"My Lady, I am sure your husband would not wish to see you in such a place," declared Spring, expecting her to be ashamed.

"The men don't get to have all the fun Major," she replied with a smile.

Spring shook his head as he walked away. He left the building and waited for Craven. A few minutes later he appeared with his jacket unbuttoned and a generally dishevelled look. His trousers were still cut open from the night before, though a bandage wrapped the leg beneath them. Yet the lady looked as fresh as she would for church, adjusting her large hat as she stepped out into the daylight.

"Captain," she said with a smile to Craven before heading

23

for the camp.

"That is how you find yourself in duels and out of favour with Sir Arthur," declared Spring.

"What is a life if not fully lived?" Craven was watching her leave.

"Is this what you call living?"

"It could be worse," replied Craven as he thought back on the night before. Yet as he turned back to the two Majors, he was reminded of why he was angry with Thorny.

"A scouting troop, no more than a dozen men you said."

"Well, what did you find?"

"A full company at least."

"Then it is as I thought."

"As you thought? Are you trying to get me killed?"

Thorny said nothing and went over to the horses. He knelt down beside the saddles and opened the sabretache on the first. He found it empty and moved on to the second one, taking out a packet of papers. He opened them up and smiled as he read the contents.

"You set us up," stated Craven as he pieced the puzzle together.

"I shared information. How you acted upon it was entirely your choice."

"And the Major's horse, you mentioned that, too," added Craven.

"I knew it would be too much a prize for you to leave behind," smirked Thorny.

"Well?" Spring asked.

"It is as we thought, a significant reinforcement of troops to battle the Bandidos. It seems the French lines of supply and communications are in complete chaos at the hands of these guerrillas. They have no idea where Wellesley is, nor where their own allies are."

"You see, Craven. This war won't just be won by big battles, but everything that leads us to them. These bandits are wreaking havoc amongst the French, but they are going to need our help in the face of these redoubled efforts by the enemy. Knowledge is power, and this disruption to French communications is depriving the enemy of it. I want you to head up into the mountains and help these Bandidos. Make sure they are able to maintain the chaos in which they have brought to the enemy."

"No. No, no, no, no, no," said Craven as he shook his weary head.

"No?" Spring lamented.

"I've done my part. I've more than made up for past indiscretions."

"Done your part?" Spring looked to Thorny in amazement.

"I was caught by Wellesley fair and square, but I've done more than my fair share to make up for that," explained Craven.

"My dear, Captain, this is not a gentleman's club, and if it were, you would hardly be a member," scowled Spring.

"You would cross blades with the enemy for wine but not for the King?" Thorny asked.

Craven shrugged, as that seemed reasonable to him.

"You know how valuable good wine is around here? We lived like kings this past night," he smiled.

Spring looked furious.

"You can do your duty, or you can face a court martial. Is

that clear?"

Craven sighed, knowing he had no choice but to submit.

"What do you want from me, Major?" he sniffed.

"You're a ruffian, Captain, every bit as ragged as those Bandidos out there. Always spoiling for a fight and getting themselves in trouble, they hate the French, but they aren't always too fond of the English either. Who better to rally these ruffians than one who is just like them?" Spring smiled.

"Plenty of spoils to be had," added Thorny.

That got Craven's attention, although he was still not convinced, and so Spring finally laid out the reality they were facing.

"Look. Wellesley has sent most of the Portuguese troops back for retraining. He's not at all pleased with them, and whilst it might be the right decision, it also leaves us thin on the ground, especially with troops who may be useful in dealing with the locals. You may not be one of them, but word of what you did for the Lady Sarmento and how you stood up to Mardel has spread amongst the population. You are a folk hero to them, in spite of being an Englishman."

That tickled Craven, who'd only done what was necessary to avoid Wellesley's wrath.

"Listen to me. You might think we won a great victory at Porto, but that was just one battle in a very large war. Napoleon wants Portugal, and he wants to drive us into the sea just like he did at Corunna. Make no mistake, as heroic a withdrawal that affair was, however much it is spun in the papers, we were firmly booted out of these lands. Whilst we were busy in the North, there were more French armies probing the borders. At Alcantara Marshal Victor smashed our forces there. Had he known how few we had, he might have continued on all the way to Lisbon! You see, Captain, Victor could not advance because he did not have the strength, but because he did not have information. Not knowing whether his flanks were supported, he was stalled. That is the power of these irregular forces. If the French cannot communicate and cannot collaborate their vast forces spread over hundreds and thousands of miles, then half our battle is already won."

"You see, Craven, you aren't being sent to do the dirty work, but things vital to the war effort," insisted Thorny.

Craven sighed, as he knew there was no resisting.

"These Bandidos are ruffians, but who better to join them than you?"

Craven almost looked insulted as Major Spring went on to explain himself.

"Come on, Captain. You are not a man to lounge about in an officers' mess and trade petty insults. You want action, and I am giving it to you. Get out there, and make life hell for the French, and who knows what you might find of value?"

He knew this was not persuasion anymore, as he had no choice, and they were merely sugar coating a dirty job. However, his curiosity was also piqued, as he imagined the riches he might find amongst wealthy French officers.

"I told you what I saw out there. That is an army coming to support the troops in the area. They've come to hunt these Bandidos, and you want me to jump into that lion's mouth with seven men?"

Spring smiled as he realised he was on board, and he went on.

"Whilst it is true that Wellesley sent the Portuguese back

for training, there are some who proved themselves and remain, notably Captain Ferreira and those Caçadores of his. The fine men who helped you pull victory out from the complete disaster of losing the Lady Sarmento."

Craven smiled, for he knew he'd screwed up. Although everything that had followed it had made up for it, and the Major knew it.

"They did all right," he joked.

"They are no ordinary troops. Ferreira leads a unit of Caçadores Atiradores. Good light infantrymen and marksmen are in much demand at present, but rarely in enough supply. Officially, Ferreira has gone back to continue his training with the rest of the Portuguese."

"And unofficially?"

"His men are celebrated in these parts almost as much as you, Captain. They have more than proven they are up to the task of facing the damned French. You will take Ferreira and his Atiradores out into that wilderness, and you will raise hell, do you hear? The French must not be allowed to crush the Bandidos, and they must not be allowed to regain their lines of communication. Do what you do best, Captain."

"Drink?" Thorny asked.

"Not until the fighting is done," snapped Spring before the others began to chuckle, and he couldn't help but join them as he finally relaxed in the knowledge that Craven was not going to resist any further.

"You're a man no officer would wish to have under his command, Captain, and yet the sort we need all at once. Good luck out there."

Spring left, leaving Thorny to hash out the details.

"Was that a compliment?" Craven smiled.

"From that man, absolutely," replied Thorny.

CHAPTER 3

"What do you mean you have no horses?" Craven demanded. He adjusted his stance and winced a little as he reached down to his bandaged leg. Before him was a well-spoken Commissaries Clerk, a uniformed civilian responsible for the supply of the Army in most things that were not ordnance.

"What's your name?" Ferreira asked, who was propped up against a pile of crates beside Craven. His nut-brown uniform seemed not to suffer so badly in the sun as the Bloody Back jackets the British were famous for. Yet he was as dusty as the rest.

"Ned Clinton."

"Okay, Ned, you see we are about to head out in small numbers to hunt whilst simultaneously be hunted by the enemy without the support of the Army. We need to get to places quickly and get out of trouble just as quickly."

"I understand that, but I cannot give you what we do not

have," replied Ned as he went through a book checking for the resources he had at hand.

"Is it so much to ask for?" Craven asked.

"Yes. We've been buying up horses from all the locals who are willing to sell, even at the most outrageous of prices. I can provide you with several days of food and water, but that is all."

It was hard for either of them to get angry with Ned, for he seemed an agreeable fellow who would help if he were able. Then Craven noticed another book that the clerk had not looked in.

"And that one? Might we find what we need in that book?"

Clinton snatched the book up protectively.

"This one is not Commissaries business."

"He's running a side hustle," Ferreira pointed out in an amused fashion.

"Is that true?" Craven pressed.

"Yes, but…not like you think."

"Oh, really?"

"The men like to gamble," added Clinton.

"Which men?"

"Well, most of them,"

"You're a bookkeeper?"

"I bet he's making a killing."

"I will if they all pay up. Army pay isn't exactly keeping up with things these days," complained Clinton.

Craven smiled. He suddenly felt in familiar company, and he understood why the man was so protective of the book. His fortune, his reputation, and perhaps even his life were bound to it.

"You, Sir, where can I find Colonel Halkett?" called a voice from high.

Craven looked about in disgust to see a British officer looking down on him from a magnificent mount. His uniform was impeccable. The man was in his twenties with bright blond hair protruding from his tall bicorne hat. He carried himself like nobility. Craven ignored him as he went back to his conversation with the Commissaries' Clerk, which is what he'd come there for.

"You, Sir! How dare you ignore me," bellowed the officer incredulously.

Craven sighed furiously. He already didn't want to be there, and the answers Clinton was giving him wasn't helping at all. His temper was short, and he turned back to the mounted infantry officer with a furious scowl.

"I will not drop everything I am doing because one stupid arse can't find an officer he should probably know the location of. That is your problem, not mine, Sir," he snapped.

The officer looked stunned, but it soon turned to anger as Craven went back to his business.

"You are rude, Sir, and act in a manner unbecoming of an officer of the King's Army!" he roared for all to hear.

Craven sighed once more. Yet Ferreira smiled at his suffering, especially as he knew exactly where this situation was going, because Craven was not one to apologise to a fool.

"You know Wellesley will have your balls if you take that fight," Ferreira smiled with absolute delight, as if egging him on to do so.

Craven sighed, knowing it was true as he looked back to the officer.

"Recently arrived, have you?"

"What of it, Sir?"

"Much as it pains me, but some of us have work to do, and it does make it infinitely more difficult when fools interrupt that work."

"A fool you say?" asked the officer in surprise. He didn't seem angry, almost as if he took it as a polite challenge, "You, Sir, are rude and unbecoming, but are you also a coward?"

Craven looked confused and finally laughed at the question.

"If not, you would stand by your word and give me satisfaction."

Craven would have jumped at the opportunity just a few months before, but the last duel had cost him dearly, and the wound was still fresh, for Wellesley had made him suffer dearly for it.

"As much as I would love to oblige, Sir Arthur Wellesley has made his position quite clear on this matter to me personally. I would not risk angering him a second time," confessed Craven.

"Duelling? A man need not risk his life to prove his skill and stand by his word, Sir!"

The officer leapt enthusiastically from his horse. Craven looked equally confused and intrigued as the man drew out a long leather bag from his saddle and finally pulled out two fencing foils.

"Let us settle this matter before all to see. Give the men a little sport whilst you are taught a lesson in humility and discipline, Sir." The officer held up the two foils for all to see.

Craven smiled, for he could now see a way to fulfil his desires without angering Wellesley.

"What will it be, Sir?"

"What's your name?"

"Lieutenant Bishop," he replied as he tossed one of the foils to Craven.

"Captain Craven," he replied casually as he studied the training sword he had been tossed. It was the common form used by all gentlemen for sport, recreation, and competition. The guard was a simple figure of eight steel type with a leather liner. The blade was of characteristically square profile, as had been used for training swords for two hundred years. The blade terminated in a nail head that was concealed by a leather button to cushion the force of impacts, for this was a sword only for thrusting, to simulate the smallsword. It was like a feather in his hands compared to the spadroons and sabres he used in battle, but he was equally accustomed to it as those other swords. A crowd had already gathered as all who had been at work or rest were drawn to the first sign of excitement. Anything to break up the monotony of army life, whether it be on the road or at camp.

He looked back to his friend Ferreira. He found he was beside Clinton who had the one book he protected above all else finally open. He was taking bets with several others huddled around. Soon enough almost a hundred men had formed a circular barrier around them as if it were an arena.

"I trust you know who to bet on," insisted Craven to his friend, as he laid the foil down onto a stack of crates so he could remove his sword belt.

"I'd not trust you with my money, but I do trust you to win a fight," smirked the Caçadores Captain.

"Put fifty Guineas on me," declared Craven boldly for all to hear, causing Ned to look up in disbelief from the book he had been so engrossed with.

"Fifty?" he checked.

Even on a Captain's pay it was more than a quarter of a year's salary, and gasps rang out from the privates who were paid less than half of the sum for a year's service. It was also more money than Craven possessed, for all they had made on the stolen wine had been thrown away on bribes to gain the finest of quarters the night before and the fine food they had feasted on. He had no idea who his opponent was, but absolute confidence in his own ability to overcome whoever he may be.

Clinton hurried to take dozens of bets as the two officers squared off against one another. Craven couldn't have hoped for a better scenario, for he fed his desire for a fight without risk of angering anyone who held authority over him. He smiled as he saluted and came to guard.

Lieutenant Bishop formed a perfect position with the form and precision of a dancer, and Craven was obliged to match him so as to not be out done. He could already see this would not be an easy contest as Bishop held himself with complete confidence and knowledge in his ability. Bishop came forward taking small and careful steps. He engaged against Craven's sword with enough pressure to feel his opponent's response, but not so much that his blade might be thrown off the line of defence should he be disengaged. It was a smart and calculated approach to an unknown opponent. Bishop lunged forward a little, drawing Craven into a parry, but his lunge was short and merely a setup to disengage. A nimble drop of the blade before rising up on the other side of Craven's as the Lieutenant completed his lunge in a new attack. Craven quickly whirled his blade about to parry in seconds, his hilt now high and tip low as it swept Bishop's thrust aside.

Craven made no attempt to riposte as he studied his curious new opponent. Bishop moved with perfect form and great speed, and he dared not be drawn into a trap set by the clearly experienced swordsman. For Craven this fight was just as important as one with sharps, for he needed to forever keep sharp and ready for such an encounter. Bishop waited in his lunge for a moment to further bait Craven, but he would not be lured into such a deception. The Lieutenant recovered to guard and waited for a moment for him to come at him. He was clearly expecting an aggressive and unrefined opponent after the insulting words that had been tossed at him. The surprise was visible on his face, though there was no fear. He studied Craven just as he always did of his opponents.

"Come on!" cried a soldier in a thick Northern English accent.

Others jeered in agreement. They'd never talk to an officer in such a way, but it was sport they were watching now, and they demanded some excitement. Craven didn't want to disappoint them, and so he went forward. He probed with light thrusts either side of the Lieutenant's blade without committing to a full lunge, but Bishop was quick to get to his parries without ever leaving an opening large enough to strike safely. He began to use double feints, quickly throwing deceptive strikes from one side to another before attacking on the third movement, and yet Bishop got to his parries with ease and quickly countered.

Craven tried striking from a variety of angles to both low and high targets, and yet Bishop's defence was excellent. He was frustrated at his inability to land a blow and snapped out a cheeky thrust to the wrist and forearm of the Lieutenant.

Bishop's arm remained straight behind his guard, and he dropped his blade over Craven's to parry it. He was going to be a tough nut to crack, and for all his frustrations, that was just what Craven needed.

The clash of steel went on for more than thirty more exchanges of attacks and ripostes made with such perfect timing it appeared as some kind of exhibition; a perfectly trained danced intended to thrill the audience. Yet neither man had met before. They merely were both trained to the same levels in the French foil and smallsword methods that were so well loved across England and Scotland, despite now being at war with said nation. Finally, on one lunge Craven's front foot slipped a little forward, and he could not recover quickly enough to escape the Lieutenant's riposte. He had to quickly traverse to escape, leaping to the side and narrowly missing the foil button as it flashed past his face. As he landed hard on his right leg, he winced in pain, feeling a gushing surge through his wound.

He recovered to guard but looked down to his wound to see the bandage was bloody. He cursed himself for it, knowing he should not have pursued a duel in such a state, yet fully aware he was painfully unable to depart from his very nature. He could feel his leg was weak and knew he must try and bring the contest to a close. He began again with double feints, trying to create an opening in Bishop's guard with a flurry of deceptions, but the Lieutenant had a keen eye and as keen a sword hand. Craven's speed was as important as his skill, but his rapidity was fading now, and he knew he must act quickly and decisively. He continued to traverse, circling his opponent so that the sun, still low in the sky, was onto his back and cast shadow over Bishop.

Timing was everything. It was the rule of fencing, but

never was it as important when fighting such a competent student of the art as Bishop clearly was. Craven moved in carefully for the kill, or the point at least. He opened with several feints as he had done before when finally he lurched forward with a powerful thrust towards Bishop's chest, forcing him to react with a strong parry. As the Lieutenant's blade moved across, Craven dropped his point under and sunk into a long and deep lunge as he reached for the Lieutenant's abdomen. As his body dropped into the lunge, the rays of sunshine that had been warming his back dazzled his opponent.

For the briefest of moments Bishop was blinded, and yet he knew he was not in contact with his adversary's blade, and could see a glimmer of movement below as the foil came for him. He whirled his blade about, creating a snapping half circle action that beat Craven's blade aside at the very last moment. Unbeknown to either man, the last three inches of the Lieutenant's blade snapped off in the parry. Craven had paid the price in his far-reaching lunge, for pain once again surged through his wounded leg, and he was unable to recover in his usual brisk fashion. In the dazzling light, Bishop could not see the button missing on his tip, but he could see the silhouette of his opponent. He immediately went to riposte in rapid fashion.

Craven tried to pull back, but his leg was like a dead weight. He moved his sword to parry, but in such a low stance his opponent's foil engaged at the foible, the weakest point of leverage and forced through his parry. The broken tip of the foil struck his upper right arm near the shoulder. The blade was so narrow as to flex for safety, but without the button and nail ahead of it, it acted as a smallsword was intended. The blade passed through his jacket with ease and several inches into his body. He growled in pain, causing him to rise bolt upright, forgetting the pain of his leg in lieu of this graver wound. Bishop was frozen in horror and let go of the foil. Craven turned away and staggered a few paces in frustration with the sword embedded in his body. The crowd was stunned into silence. Bishop clearly had no malicious intent and was the most distraught of them all. Even Ferreira rose up from his characteristic slump against anything he could find to rest against. Bishop finally found his voice as Craven looked down at the blade protruding from his body.

"Captain, my sincerest apologies, I meant no harm."

Ferreira went to Craven just as he got both hands around the foil and wrenched it from his body. Blood spewed out after it, and he tossed the broken foil down in disgust.

"Sir, I only meant for a friendly contest," added Bishop.

"Get out of my sight," growled Craven.

The Lieutenant dared not speak another word. He gathered up the broken sword and led his horse away. He looked genuinely saddened by the affair, but also not wanting to bring down the wrath of his superiors, he went on his way.

"All right, show's over, get back to work!" roared a Sergeant. The crowd soon separated as Craven staggered back to his sword belt and slumped onto a box beside it. Several of the men settled up with Ned Clinton.

"Let me take a look," advised Ferreira.

"What the hell do you know about wounds?"

"Enough."

"Never been scratched, have you?" Craven spat.

"No, not stabbed, nor cut, nor shot. Because I don't look for battles which I need not fight."

Craven shrugged, knowing that was true. He had brought this upon himself, but he'd certainly not admit it to anyone.

"It's not as bad as it looks."

The sound of Ned's treasured book closing drew both their attentions.

"Fifty Guineas? You had to have complete confidence in victory. You know, Captain, I have heard of you, and knowing what I know, I would have bet on you, too, if I were a gambling man," he said with a smile.

Craven couldn't help but grin. In spite of owing the man a significant sum of money, he was an agreeable fellow.

"You know, Captain, there are some men who bet beyond their means thinking they'll die on the battlefield before need of paying it back. You aren't that sort, are you?"

Ferreira laughed.

"Captain Craven will outlive us all. He may gather scars along the way, but die? He wouldn't give the Devil the satisfaction!" Ferreira laughed again, even louder.

"You don't have the money, do you?"

"No, I don't, but you'll get it. I assure you."

"Yes, yes I will. I'll have whatever supplies that can be spared sent on to you. Good day, gentlemen." Clinton merrily went on his way to return to work.

Craven didn't much like the way Ferreira looked down at him, but he knew he was justified in doing so.

"Don't say it," he snarled.

"You are a fool, but you're a funny fool."

Craven looked down at his two bloodied wounds and merely shook his head.

"Well, that's shit."

CHAPTER 4

Craven sipped on rum whilst Matthys sewed up the wound on his arm, and Ellis worked on the hole in his jacket. The Captain already had his repaired trousers back on. He looked weary, but the rum helped as they finished their work. They were outside the cottage they'd bribed their way into with the treasure they brought back the night before. Four horses were tied up outside whilst everything else was gone, even the cart.

"We're a rifle short, lost in the fighting last night," declared Moxy.

"I'll go without. I can't shoot with this arm anyway," replied Craven.

"Or hit anything if you could," jabbed Birback.

"You've got to start taking it easy, or do you want to die by a thousand cuts?" Matthys asked.

"Why were you fighting anyway? Didn't you anger Wellesley enough the first time?"

"It wasn't a fight, Charlie, just good sport with foils," he wheezed wearily.

"Foils?" She looked to Ferreira for clarification. He was sitting on a chair he'd dragged from the cottage and enjoying some of the rum intended to sooth Craven. At first, he said nothing until her piercing gaze demanded it.

"He's not wrong. The blade broke on a parry, and it went unnoticed."

"That is not going make Wellesley any happier about it, though, is it?"

"What? Why do you keep talking about Wellesley, what matter is he now?" Craven demanded angrily.

Charlie pointed back towards the camp. The General himself was approaching with several of his staff, all mounted.

"Christ, that's just what I need."

He shot up just as Matthys tied his stitches and followed him up.

"Wait just a moment," insisted Matthys as he cut the threads. He looked for his jacket, but it was not finished, not that he cared that much. Craven soon recognised one young officer riding at the back of Wellesley's small party. It was Paget. He couldn't help but smile as he saw the young officer who had certainly earned his spurs when they served together. Wellesley stopped before him and glanced at his ragged composure yet made no comment on it.

"Are you fit for service, Sir?" demanded the General.

Craven looked past the General to Major Spring. He knew he already had work to do, and was reminded of the huge debt he had now incurred.

"I am always ready for a fight, Sir."

"Do you know what battles are, Captain?"

"No, Sir?"

"They are misery. They are expensive and the most melancholy of affairs. Next to a battle lost, the greatest misery is a battle gained. Do not be so eager to fight, or you shall die a disappointed man."

Craven smiled. He didn't understand Wellesley's meaning, and yet he'd never had to stand before the might of one of Napoleon's grand armies. They got lucky at Porto, and everyone knew it. Casualties had been low, and there had been much to celebrate, but it was clear Wellesley knew the real hardship had yet to begin.

"Let us not forget the great Sir John Moore and Corunna," added Wellesley.

He spoke of the deadly retreat of the British Army over the last winter, pursued by none other than Napoleon himself. Two hundred and fifty miles of trudging through snow and ice clad mountains. Corunna, the battle which finalised the withdraw, and ultimately cost Moore his life, following in the footsteps of thousands of his troops. Yet the army escaped before Napoleon could drive them into the sea as he intended. It was a bitter episode that Wellesley was ever aware of the risks of a repeat of such dreadful times.

"It was the light infantry who truly excelled themselves in those dark days. Men like yourselves, keen, eager, and capable in all situations. And that is what we need of you now," declared Wellesley.

Craven nodded in agreement, thought he was hardly feeling enthusiastic, let alone eager, and Wellesley could tell.

"You do not approve of your new assignment?"

Craven was slow to respond, and Wellesley leapt from his horse. He pulled out a map from inside his coat and unfolded it before Craven's eyes.

"You see, Captain, the enemy still threatens us to the North, but we want to go South. Right now, we have been forced to stop at Abrantes on the Tagus, forty miles inside of Portugal. We must replenish our supplies if we are to continue the advance, but equally importantly, we must rendezvous with the Spanish. General Cuesta. He has perhaps thirty thousand troops under his command; ready and able men willing to stand and fight for their country, or so we are told. But alone they are weak, and so are we. The French have more than us, they always have, and if they can put them all in one place, we really will be in a spot of bother. What stops that from happening is the harassment of their communications. If they do not know where their enemies or their allies are, they move without rhyme or reason, if at all. To make matters worse, I have had to send back our Portuguese allies so that they may be properly trained. The men are very bad. The officers worse than anything I have ever seen, though you seem to have found a good one, Craven," he said, looking over Craven's shoulder to Ferreira.

Wellesley spoke loudly enough that the Captain could hear, and yet he didn't draw even the slightest of responses, for he had as much contempt for his countrymen as Wellesley. Hardly surprising when he was an officer of an elite sharpshooter unit who had distinguished themselves, though Ferreira had been that way long before such exploits.

"I need you to do what you do best, raise hell, Craven. You are no conventional officer, and that is precisely what is needed here. I need an officer who thinks on his feet and can handle any situation, no matter the resources he has at his disposal. We push on to Spain and perhaps all the way to Madrid. I cannot spare an army to help the Bandidos, but you have some unique talents, Captain. You have achieved what any other man would require an army to do, but you achieve it with a handful of rascals. What do you say?"

Craven smiled as he looked to Major Spring once more, knowing he had no choice. No man turned Wellesley down, and he was in dire need of money.

"I will have command, Sir?"

"Yes, though there are other small British forces operating in the region and you will all ultimately come under the command of Major Thornhill, though his presence will be sporadic. Largely, you will be left to do your work. Hunt the French, be the thorn in their side, but always remember there will be no support should you get into more trouble than you can handle. Fight hard and think even harder. You will need your wits about you, or heaven forbid you will become the hunted."

"Horses, Sir. If we are to operate in hit and run actions, we will need to be fast."

"I cannot spare them, but you may take from the enemy anything of use. It is not an easy task, Craven, but it is one vital to the war effort. You like to use your sword, perhaps a little too much. Well, I am giving you the opportunity to use it plenty, and with my blessing. Draw that sword, but not for your own ambitions and angers, but for Country and King. What do you say?"

"If we do get into trouble? I've seen the army that has been sent to deal with these Bandidos, and there could be many more coming. If we do meet them head on, what then?"

"Use your brain, your wit, your charm, and any other tools which you possess. You must find a way. The movements of our armies and the size of those we will face depend upon it. This is not a punishment, Captain. It is true that I first sought to discipline you for your grave offences and poor conduct. There is many a gentleman who would see me send you home and raise a glass of wine in delight at such news. But no, I say to them, for I would not send a fighting man home, not when there is so much fighting to be done. You proved your critics wrong, Captain, now ram the point home, and show them what you can do!" declared Wellesley before leaping back onto his horse.

"You'll need officers to act as captains to the Bandidos, for that is what they call their leaders. They will not respect a ranker, but even a young officer with a strong will can manhandle them. Ensign Paget proved a formidable soldier beside you, Craven, and I know he is more than eager to return to your side. I will also leave you with Mr Nickle. Two fine young men who will be the sort of leaders you need. Good luck to you, Sir," he added before quickly getting back on his way.

For Wellesley seemed to want to be everywhere. Managing so many of the small articles that many other leaders did not. But that also meant there was no escape for Craven, who had largely managed to escape the attention of Generals for so long. The rest of the group soon gathered around, waiting for news on their next move, as all had been listening in to Wellesley.

"What have you got us into?" Moxy asked.

"It was not Craven who got us into this," replied Matthys.

"He'd never have known of us had Craven not been caught duelling," protested Moxy.

"Believe it or not, but we are soldiers, and this is a war.

Nobody forced you to come out here," replied Craven as the two newly arrived officers tied their horses up beside the house and came back to join them.

"You signed up for this, same as the rest of us," replied Matthys.

"To come here, sure, but not to lead the way and get my head shot off."

The newly arrived man with Paget could barely believe how the men talked to Craven, and yet it was clear Paget had briefed him on it, as he made nothing of it.

"Mr Nickle, Sir, at your service."

"Mr?" Craven looked at his uniform, which was a perfect match for Paget's, being a little too short in the arms and tight in the body.

"Jonnie here is a volunteer, Sir," insisted Paget.

Craven shook his head in surprise. "A volunteer?"

"Not like the home services, Sir, but a volunteer officer."

Craven still looked confused as he had no idea what that meant.

"You have not heard of these men, Sir?"

Craven shook his head at Paget.

"A volunteer, Sir, is a man with the education and capability of being an officer, without the means to purchase a commission. I serve as a common soldier but mess with the officers until such time as an opening becomes available that I might be commissioned," declared Nickle.

"And yet you wear the uniform of an officer?" Matthys asked.

"I have loaned it to him. Jonnie deserved better than roughing it with the men," replied Paget.

As one of the few officers there, he didn't get the warmest of responses. Craven weighed him up for a few seconds before finally replying.

"Wellesley said I need officers to lead these Bandidos, are you up to the task?"

"Why yes, Sir, I have studied all the books recommended for an officer in the service," replied Nickle enthusiastically.

Craven looked to Paget for his endorsement.

"I've known Jonnie for many years, Sir. You can rely on him."

"Then listen up. We are going into bandit country, where the French aren't our only concern. These Bandidos attack the French, but they are not to be trusted. Wellesley wants you to lead some of them, and so you must gain their respect. You will not go by Mr and Ensign any longer. You will be addressed as Lieutenants, is that understood?"

Neither man could believe what they were hearing.

Matthys leaned in over his shoulder. "You can't just give them field commissions," he insisted.

But Craven replied for all to hear.

"This is not a commission, and you will receive no further pay. I may yet be able to secure you both commissions in the 18th Portuguese Line, but I make no promises. This is not a promotion; it is a façade. When we get out into the wild you need to command respect. If the locals see two naive young men trying to play soldiers that run amok. As far as they are concerned, and everyone amongst us, you are both Lieutenants and will act as such, is that clear?"

Both looked as excited as one another as though it were a dream come true. Craven knew he was stepping far beyond the remit of his rank and position, and yet that is precisely where Wellesley was sending them, out into the unknown and the wild. He had little care for rules and military discipline out there. He could see his companions were far less enthusiastic about the prospects of such a dangerous expedition. Only Charlie was raring to go, and Moxy looked the angriest of them all.

"I know this isn't what any of you wanted, but it is what it is."

"What happened to making our fortune?" Birback demanded.

"War happened," replied Craven.

"Any chance to kill the French is a good day," added Charlie.

Paget looked confused, as he still didn't understand her bitter hatred of the enemy. To him it was a noble war as if they were feudal knights abiding by some quaint rules of conduct. Despite all he had seen, he still clung to that notion. That dream.

"I won't force any of you to go. These are my orders, and I will sign papers to send any man home should he want it," declared Craven sternly as he looked to Matthys for an opinion.

"This is what we came here to do, no matter what anyone thinks. There won't be any money to be made if we lose this war," he affirmed without hesitation.

"We came here to make some money, so let's make it," growled Birback.

Moxy didn't look happy about it and sighed before nodding in agreement.

"Yes, any way I can kill the French," replied Charlie angrily.

Caffy nodded along in agreement. He would go and do

anything Craven wanted of him, eternally grateful for what he had done. Ellis looked completely indifferent.

"What'll it be?"

"We have our orders," he replied dryly.

Ferreira looked as relaxed and carefree as ever.

"Can your men ride?" Craven asked him.

"Of course," replied Ferreira indignantly. Though Craven had to ask, as many common soldiers could not.

"All right, then, gather around!" he roared as the rest of Ferreira's men arrived and stopped well short of the gathering. They waited for Ferreira's signal before circling in.

"Listen up." Craven rubbed his chin, thinking of all the hurdles that lay before them.

"This thing we are going to do, which Wellesley has asked us to do. It is dangerous. A French army is in the mountains hunting the Bandidos and anyone who supports them. There may be other dangers, too. We do not have enough men or rifles to win in a straight up fight. We have to be smart, and fast. We must be mounted, so that we may get out of trouble as easily as we get into it, but there are not the horses to spare. We will have to take what we need from the enemy. We will have to lean hard on Captain Ferreira and his men for their knowledge of the local language and terrain. Remember we are hunting the enemy, but on friendly ground. All but Nickle here was there at the Lady Sarmento's home when we got the people to rise up with us. That is because they believed in what we were doing. We must maintain that relationship. If the people turn against us, then we are finished. We need their help to beat the French. And somewhere out there is a Major Claveria. The man responsible for this." Craven pointed down to the patched-up hole in his trousers.

"You already picked a fight with him, Sir?" Paget asked.

"We had a bit of a clash last night, yes," smiled Craven.

"Last night? How close are they?"

"Maybe twenty miles or so when we encountered them."

"That close?"

"They won't venture any further West, for they do not have the numbers to face an army. They may not know the location of Wellesley, but they know scouts patrol this area. They have come as far as they're going to come, and perhaps in light of our attack, they may stray further East. Gather up what supplies you need. I have some provisions on their way, and we depart as soon as they have arrived."

For a moment nobody moved, as few imagined such a task being laid at their feet the day before.

"Well come on, move it!" Matthys roared.

The group soon split up, though Paget and Nickle hung close to Craven, having no tasks to undertake.

"Sir, what is it that makes her, ahem, I mean him, so angry?" Paget asked he watched Charlie walk away with a murderous expression on her face. It was clear he had not been forthright with his friend about who Charlie was, and Craven appreciated it, as few were understanding of her situation.

"Charlie's…wife," replied Craven as he chose his words carefully in present company.

"You said it was dysentery?" enquired Paget.

"That was just the last straw. Charlie lost everything at the hands of the French and hates them for it, and nobody can hold that against him."

Paget didn't know what else to say for it was a grim tone

to have set.

"Sir, it is good to see you again," declared Paget.

"Likewise, but I thought you'd have moved on to bigger things. Shouldn't you have a company by now?"

Paget laughed.

"Honestly, Sir, your version of soldiering is a lot more fun than the alternatives."

"Fun? Is that what you came here for Mr Paget?"

"Why yes, of course. Is this not the most exciting undertaking since Nelson took on the French at Trafalgar?"

Craven smiled, and it pained him to admit it, but he had begun to enjoy himself, but as he looked back towards the mountains, he was reminded of the huge task that lay ahead.

"Last night, that was fun, but where we're going, I don't know. Wellesley is asking a lot."

"That is why he chose you, is it not so, Sir?"

"Perhaps," nodded Craven, "Or perhaps we just get given the worst of jobs."

"Why would Sir Arthur make you suffer so?"

"Because he's a troublemaker," injected Ferreira.

"Is that true, Sir?" Nickle asked.

"It could be," smiled Craven.

CHAPTER 5

Craven rode at the head of his small column beside Paget. The remaining horses all carried supplies in the rear. It was a welcome break for the Captain's injured leg, though he still felt sharp pains in his shoulder as they made their way over the hard ground, retracing their steps from the day before; for they were once again heading for the same location. The rolling hills stretched out as far as the eye could see. The fields were dry and sun bleached, nothing like home for either of them. They were just leaving a small stone hamlet, one of thousands like it looking out over shallow valleys. There was no shade for troops on the march, and even in small numbers they kicked up a dust cloud which followed them everywhere they went, at least until the rain came once more. There only seemed to be two conditions on this campaign, scorching heat and torrential rain.

"Sir, if I may, you said we're heading for the last place you saw this Major Claveria?"

"Yes. What of it?"

"Did you also not say he is in too great a number for us to do battle with?"

"Yes."

"Then why are we heading right back to him?"

"Well, because he is either there, in which case we shall know his location, or he is not, and we shall have lodgings for the night."

"Why would he not be there?"

"Because we know his location now. He has strength, but not so much that Wellesley could not crush him if he so desired."

"I also heard of some great hoard of wine which you took from him, wine belonging to Marshal Victor?"

Craven chuckled.

"Yes indeed, it was passing through and under the protection of the Major, which will surely pain him greatly when the Marshal hears of it. But like everything else French which tries to pass through these lands, it will be met with the utmost and most vigorous of resistance. The Bandidos have seen to that, and we have further cemented it. That is why we are out here."

"I look forward to it," replied Paget with an enthusiastic smile.

"Why did you really come out here with us?"

Paget looked confused.

"You can't have chosen this. This is a dangerous task, and with your rank and wealth, you must have had a great many opportunities before you. You could be rising through the ranks of one of the finest regiments in the Army, or acting as aide de camp to a General."

Paget remained silent.

"Well come on, out with it," insisted Craven.

"I came out here, to Portugal I mean, to look for something. I'm not sure I ever knew what I was looking for, but surely it was something I did not have in England. I have led a good life so far. A rich life in so many ways, but that life is not always as exciting as you might think. Lavish dinners and hunts, weekends away in the country. I never had to work, you see. But coming here things were little different. Of course, there is an enemy to fight, but not much else had changed. An officers' mess can be a wicked den. I once made a bet with you that all English gentlemen were good and pure. Timmerman showed me otherwise, but he is not the only one. Yet with you and those who follow you, there is no pretence. No games and trickery, nor endless attempts to one up one another. It is altogether a warmer experience, however rough around the edges."

Craven began to laugh.

"So, you like to rough it down here with us?"

"I like the simplicity of it. Many men who claim to be honourable will stab you in the back at the first opportunity. But I rather believe any of us here would have the decency to stab you in the front."

Craven nodded in agreement as he looked back to those who followed, when he spotted Nickle, the one man amongst them he wasn't familiar with.

"And him?"

"Jonnie? He is a fine young man. A year older than I, but not so fortunate as to have born into the comforts I did. I am helping him as best I can, but I fear he is too good a man for this army."

"The army, or the officers?"

Paget shrugged off the question, but it was clear they understood one another. The sun was low in the sky as they came up over a crest to the find the place where they had last fought the French. Craven smiled as he saw one of the French cavalry carbines lying in a bush and was reminded of the excitement of the night before. He brought the column to a halt, knowing him much risk potentially lay ahead.

"Get off the road and wait for us here. Paget, you're with me," he ordered. He kicked his heels in and spurred the horse on further as he went forward to scout out the farmhouse. Paget excitedly followed on. It wasn't long before they came up over a ridge looking down to the farmhouse where they had first observed the enemy, but to Craven's joy, there was no sign of the enemy, or anyone else.

"All right, it looks like we've got lodgings," declared Craven.

A fire raged in the house as the sun went down, and the group made merry in the comforts of four walls once more. Ferreira stepped inside to join them as laughter echoed about the room.

"Will you have your men join us?" Craven gestured about at all the space they had available.

"My men have taken the barn for the night."

"They're welcome to join us."

"I appreciate it, but they are quite contented," he replied and took a seat opposite Craven, who poured him a glass of wine. Ferreira took a sip of the wine, and his eyes widened in amazement.

"You really did steal the Marshal's stores?"

"Of course, though this is the last of it. So, enjoy it while it lasts."

"Sir, I meant to ask, what the devil have you been up to these past weeks? It has been a month since I saw you last," declared Paget cheerfully.

"Marching, like the rest of the army."

"Yes, this far South, I would have thought we would have pressed our advantage and gone on to Salamanca?"

"Indeed, and that's probably what the French were thinking, too. Wellesley has got them all in knots, not knowing who is where, on their side or ours," replied Craven.

"I don't understand. We have the finest army on God's Earth, why do we not go straight towards the enemy?"

Ferreira burst out into laughter, and Craven soon chuckled along in response.

"What? You do not believe we have the finest men in uniform?"

"I know we do not, and so does Wellesley."

"He cannot?"

"The scum of the Earth he calls them. Behind closed doors at least. That's what I have heard, and he makes little secret of that belief in person," replied Craven.

Paget looked aghast.

"Wellesley is shaping these men into soldiers, but never underestimate Napoleon. He committed to making large professional armies long before we did, and he always has more. Back in England with the English Channel dividing us, and the Navy keeping watch, we could sit pretty. March to our hearts content, safe and secure. But out here, things are not so certain nor secure. Wellesley plays this war like a game of chess. He doesn't rush in like a fool," pondered Craven.

"And yet you do?"

Ferreira spilt a little of his wine as he chuckled whilst trying to take a sip. Craven didn't look impressed.

"I'm, sorry Captain, I meant no offence," insisted Paget.

"I am not a General, am I? Just a fool on a fool's mission."

"If Sir Arthur is playing chess, do you trust he is the better player?"

"We'll know soon enough."

As they made merry in the warm farmhouse, Birback sat eight feet up in a tree looking out over their lodgings. Beyond the house he could just make out the silhouette of Moxy sitting with his back against a tall bush, his rifle resting across his crossed legs. Though he'd never have spotted his comrade had he not known where to look, for upon a glance the Welshman just looked like shrub. Further to the North was one of the Caçadore sharpshooters, standing in the shadow of a tall tree. Birback was watching the scene intently, eagerly awaiting anyone who dared to cross their path. He had to wait another hour, but sure enough they came. He spotted a glimmer of movement and could see it was the Caçadore signalling before he vanished back into the shadows.

"Not again," smiled Birback. His mind quickly shot back to the time he was caught off guard. The night Lady Sarmento was taken, and the spark which set off the fire which had become their life ever since. He was desperate for some payback, no matter who it was against. He could see several men with muskets scrambling about in a treeline. They finally stepped out into the faint moonlight as they covered the ground towards the farmhouse.

"All right, here we go," Birback whispered. He lowered himself slowly out of the tree and gently cocked the hammer back of his rifle. He watched them carefully as he moved up to the horses tied to a fence near the house. They provided the perfect cover for him as the enemy advanced. There appeared to be just five of them. He kept looking about and scanning the treelines for more, but he could see Moxy was already on it.

"All right, you sons of bitches," whispered Birback.

He brought his rifle to the shoulder and took aim, waiting for them to appear at the opening between the barn and house. He had to wait a little while as they clearly moved cautiously, but soon enough they came into his sights. His finger reached for the trigger and began to tremble with excitement. He wanted nothing more than to take his shot, smell the sweet aroma of powder before drawing his glistening blade in the moonlight to rush in there, and yet some how he managed to contain himself. He watched as the men came into the light cast out by the roaring fire. They wore long cloaks and large rimmed floppy hats as if to conceal themselves. Two went for the main door of the farmhouse whilst the other three went to the barn. The first two rushed inside whilst the other three pulled open the door to the barn only to be met with the audible click of rifle cocks being drawn back by Portuguese waiting inside, priming their weapons ready for a volley. Their attackers froze in panic.

Craven's voice could be heard roaring as the other two attackers backed out of the house. Birback rushed out from cover and towards the group, eager to get involved. The five mysterious men had already lowered their weapons in the face of such overwhelming odds, much to his disappointment.

"Lay down your weapons!" Craven ordered.

"We are not the enemy!" yelled back one in a Portuguese accent, taking off his hat to show his face, as if that would mean something to them.

"If not the enemy, then why then do you attack us, and in the night?"

"These men are not Frenchmen. They are locals," Ferreira intervened.

"Yeah?" Craven stepped nearer to the one who had spoken, assuming he was their leader. He had his trusty sword in one hand ready strike anyone who made a move, but the truth was it hurt his injured arm to even extend it out toward him, "Start talking. Why are you here?" he demanded.

"Senhor, we believed you to be the enemy, as they are in this area," pleaded the man.

He looked more closely at the muskets they carried and could see that every single one was a Brown Bess as he was intimately familiar of seeing, if not using.

"English muskets?" Matthys asked.

"They could have stolen them, killed the men carrying 'em," insisted Birback as if desperate to get some response that would give him the fight he had expected and desired so much. He pushed forward as if to start the fight, but Craven blocked his way and pushed him back.

"Hey, enough!"

Birback didn't look impressed, having clearly gotten attached to the idea of a violent night, although as he looked around at the others, he found little support and was forced to back down. Craven studied the men closely. Beneath their cloaks they dressed as peasants, though their boots were all of French manufacture, and two carried French cartridge boxes.

"You fight the French?"

"Sim, Senhor."

"Not alone, though?"

The man shook his head.

"Who is your captain?"

"Fantasma," grinned the man.

Ferreira burst out with laughter, but Craven waited for him to regain his composure and explain himself.

"The Ghost? Really?" he asked the Bandido.

"Sim. A great warrior, an Englishman, like you." The man was looking at Craven.

"Must be one of the other officers Major Thornhill mentioned?" Matthys asked.

"Yes, Major Thornhill," repeated the Bandido.

"Thornhill, he is the Ghost?" Craven asked.

The man smiled as he shook his head. Craven was getting tired of the whole conversation.

"All right, you will take us to this Ghost at first light, is that clear? You'll stay here until then. There is space in the barn."

"Thank you."

They withdrew into the barn where the Caçadores glared at them with contempt as if they were the worst kind of scum. Craven knew they were proud men, but he'd expected them to treat their fellow countrymen with more respect, especially as they too fought the French.

"Watch them, with both eyes," he said to Ferreira.

"You don't trust them?"

"No, I barely trust you," replied Craven with a wicked grin.

"You know we are nothing alike? They are nothing more than criminals who see an opportunity to make some money and steal anything they can."

"And we aren't?" Craven smirked, patting his friend on the shoulder.

"At least we get a uniform," Ferreira smiled back at him.

Craven nodded in agreement as they went back to the comforts of the farmhouse, but not before one more glance into the barn where they could see six of the riflemen watching the newcomers with suspicion. They soon took their seats at the table once more.

"Did you really steal Marshal Victor's wine?" Ferreira asked.

Craven sighed at being asked once again.

"Is it so hard to imagine?" he gasped.

"Not for you, I suppose not. I'm just not sure some barrels of wine are worth risking one's life over."

"And what is, a few shillings? A flag?" Craven sounded weary.

"We do not fight for reward but for duty."

Ferreira could barely contain himself as he burst out into laughter.

"You think honour and duty are amusing, Sir?" Paget asked as if offended by his reaction, and not at all bothered by the seniority of his rank, especially him being Portuguese.

"I think it amusing that it is acceptable to risk one's skin for duty but not for wine, yes."

Paget looked put out, and Nickle was clearly way out of his comfort zone, too, as Craven laughed along with the Portuguese Captain; the two younger men having to wait for them to get over it.

"Ah, good times. So, do you think we can trust them?" Craven asked Ferreira, gesturing towards the barn and the Bandidos who were being watched so carefully.

"Would you trust criminals and robbers with anything of yours?"

Craven shook his head.

"These Bandidos, some may have become what they are because of the French, but many were always that way. They rob, kill, and steal for a living."

"Then why would we associate with then? Why would Sir Arthur use such men?"

"Because, Paget, we need them. We are too few, and they are willing and ready to fight," replied Craven.

"They also know the land. Every road a messenger may take. Every shelter the enemy may take," added Ferreira.

"You sound like you respect them?" Nickle asked in horror.

"Yes and no. You'd be a fool to not recognise what they are capable of. Sometimes there is the way things ought to be done, the way you want them to be done, and then what works. Take the Captain here. By all conventions he should have been demoted and put to work or sent home. But here we are," replied Ferreira.

"So, you are saying the rules and morals are flexible?" Paget asked.

"I believe the Captain is saying life is not as simple as it would first seem. We all have expectations of how it will unfold and how we want it to develop, and yet we are all forced to adjust and evolve," added Craven.

Paget didn't look convinced.

"You don't agree?"

Paget did not respond, but his frustrated expression betrayed him.

"Think back to when you got your commission. When you first mustered, and when you came out here to this Iberian Peninsula with so many ideas in your head of what you would achieve and how far you would go. But ultimately, when it came down to it, you chose to come with us, with me. I am everything you despise in an officer, and yet you chose to stick with me once more. You didn't have a choice the first time, and you did not know me, but this time? Something tells me it was not Wellesley who insisted you come along?"

Paget looked a little red-faced as if he'd just been caught in the act.

"It's okay, you can admit it. You've had the strictest of upbringings, and coming out here with us gives you a chance to break free of those shackles."

"It's not that, Sir," he muttered.

"No, then what?"

"I still don't agree with your methods, but you do get results. I wanted to return to your side because I think you can make a difference, and that I can make a difference by your side in a way I never could elsewhere."

"The smile soon slipped from Craven's face as he could see the sincerity in the young man's words.

"Is that what you think Craven is doing here?" Ferreira asked.

"Maybe he never set out to do so, but nobody forced him to cross the Douro and hand such a spectacular victory to

Wellesley." Paget turned to face Craven who appeared utterly stunned, "Beneath that rogue is a good man. I have seen him."

Craven smiled.

"All right, enough of the nostalgia. Porto is now long in our past. Let us turn our heads to tomorrow and the coming weeks," he replied, directing the conversation away from him. He poured the last of their wine out and sighed, "The last of it."

"Then we shall have to find more Frenchmen to take it from!" Ferreira held up his glass in salute.

CHAPTER 6

Craven kept a keen eye on the Bandido leader. He had been separated from the rest and was leading the way thirty paces ahead of them. Moxy and Birback were by his side. They'd been on the road for several hours and were all starting to feel a little uneasy about where they were being led. With most of them on foot and a few horses carrying equipment, they would be easy pickings for a cavalry scouting party, ideally suited to harassing a small unit on the road and without support.

"Sir, what if they are leading us straight back to this Major Claveria who you angered so gravely?" Paget asked.

Craven grimaced as the same concern had plagued him for the last hour, though he dared not express it.

"Well, Sir?"

"I don't believe the locals would work for the French. They despise them."

"But for enough coin? And Mardel, he fights for the

French, does he not?" Paget pondered.

Craven nodded in agreement though he didn't look happy about it.

"And would it not be a clever strategy to leave a trap at the last location you had encountered the Major?"

"If the Major had any idea we were coming after him, but he believes he is in charge. He has the numbers. He thinks he is taking control of this region."

"Is he not?"

"He's going to try."

"And you think we can stop him?"

"Not in a straight up fight, no."

"Then I beg you, Sir, tell me how!" Paget asked with enthusiasm and curiosity. His concerns over a potential trap melted away as he became captivated by the Captain's strategy.

"Not every battle is won on the field. Wellesley would tell you that. It is everything that happens well before and around that battle. Information, manoeuvres, harassment of supply lines on land and sea; misdirection and interference that is what we have been sent here to achieve. To cause chaos."

"But how can we do that with so few of us? We are barely more than twenty men?"

Craven smiled as he could see Paget could still not see past the straight up battles he had envisaged.

"When we rescued the Lady Sarmento, we were far fewer, were we not?"

"Yes, Sir, but so was the enemy."

"And at Porto. How many of us did it take to gather those boats and get across the Douro?"

"Less, but we still needed an army to defeat the French."

"To win the battle, yes, but in everything else it required but a few men in the right place, and that is what we shall do here. When the French send out dispatches, we will stop them. When they go to forage, as we know they do. The French are told to live off the land, taking and stealing anything they want. When they go to this, they shall find us waiting for them. We will chip away at them as the chisel does to the wood block, and we shall whittle them away until they are shaped by our own hands."

Paget smiled at the prospect, but it was still clear he had no idea how it could be achieved.

"I do hope you are correct, Sir."

"My dear, Paget, this is what we trained for. Most of us served in the Manchester and Salford Independent Rifle Regiment. We trained to fight the French in an irregular fashion should they ever successfully invade England. We were not intended to stand in line, but to plague the enemy off of the battlefield."

"And you believe these strategies can work?"

"I know they do. You must know your history, Mr Paget, and how we lost the Colony in America. It might have been the big battles that will be remembered, just as they will be in this war, but it is the little battles that make all the difference. The Americans won their war, but they were also fighting with the support of the local populace, or a great many of them at least. We now have that strength. Napoleon has ensured the peoples of Portugal and Spain despise him and his despotic Marshals. We have the support of the people, and through irregular tactics we will make this Peninsula a living hell for the French."

The group ahead of them came to a standstill, and Craven

felt his hand instinctively reach for his sword, though even as his fingers began to clench about the grip he could feel pain once again soar through his arm. The bushes ahead of them rustled, and two men stepped out, causing many rifles to be lifted on Craven's side in readiness, though they soon settled down as they recognised British red jackets on their backs. Both men wore light infantry, signified by their the wings on their redcoats, though they wore no shakos with the bugle and green plume which would further identify them. Instead, they wore floppy felt hats the same as the local peasants, and their jackets were faded and coated with a layer of dust so that at first glance they looked little different to the locals. For a moment Craven paused to consider the possibility they were enemy in disguise with captured tunics, but he knew any foe would try far harder in their disguise than the two ragged men before them. Moxy strolled casually back to them whilst cautiously looking over his shoulder several times.

"They're with us as far as I can tell."

"Do you trust them?"

"They know who Major Thornhill is. How could they know otherwise?"

Craven nodded in agreement.

"All right, lead on."

He let go of his sword hilt, through lifted the scabbard into his bridle hand so that the grip was close at hand should he need to draw it. They were led through some narrow tracks between several lines of trees. They were lightly beaten trails and not easily identified. Soon enough they came to a clearing where British soldiers and Bandidos alike were resting in the shade. Two officers at the far end of the clearing were deep in conversation with their backs to them. Craven released the grip of his sheathed sword; content in the knowledge they were amongst allies. There were little more than a dozen redcoats amongst them, the rest being local troops, though they appeared more like bandits than professional soldiers. The iconic Brown Bess musket was the only uniformed piece of equipment amongst them. The rest of what they wore and carried was a ragtag mix of French, British, and civilian gear.

Craven rode to the centre of the clearing and dismounted to take the final steps to address the two officers. As he approached, they turned around. Craven's pulse raced as adrenaline pumped through his body. He recognised the man immediately, for it was none other than Timmerman. Craven snatched his sword from his sheath, forgetting his wound entirely in the face of such a threat.

"Sheath your sword!" the other officer roared.

Craven had not even realised who it was as he maintained his focus entirely on the man who had sought to do him so much harm.

"Captain, sheath your sword!" the other officer cried.

Craven had still not taken his eyes off of Timmerman, but he recognised the tone of Major Thornhill, who he finally turned to, breathing heavily with a furious expression as if he had been betrayed. He took a step towards Timmerman who hadn't even reached for his sword in response.

"Craven, put your weapon down!"

He was finally forced to look at Thorny as he stepped between the two of them.

"I won't say it again, Captain. I am in charge here and under the direct orders of Wellesley himself. You will do as ordered!"

Craven scowled at Timmerman, willing him to make a move so that he may retaliate, but the villain looked as calm as could be as if relishing Craven's fury and discomfort.

"What the hell is he doing here?"

"He is here on Wellesley's orders, the same as you. So, unless you want to face a court martial, you will sheath your sword, Sir!"

"He should not be here. Nothing good can come of it," snapped Craven who would not take his eyes off of Timmerman.

But Thorny would not budge. Craven growled angrily as he tried to take a step forward but froze when Thorny boomed in his face.

"You forget who you serve, Captain!"

"For Country and King, Captain," smirked Timmerman.

Thorny took a step closer to Craven and blocked his line of sight to his hated enemy.

"Think about what you are doing here, Captain. This isn't about you and him. It doesn't have to be. We have a lot of work to do here, and you need not do it together."

"I won't serve under him," growled Craven quietly.

"And you won't have to. You will run your own outfit. You report directly to me."

Thorny clearly sympathised with Craven's position. Craven didn't look happy about it, but he knew he didn't have much of a choice, and so finally he sheathed his sword.

"What is he doing here?" he asked again with a less aggressive though obviously frustrated tone.

"The same thing you are," declared Timmerman. He held

out both his hands before him to draw attention and address them. Thorny stepped aside, confident Craven's hunger for Timmerman's blood was abated, at least temporarily. Timmerman went on with a cheerful tone as if he were addressing an eager crowd.

"We are all here to fight the French, are we not?" he roared for everyone to hear.

Craven shook his head for he could not believe what he was hearing.

"You didn't come here to fight the French," he spat back.

Thorny stepped in once more, but closer this time so he may whisper and not be heard by all those who were watching them.

"Careful now. These locals are fighting for us, and they need to know we are fighting for them, too. Nobody is asking you to like Timmerman, but you will not raise issue here. There are larger things at play than your petty quarrels, do you understand?"

Craven looked furious, and yet he knew there was nothing he could do. One word of misconduct in the eyes of Thorny, and he'd be in a whole new world of trouble. He nodded in agreement to Thorny, knowing he had no choice.

"Aside from the Major and the handful of troops here, these men now follow you. How you run this is up to you. All that matters is you harass the French in any way you can. You stop messengers getting to their destinations. You intercept supply lines and scouting parties. The harder you make it for them, the more resources they will waste here. This is not a gentleman's war, and that is why you two are here." He gestured towards Craven and Timmerman, "I will be around often to gather any information you might have and provide my own. Good luck to you."

He then walked away to find his horse.

Craven glared at Timmerman. He could feel both his fists clench. He wanted nothing more than to go to war with him. Somehow, he found restraint and paced towards the man who'd try to kill him more than a few times. He stopped within range of a punch.

"Whatever you think you are doing here, think again. If you come for me, it will cost you everything," he growled.

Timmerman smirked as if relishing the moment.

"Don't think for one second this is over. I came here to settle a score, and that is just what I will do. I shall have my satisfaction. Not today, though, but soon," he replied before whistling to gather the few men he had to him as they left. Craven watched him go with disgust.

"Well this just got a lot more dangerous," said Matthys who was standing behind the Captain.

"That bastard will not stop coming after us."

"Us? I've got no argument with him," replied Birback.

"A problem for another day," added Matthys, looking around at the suspicious faces of the Bandidos that had been left in their care.

"How many of you speak English?" Craven shouted.

"I do," replied the one who had pleaded for his life back at the farmhouse.

"Yes," another added.

Craven gestured for them to come forward.

"What are your names?"

"Nuno," replied the one they had already met. "Pero,"

replied the other.

The men looked remarkable alike.

"Brothers?

"Yes," replied Pero.

Craven nodded in appreciation. They had a sharper look about them, as if they were far more intelligent and capable than the rest of the camp, and their language skills would be invaluable to him. He signalled for Paget and Nickle to step forward and join them.

"Lieutenants Paget and Nickle. You will divide your men in two and each come under the command of these officers. You will answer to them and act as sergeants to the two groups, is that clear?"

"Yes," smiled Nuno enthusiastically, but Pero clearly did not share his elation.

"What is it? You are not pleased by the promotion?"

"Sir, there are men who have been here longer who might not like it."

Craven looked about the group. Many of them were looking on with suspicious eyes towards the newcomers. He suddenly drew his sword from its scabbard and held it before them. He pointed it at the group, as he circled about directing it towards each of them. Just holding the sword parallel to the ground was exhausting for his wounded arm, but they didn't know that.

"Translate for me, will you?" he asked Nuno.

"Let me be absolutely clear. You now work for me, and in turn you serve whomever I tell you to serve. You may not be regular soldiers, but you are soldiers, nonetheless. These two men are now your Sergeants, and you will treat them with the respect of that position, am I understood?" he roared and then waited for Nuno to repeat it in Portuguese.

One or two looked displeased, but most nodded along as if they'd accept anything Craven had to say.

"I believe you are no strangers to war. Neither am I," he added.

The sun was low in the sky now, and they were weary from the road. Even though he'd been mounted the entire time, he was certainly saddle sore.

"Get some rest, for tomorrow our work begins. That'll be all."

The Bandidos carried on much the way they had been when Craven first arrived. They had no discipline, but they all had the eyes of killers. Several fires soon lit up the clearing as the sun went down, though the groups very much kept themselves to themselves. A clear division between the Bandidos, the Caçadores, and Craven's small posse, which still had no official title, for their connection to the Portuguese line regiment Craven had been hired to instruct was tenuous at best. They wore different uniforms, carried different weapons, and were far from their outfit. The thought was clearly on the mind of the young Mr Nickle also as he posed his question.

"Sir, if I may ask, to which unit do we now belong?"

Craven shrugged as he wasn't completely sure himself.

"Captain Craven's," replied Paget.

"Yes, but what regiment or detachment?"

"We have none," replied Matthys.

"How can that be, Sir?"

"Do you know how muddled this army of Wellesley's is? At Porto he commanded over something called the battalion of detachments. The ranks are filled by foreign troops of all kinds. Not just Portuguese, but Spanish, German, Dutch, even French. Some of these émigré units fight as one, some mix amongst our ranks. There are detachments of all sorts attached to large units, staff and experimental corps, observers and intelligence officers and their staff. The Army is made up of much more than the regiments whose names you read of in the newspapers."

"But we must be something."

"We are whatever we need to be."

Nickle looked more confused than he had before he first asked his question, but he pressed no further as they turned their attention to the clash of sticks. Charlie had been teaching their methods to Caffy, and the two had now progressed to a light bout. Caffy looked strong and determined, but lacked the finesse of a fencer. Yet each time Charlie laid her stick about his flesh, he appeared to learn something new, and she gave further advice after every hit. As every minute of the exchange passed, the former slave made his movements smaller and more precise. He was learning quickly and was soon able to parry most of her strikes. After one prolonged exchange where she could land nothing, he finally came back at her with two quick ripostes, which though did not get through, they came close to breaking through her guard, for he could generate a lot of force in a short time. The Bandidos watched on in amusement, as if thinking it a game and not the practice for combat.

"Good, that's very good," she declared, saluting with the stick to end the exchange.

"Now, young Paget, what have you learned of fighting in my absence?

Craven got to his feet to stretch his stiff legs. The day off his feet had done his leg some good as it was not giving him such sharp pains as he placed weight on it. He took the sticks from the two fencers and threw one to Paget. He caught it confidently despite being rushed off his feet. The two officers came to guard, but Craven's arm wobbled a little under the weight of the light singlestick. He quickly changed to his left arm before the Bandidos noticed. He dared not show weakness to such a cutthroat crowd who he would spend many days and nights beside.

"It's good to train both hands. What kind of swordsman can only fight with one hand?" Craven smiled, prompting Paget to change to his left also. The young Ensign didn't seem bothered by the change and switched as if he'd done it many times before.

"My foil instructor said the same," he replied confidently.

Craven was glad to place his wounded arm far from danger, tucking his right hand down against his hip and formed his guard. He made a few initially cuts as if to warm up, and Paget parried those with ease.

"You've learned to respond to cuts well," declared Craven.

"I didn't have much choice. I don't much like being hit with a stick."

Craven chuckled in agreement.

"You already knew how to use the point, and now you can use the edge, but there are other ways to strike, other ways to get inside an opponent's guard," declared Craven as his teachings began.

"With a beat?" Paget demonstrated by quickly, snapping a short cut into the tip of Craven's blade to push it aside and create an opening to strike.

"Yes, you would know this from foil, but there are other less delicate and gentlemanly ways."

Paget looked curious, and Craven's blade suddenly lurched forward. It engaged against his with significant strength and forced his sword down. Craven stopped his cut on Paget's head, making contact to show he could, but stopping short of doing injury.

The young man looked both bewildered and fascinated.

"What was that?"

"It is called forcing. Your beat knocks an opponent's blade aside, but forcing merely pushes through it. If an opponent holds a weak guard, or their feeble is low," he went on, referring to the last half of the blade towards the tip, "Then you may simply push through it and strike them where they thought to be strong. Now you try."

He held his guard a little lower and a little languid. Paget engaged and repeated what he had seen, his stick stopping on Craven's brow.

"Just beware a disengage. Forcing beats a weak guard, but if a man holds a weak guard with the intention of disengaging at the moment of contact, you must be very wary. Now, there is another way we may push a blade aside and create an opening, and we call it bearing. When a man is strong in guard and means not to disengage, we may use this technique." He began to show as he explained it.

"Engage as if to thrust, so that they maintain pressure in defence, and yet our intention is not to strike them in this action. We lunge forward, and they believe they have parried, but our intent is to get inside their guard."

Paget looked confused, and then shocked as Craven's

blade suddenly appeared inside his guard and before his face.

"Once we are extended forward, rotate our blade, and strike inside," he described.

"It's like carte over the arm, but for cuts?"

Craven nodded in agreement. "Very much so, but we must close with the lunge and displace before we go to strike. You can also use this method to disarm, but be cautious in closing, as you are of small stature. You are quite fine with a blade, but you would not wish to come to blows with a ruffian far bigger and stronger than you."

"Yes, Sir. Do you think we will have much need of swords in these mountains?"

"More than ever. There will be no big battles for us to fight. Small engagements and skirmishes amongst mixed terrain, never was a sword more useful, or a pistol. Did you bring one?"

"No, Sir."

"Yeah? Me neither, that is something which we must remedy. It is frankly amazing to me that this army does not provide its officers with a robust pistol, for we surely have great need of one."

"The Army does not provide much, Sir. I had to pay for everything I wear and carry. But I only purchased what was required of me. Never had there been mention of a pistol."

"It wouldn't be the first time the Army sent men to war without being fully prepared. A good snapper will get you out of a tight spot and can be a handy companion to the sword, especially when you find yourself facing more than one opponent."

"Snapper?"

"Snapper, bulldogs, pistols," smiled Craven.

"I have the money to purchase one," he declared proudly.

"Do you see any merchants here? No, we will take what we need. The enemy will provide like the land provides for them. Now, let's put your skills to the test, shall we?"

Craven retreated to wide measure and saluted Paget before beginning a bout.

"One would think this war would be won by the sword the way they continue," said Nickle to Matthys who watched on.

"Gunpowder is the way of war, but never underestimate a fine blade and its skilled user. The day of cold steel is not over yet," replied Matthys.

The friendly contest went on. Craven was impressed with Paget, but he soon felt pain in his right arm once again as it instinctively was thrown out behind him when lunging. He drew back and saluted to call an end to the bout.

"That's good. Stay sharp, you're going to need it," declared Craven as they sat back down beside the fire. There was concern and anticipation from most sitting about them and little conversation as they dwelled on what obstacles they may face the next day.

"Get some rest. You're going to need it."

CHAPTER 7

"Wait for it, wait…" whispered Craven.

He watched carefully from behind the cover of a dense bush onto a narrow valley track below. Heading his way were eight Frenchmen on horseback, a scouting party. They meandered along the track in ignorant bliss of the danger ahead. Craven almost felt sorry for them, but as he looked to the familiar faces around him, he was reminded who he was fighting for and those worries faded away. The light cavalrymen wore none of the armour of their brutish heavy counterparts who were clad in steel cuirasses and helmets. Craven was eying up their horses before the riders had even fallen from them, as he urgently needed mounts for his troops.

He looked along the lines of his friends and allies to see they were all ready. Each man had a rifle or musket at the port, ready to cock the hammer and join the fight. He looked to Moxy and nodded to give the signal for his finest shot to go first. He watched as the Welshman quickly braced the stock against his shoulder and took aim. He took one last glance to Craven to ensure he had not changed his mind, but the Captain's expression was all he needed to see. He took aim at the nearest cavalryman and squeezed the trigger.

The shot echoed about the quiet valley, causing birds to rise out from the trees and flee in a panic as the first Frenchman was downed. A puff of sulphur wafted past Craven's face, the acrid steam lightly burning his eyes. It was a smell he'd come to quite enjoy, for it almost always pre-empted some excitement or action. One of the Frenchmen cried out in panic, but a volley of fire hailing down on them from both sides soon drowned him out. The valley quickly filled with powder smoke, as it seemed to cling to the trees around them. Several drew swords and pressed forward, but they were soon met with a volley that killed two, and the others began to turn tail under the weight of fire. Craven kept a keen eye on the Bandidos to be sure they were doing their part, and to a man they were in the fight as much as any other.

The cavalry was now in full retreat, but they were not allowed to get away with their lives. The Caçadores shot them in their backs with exceptional accuracy. In little over a minute the valley was silent once more, but cheers from the Bandidos who shouted and whistled with a frenzied excitement soon replaced it.

Nickle rose up and stepped out of cover to look down at the carnage. Many of the horses were killed or wounded from the battle, and it appeared as though no wounded remained.

"Did we need to kill them all?" he gasped, as he looked down at the bodies.

"This is war," replied Craven.

"But prisoners and wounded?"

"If we take any, they will be handed over to Major Thornhill, but we cannot manage prisoners. This isn't a battle. It is a hunt, and they are hunting us just as we hunt them."

But Nickle still shook his head in horror at the scene. It was clearly the first time he had seen blood spilled, and it was a long way from the honourable stand up fight he had expected.

"Grab anything useful and any horses that aren't lame. We move out in two minutes!" Craven ordered.

"We are just going to leave the bodies?" Nickle asked in a shocked tone as the rest of them rushed on past to take from the bodies what they could, but not Craven. He stayed back to survey the scene, especially as he could see the internal crisis Nickle was facing, not that he much wanted to have to deal with it.

"Do you know how far the sound of gunfire travels? Have you never been hunting?"

Nickle nodded.

"You can hear a musket a couple of many miles, so now imagine a volley. If there are more of them within a few miles of here, they will be coming for us, and soon."

"You think they are that close?"

"I don't know, but until I do, we will assume the worst."

"Only three of the horses are worth keeping, and there were no messenger bags," panted Matthys as he rushed back up the hill to report to Craven.

"Then they were looking for the Bandidos?" Nickle asked.

"Or Fantasma?" theorised the Sergeant.

"Timmerman? They'd be fools to go after him with so

few."

"If they even know who he is, or what he is. Perhaps they think he's just one more bandit captain?" Matthys asked.

Craven nodded in agreement.

"We should move out," insisted the Sergeant.

Craven whistled loudly, grabbing the attention of all below.

"Let's move out!"

They moved off at speed. Craven recovered his horse that he had left nearby, and as he climbed onto it, he found Birback approaching with one of the captured mounts. Charlie and Moxy were on the other two.

"That's a start," he declared as he led them briskly on their way, those on foot being forced to jog to keep up. When they came to the next ridge, Craven stopped and ushered the rest past as he handed his horse to Ellis. He took cover whilst drawing out his spyglass. Paget and Matthys took up position beside him. They were far from the sight of the ambush now, but still close enough to see anyone who approached the site. They didn't have to wait long before a cavalry troop reached it. Several officers accompanied them, and Craven smiled as he recognised Claveria.

"Son of a bitch," grinned Craven.

"We should have stayed and taken them, too," growled Birback who was towering over them.

Matthys looked up angrily before pulling him down into better cover.

"What? We took them easy," he complained.

"We have no idea what their numbers really are. If we make one mistake, it could be the end of us all," insisted

Matthys.

"You can see them, what, another twenty soldiers?" Birback protested.

But the rest of them said nothing as they watched the scene unfold, and as if perfectly timed in order to spite Birback, more troopers soon galloped onto the scene.

"You see? And where they are, there will be more," said Craven.

"How can you know this, Sir?"

"Because we trained for this, Paget. Precisely this. How to take on an invading force with superior numbers, using limited resources. We may not be defending England, but it is the next best thing. We won't beat this enemy head on, and we can't afford to." Craven finally sat down and faced away deep in thought.

"What is it?" Matthys asked.

"We have both too many and too few. Our numbers are wasted in these small skirmishes, but we have too many to be flexible."

"What are you thinking?"

"I wanted one victory fighting as one. We got that here. But it is time we divided our forces. We need to cover a lot of ground. Gather information and cause trouble all over."

"Do you think they're ready for that?" Matthys was looking back at the Bandidos, still unsure how far they could trust them, and the young officers who were expected to lead them.

"They have to be," replied Craven.

"How do you want to do this?"

"In stages. We divide into two for the next couple of days.

So long as things go smoothly, we will split further."

He took a quick look back towards the enemy who were clearly still looking for them, but wary that they may still be in the sights of the ambush. Craven got back to his feet and scrambled back down over the verge to join the others as they gathered around, and most looked gleeful following their success. A number of the Bandidos carried French sabres now, either in their hands or already having put on their lavish belts. They would be a handful to carry on foot, but Craven appreciated the enthusiasm, and he would never ask a comrade to part with his sword.

"Listen up. It won't take them long to come after us, and I won't be chased all over Portugal hounded by those bastards. They may think they are hunting us, but they couldn't be more wrong. We are splitting up. Ferreira you and your riflemen will head North with Paget's squad. Nickle, you and your men will stay with us and head South-East. Cover your tracks when and where you can. Take any chance to do the enemy harm that does not risk your own. We meet back at the clearing at sunset. Remember what we are doing here. We make life hell for the French. We need not beat every force they have, but keep a lookout for messengers and scouts, those are our priority, everyone clear?"

Paget didn't look happy about leaving Craven's side. Craven wouldn't say it, but he needed a trustworthy and steadfast officer to lead the Bandidos beside Ferreira, and he knew he would have to keep a keen eye on Nickle, who didn't seem to have the stomach for their work.

"Stay safe and raise hell, good luck." Craven took the reins of his horse and led his party onward.

"That was a good start," declared Matthys.

"And I thought you didn't like killing?"

"I don't, but this is what must be done."

"Must be? How come?"

"Napoleon is the biggest threat to England since the Spanish Armada, but far worse than that, he claims to be a revolutionary whilst acting as a conqueror. He would have the whole world under his lifelong rule if we did not stand against him."

They'd been marching for two hours when Craven suddenly came to a halt as though he had spotted his prey. There was a glimmer of movement beyond a line of trees ahead. His gaze was locked as he tracked the movement. It was a Frenchman on horseback. He was alone and moving at great speed with all urgency.

"A messenger," said Craven before digging his heels in.

The others on horseback had not seen him break formation as they were at a bend of a narrow cart track. "Craven!" Matthys yelled, but it was no good. He was at full tilt now, soaring towards his target. Matthys rushed back to Charlie, Moxy, and Birback, pointing in the direction Craven had gone.

"He's gone after a rider!" he yelled frantically.

"A messenger?" Charlie asked.

"Or a trap?" Moxy added.

"Which way did he go?"

Matthys pointed for her. Charlie raced off after him, whilst the other two seemed unbothered. As she got to open ground, she could see the treeline the Captain was heading for. He had a sizeable lead on her, but she caught her first glimpse of the Frenchman. She could see flashes of his bright green tunic and tall red plume on his cavalryman's shako.

Craven was well ahead of her and close to intercepting the rider who caught a glimpse of him and spurred his horse on to an even faster pace. Craven would not let him go and burst through a shallow bush and onto the trail, now just twenty feet from the Frenchman. He drew his sword as he slowly gained on the man. The Frenchman took out a pistol and fired back at Craven, who hunkered down low for the protection of his horse. He felt the shot whistle past his head and timber crack behind him as the lead ball struck a tree. He smiled, knowing how close the shot had come to striking him, but also how defenceless the Frenchman now was, and yet he was not done yet. He drew a sabre as Craven gained ground, though he dared not slow down as he could see Charlie in the distance.

Craven came up on the Frenchman's left side where his opponent would have little reach and struggle to manoeuvre his sword. Even so the man made a cut as best he could. It was awkward as his body was crossed to do so as he held on to his galloping mount. Craven parried the blow, but even though it struck lightly his own arm was battered down, for he still did not have the strength to ward off the blow. His sword arm dropped down, his sword trailing beside his leg. He grimaced in pain, but also frustration. He pulled his sword back up and rested it across his saddle. Switching hands, he took his sword in his left and reins into his right. He slowed his pace just a little and backed away from the galloping Frenchman, before advancing to his right side.

Coming alongside the man they now had their sword arms opposing one another, allowing the Frenchman to use the full power of his heavy curved sabre. Yet Craven took the blow this time, his robust Ferrara blade stopping it dead. He replied with a thrust towards the man's chest, but this was parried with quick reactions. He followed it with a cut at the back of the man's neck, knowing how difficult it would be to parry, and yet the cavalryman lifted his hilt. He let the blade drop down over his shoulder and back, bracing the blade, and stopping Craven's cut. With the blade coiled up and ready to strike, he swung a huge horizontal cut, which would decapitate in one if it met Craven's neck. Yet the Captain ducked under. The curved blade skimmed his horse's mane whilst in his lowered position, he extended his point and drove a thrust into the man's body with a perfect timed thrust. The man cried out as he was hit. His sabre dropped to the ground, and he fell from his saddle, his horse soon coming to a halt nearby.

Craven circled about his opponent before leaping down from his horse. Charlie raced onto the scene, sabre in hand, and ready for a fight.

"Is that it? No more?" she asked wearily.

"That's it," declared Craven as he towered over the body. The man had already expired from the deadly thrust which had entered under his ribs and driven up to the heart.

"We're not going to get anything out of him," complained Charlie.

"We don't need to. Our priority is to interrupt their lines of communication and do what damage we can. We are fighters, not spies." Craven reached for the sabretache and opened it to find papers. He opened them and looked over curiously.

"What do they say?"

"No idea, they're in French." Birback and Moxy finally arrived on the scene.

"Impeccable timing," jabbed Craven.

"Maybe let us know before you set off after an enemy only you have seen?"

But Craven was already shaking his head.

"It would have been too late, Moxy. This man was riding like the wind. Whatever he was doing and wherever he was going was important."

"You sure he wasn't just running from us?" Charlie asked.

"No, he couldn't have seen us. He was already flying before I was on his trail." He went to grab the horse he'd claimed, "Come on. Let's keep moving."

Three hours had passed when the group once again found themselves lying in wait for the enemy, but it was not a scouting party, but a foraging one this time. More than a dozen men were gathering firewood ahead of them. Some picked up kindling and branches from the ground whilst two wielded axes as they chopped up several large branches.

"Infantry, they must be camped nearby," whispered Matthys.

"And if we open up, they will come for us. What if they have cavalry, too?"

"Moxy, we'll be long gone before they can muster, and they'll not want to move far from camp with only a few hours of light left," insisted Craven.

"Neither should we," said Matthys.

Craven gestured for Nuno to come to him.

"Can you guide us back in the dark?"

"Yes, this is my land. I could guide us blindfolded," he bragged.

"And the enemy?"

"They dare not travel by night for fear of getting lost. The Bandidos and even the locals here will take everything from them given half a chance."

"You want to do this? Have we not had enough success for one day?"

"Opportunity awaits, Matthys, and we have powder to burn," smiled Craven.

"If we are going to do this, we should be fast. No time to loot the bodies."

"There's not a lot worth taking anyway." Craven looked back at them. A couple had muskets slung on their backs whilst several others carried short swords on belts, the briquet as they were known.

Matthys didn't look satisfied, but knew there was no arguing with Craven.

"All right, let's get this done quickly."

Craven nodded in agreement before gesturing for the others to take up position.

"When you're ready, Moxy," Craven indicated for him to once again mark the start of the action. He took aim at one of the two with a musket on his back. Yet as he aimed, Matthys watched in horror as an officer with a dozen cavalrymen rode into view only a hundred feet further away, but Moxy had not seen them as he focused on his target. Matthys opened his mouth to call the attack to a halt, but Moxy pulled the trigger before he got a word in, eager to get it over with quickly.

"Damn it!" Matthys quickly got his rifle to his shoulder and took his own shot. Moxy looked up with a smile in celebration of his shot. That was the moment he spotted the cavalry, and the smile was soon wiped from his face. The area erupted into fire and panic as the French cried out. They were quickly silenced by a savage salvo from the rifles and muskets combined, but the cavalry drew swords and raced on towards them.

"Time to move!" Craven roared.

The skirmishers quickly fled from their positions, having no time to reload.

"What was it we were taught, the sword is superior to the bayonet? Nobody ever said anything about cavalry!" Moxy cried out.

"I don't think our esteemed master considered it!" Matthys replied.

They ran over to the rest of them to find two Bandidos holding their horses for them. Craven, Birback, Moxy, Charlie, and Matthys leapt onto the mounts as the others fled for their lives. Some tried to load their weapons, but it was no good whilst they scrambled away as quickly as they could.

"There, up on the rocks!" Craven yelled, as he saw an outcrop with a steep ramp on one side and a sheer drop in front. It was less than twenty feet high, but enough to impede cavalrymen. Nuno led the way as they rushed to the ramp, with those mounted having drawn their swords as they ushered them on.

"Come on, move it, move it!"

Those on foot reached the top of the rocks as the French cavalry soared up over the edge where they had made their ambush. Craven and the others on horseback formed up at the base of the ramp with their swords at the ready. The French charged forward, and more joined them, but they'd got only halfway when the first gunshots rang out from above. One

Frenchman was struck down, and then several more shots rang out. Two more went down, but they were almost at the base of the ramp now. Craven switched his sword into his left hand once more and held it up before him. The last thing he wanted to do was be caught stationary against a charge of horse.

"Charge!" he cried out.

Moxy's eyes opened wide in horror at the command, and he hesitated, but not Matthys. He knew what must be done, just as Craven did. They kicked their heels in and spurred their horses forward as the mounted infantrymen met the cavalry head on. Two more shots struck the Frenchmen and whittled down their number, but there was no denying there was going to be a clash of cold steel.

Craven approached with his sword stretched out in front as if it were a lance and headed for the most lavishly dressed officer amongst them. There were both cavalrymen and mounted infantry officers amongst their party. He took the opponent's sabre as he approached with the edge of his blade, pivoting it over his head and smashing the ward iron of his sword hilt into his face as he rode on past, knocking him from his horse.

He circled around to make another pass, but another was already approaching him, as they were outnumbered. Few of their comrades dared take a shot for risk of hitting their own as they watched on from the safety of the ridge and reloaded their weapons. All for Caffy, who was scrambling down and rushing towards the melee with a rifle held in both hands at the muzzle as if it were a club. He spotted Charlie desperately fighting off two cavalrymen. Her blade moved like lightning, but she could not land a blow as she was forced to parry from one side to another.

Caffy rushed up to one and swung his rifle, smashing him in the face and knocking him from his mount. Before he could finish his man, another cavalryman strode forward and slashed down against his back. The deeply curved blade slashed into his back, opening a long wound from shoulder blade almost to his hip, and he dropped down to one knee in pain. His rifle fell from his hands.

"Caffy!" Charlie cried in concern as she saw his uniform ripped open, his bloody wound, and the cavalryman looming over him for the kill. It was enough to shock him back into action, and he rose up before his attacker, lifting his sabre for another cut. He was a tall and powerful man and didn't run like many would before such a deadly and terrifying sight. Instead, he went forward and closed the distance. He raised his left hand up to stop the hilt of the sabre as it descended towards him whilst delivering a short and sharp punch into his attacker's sternum, taking the wind out of him. Caffy took hold of him with both hands and lifted him out of the saddle. It was as if he were a giant throwing a mere mortal to the ground. Yet still another came at him. He spotted a sabre on the ground from the man he had just thrown and took it up, parrying the thrust of his opponent as he galloped past. He grabbed hold of the horse of the man he had just tossed aside and leapt into the saddle, ready for the next pass.

Craven could see Moxy was struggling to fend off blows. He manoeuvred around his current opponent for a better strike, but he quickly repositioned and came at him again before he could reach his comrade. Craven parried a thrust with his sword, taking hold of the blade with his bridle hand. He slid his sword onto the reins of his opponent's horse under its neck, and with one quick cut severed them completely as his opponent wrestled for his sword. He let go of it but quickly took a few paces past, delivering a brutal back stroke across his shoulder blade whilst he was unable to wheel about, having lost control of his mount. It freed up Craven, who galloped on and thrust his sword through Moxy's attacker.

"Thanks," sighed Moxy.

They turned just in time to see Birback smash his sabre down so hard onto the head of one of his opponents that it split his hat in two, and upon meeting his skull, split his blade in two at the shoulder where the guard began. The cavalryman was stunned but soon attempted a riposte with the point. Birback caught the blade with his hand. It ran a little against his palm before coming to a stop, blood dripping from the wound, but he had it clamped tight, and pulled his opponent in close, punching him in the face with what remained of his own hilt. The force was enough for him to drop his sword and turn tail.

Those still able to were now withdrawing, and a cheer rang out from the Bandidos on the crest of the ridge, led by Nickle who was celebrating a fair and square victory in battle which he had sort. Ellis beside him took a last shot at the enemy as they fled. The French officer who Craven had knocked from his horse had found it again. He turned back to look at them with disgust, carefully studying Craven and his comrades as if to make a note. His face was bloodied, and he looked furious. Craven merely lifted his sword and saluted as if it was the end of a round. The Frenchman kicked his heels in and continued the withdrawal with all those still alive.

"Everyone okay?" Matthys asked, who himself had a cut

across the side of the head.

Charlie had been thrust in the left arm, but she brushed it off as nothing. Birback was already wrapping a cloth about his bloody hand. Caffy nodded in agreement as if to ignore the wound on his back, but they had all seen it. Only Craven and Moxy had come out of it all without a scratch.

"We should keep moving. They could be back with much greater numbers," said Matthys cautiously.

"What about your wounds?" Charlie asked whilst ignoring her own.

"They'll have to wait. We need to be long gone from here."

Caffy leapt down from his captured horse, the Frenchman's sabre still in hand. He led the animal to Craven and offered him the reins as if it were a gift.

"What is it?"

"This horse, Sir, to do with as you please."

Craven shook his head in surprise.

"The horse is yours, and not because I say so. You earned it."

The former slave look in shock, but accepted his Captain's command.

"And this?" He held up the Frenchman's sabre.

It was an infantry officer's sabre, well suited to the role they usually fulfilled, and yet far more elaborately decorated than the Independent Rifle Regiments type which most of them carried.

"A fine sword, keep it, but you will need to find a scabbard."

Caffy looked upon it as a great treasure as he collected his rifle and climbed onto his new horse.

"We've done more than enough for one day. Let's be on our way!" Craven looked at the others gathering anything useful from the dead when he caught glimpse of Nuno taking a gold pocket watch from one of the fallen enemy.

"You can really get us back in the dark?"

"Of course, that is the easiest job in the world," replied Nuno merrily.

CHAPTER 8

"Huzzah!" Paget roared as he spotted Craven leading his unit into the camp. Several fires raged whilst the smell of meat cooking in the embers wafted across the weary who were returning. The smell was salty, smoky, and mouth wateringly delicious. Paget's smile soon left his face on him seeing the wounds and blood amongst them.

"Are you okay, Sir?"

"A few scratches but we're all accounted for," replied Craven as he leapt from his horse.

"You look like you've been through quite a fight," declared Paget concernedly.

"I guess Thorny was right. They really are on the hunt," said Ferreira.

"How so?" Paget asked.

"Look at them, no scouting party or messengers did this," he replied, tossing a canteen across to Craven. The Captain took it and threw it back expecting water, only to find it was wine. He coughed as it poured down his throat, but he soon had a broad smile on his face and quickly took another gulp.

"Wine? How so?"

"If you cannot find wine in my country, then times really are dire," he replied dryly.

"Please, get some food," insisted Paget as Matthys and Charlie saw to the wounded. She sat Caffy down and helped him out of his jacket and shirt. He was strongly built, even more so than Birback who they all treated as the bull in the group. Though he had all the marks of a very hard life. His back was a series of scars from the healing of lashes, and various other scars marked his body.

"That is a life well lived," smiled Birback.

Charlie took it as an insult and glared at him.

"What? I mean it. A man with marks like that is not afraid to live."

"There's nothing to admire about lashes," replied Craven.

"No, but the rest are. How many men have you killed?"

Caffy did not reply, but it was clear his answer could make many a woman and man blush.

"Here." Matthys tossed Charlie a sewing kit.

The rest of them were glad of the rest and quickly helped themselves to the food and drink.

"Much to report?" Craven asked Paget.

"We destroyed a French patrol, Sir," he replied enthusiastically.

"Good, that's good work," he nodded.

He was clearly exhausted, but the wine was a welcome relief, and he took a seat on a fallen tree trunk being used as a bench.

"What of you, Sir? It appears you had quite the excitement?"

"We certainly had our fair share of action, more than fair."

"Do tell, Sir," encouraged Paget as Ferreira sat down nearby.

"Close call?"

Craven nodded.

"But you all came back alive, how close could it be?" Paget asked.

"Like Thorny said, the troops are here to root out the Bandidos. They came here in strength, and they mean to do just that."

"But not with us here?"

"That was too close today. We must have been right on the fringe of their camp. We were lucky."

"We can't be taking those chances, or we won't make it through a week," insisted Ferreira.

"What? This is Captain Craven. You know what he can do."

"No, he's right. We have good fighters gathered here, but there is only so much one man can do. They have more, and that is a fact."

"Then what do we do, Sir?" Craven sighed as he thought on it.

"Be everywhere," Ferreira posed.

"Everywhere?" Craven asked.

"That's right. Hit them anywhere and everywhere."

"So they cannot concentrate their forces?"

"Yes. They can never gather in force and go after one

element when they are being attacked on all sides. They live off the land, so they never stay anywhere for long. They have a large base camp, but what if they had to divide that camp across many miles of these hills?"

"That'll spread us pretty thin," replied Craven.

"The fewer there are, the easier it is to hide."

"Yes, the way the Bandidos fight," insisted Paget.

"Are they up to it?" Ferreira asked as he looked at Nickle and the two Bandidos sergeants.

Craven looked to Paget for answers, he having a different perspective having spent the day with Pero.

"They're no gentlemen, but they are fighters."

"And you would trust them?"

"Not particularly, but they hate the French, that is for sure."

"I fear they hate any and all authority," replied Craven.

"Don't you?"

"Yes, but the difference is I never took up violent arms against it," he said wearily, looking to the rag-tag group of locals that he knew were mostly nothing more than common criminals using the war as an opportunistic moment to operate with some authority and legitimacy.

"Why the concern, Sir? Did something happen out there?"

"No, but I need to know they are on side. We must divide our forces once again, and that means you going out there with them. We need to know they can be relied on and won't turn tail or rob you, and leave you for dead at the first opportunity."

"I can't imagine they could do such a thing," protested Paget.

"I can. I've seen a whole lot more of people, and trust me,

there are many as cutthroat and untrustworthy as that."

"But these men have given us no such cause for concern?"

"No, because we've been equal to their number, and they know we can fight. But what happens when the numbers are in their favour?"

Paget had no answers.

"Why must we divide our forces, Sir?"

"He's right. There are others working in the area. Timmerman is surely lighting fires all over," insisted Ferreira.

"Maybe, maybe not. But we spent the day adapting to enemy movements. I say we start controlling the land. I want accurate maps and numbers of enemy positions and movements. We will operate in four squads from now on. I want to know everything there is to know about the land and the enemy."

"You want those Bandidos out there with nothing more than one young officer to manage them?"

Ferreira clearly didn't mean to insult Paget, and yet the young man couldn't help but be put out by the sentiment. That somehow, he was not capable of managing them.

"They won't be alone. Matthys will go with Nickle; he will keep order and watch his back. Paget you will take Caffy."

"I am more than capable of leading, Sir."

"Yes, you are. Caffy won't be there to lead, but to watch your back. He's a loyal man and a strong fighter. He will keep you safe."

"Do we really have a plan here?" Paget asked in frustration.

Craven shrugged. "I wish I could say it was so simple. That I could give you one objective or that success could be easily measured, but I cannot. Wellesley sent us here to disrupt and distract from the army he now leads into Spain."

"Then how do we measure our success? When is our task done?"

"Every messenger we stop. Every scouting party we ambush. Every supply train we take. All the things which take from the enemy in information and resources."

"But when does it end?"

"When the French are back in France," scowled Ferreira.

Craven laughed, but it was clear their Portuguese friend was not joking. They all fell silent as the two Englishmen reflected on what it must feel like to be defending one's own country and to know how much it hung on a knife's edge, as the threat of Napoleon and his grand conquering armies which often seemed unbeatable and unstoppable. For that was the ever-present threat. The French Army on the battlefield was a terrifying and relentless force, and everybody knew it. As they reflected on it, they were each handed a bowl of some form of soup or stew. Whatever it was it smelled delicious after a long day, and as Craven sat back, he could see the different groups were beginning to relax around one another after their initial successes.

"And Timmerman, Sir? Do we still have to worry about him?"

Taylor scowled as he was reminded of the hateful man who plagued him wherever he seemed to go.

"Always be wary of him, but he's under the eye of Wellesley now. If anything were to happen to me, and he was even slightly suspected of involvement, Wellesley would destroy him."

"You think we are that valuable, Sir?"

Craven laughed. "No, but I know what a hard task master Wellesley is. He has made his position quite clear, and if Timmerman breaks it, there will be hell to pay. For he cannot have officers running wild under his command."

"And yet he lets you?"

Craven recoiled back in surprise, and yet Ferreira chuckled.

"It is no secret, Sir, that you are what you are," explained Paget.

"And what am I?"

"The worst officer and the best fighter I know."

Both Captains roared with laughter, and yet Paget clearly meant it sincerely.

"I mean no insult, Sir."

"You're not wrong!" Ferreira yelled as he patted the young man on the shoulder.

* * *

Paget rubbed his chin as he looked out at a dust cloud rising up from beyond the hill before them. Caffy was knelt down beside him. The hulking man made him look like a child in size, and yet he clung on to the Ensign's every word, following his orders as if he were Craven himself. Paget couldn't help but feel nervous. He was a long way from help should anything go wrong and had so few men at his disposal. He'd never felt so vulnerable, and yet his pride spurred him on to keep doing what he was ordered to do. Soon enough three wagons came up over the crest ahead.

Two horses pulled each, with two soldiers aboard each of them. One carried a musket for defence whilst the other was a driver, and he carried a short sword, too.

"This is it," smiled Paget.

Caffy did not even think to question his commands as he gestured towards Pero to have his Bandidos ready. They were in one line alongside the track that the carts were travelling. Paget's small group was hidden amongst the scrub and bushes beside the road, their muskets at the ready, and Caffy with Craven's rifle. Paget drew out his sword into his right hand and his pistol with his left, so he would be as ready as he could be. For so many officers only held one weapon at a time, and Craven had ensured he didn't fall into such a trap.

"Wait for it," he whispered. He felt his pulse race, and he took long deep breaths to try and settle his nerves. He crouched down low so as to not be seen as the carts drew nearer. Cocking his pistol, he watched them like a hawk. Yet as they drew nearer, a man on the front cart tapped the driver on the shoulder and pointed out towards the foliage where the ambush party awaited.

"Damn!"

He could see the drivers picking up muskets as they looked on at the position with suspicion when one of the Frenchmen cried out and seemed to point right at the Ensign.

"Fire!" he roared.

Caffy got off the first shot, hitting the man who had raised the alarm. A burst of fire rang out from the Bandidos, and three of the enemy were hit before the Portuguese rose up to advance on the enemy. The driver of the first cart seemed to panic upon sight of them and grabbed for the reins. Paget took aim with his pistol and fired. It was a long shot for the short-barrelled weapon, but he took the chance. He didn't want to risk the enemy escaping, for nobody could reload quickly enough to get a second shot if they got their horses moving. The ball missed the body of the driver but struck his hand, causing him to drop the reins and reel in pain. Paget couldn't believe his luck as he rushed forward with the Bandidos.

The other drivers realised they were trapped. They could not move around the one now blocking the road and so took aim. Three shots rang out, and two of the Bandidos were struck, but the others had closed the distance quickly and attacked the Frenchmen ruthlessly with their muskets as clubs.

Paget rushed at the driver of the last cart. He had drawn his briquet to fight and held his sword in a strong guard in anticipation of a powerful blow, as Paget rushed in against him. He remembered Craven's latest lesson and engaged against the blade, pushed it forward and away from the area it defended, before rotating his own hilt and cutting inside the man's guard. The man looked stunned to see the spadroon flash before him as it slashed him across the cheek. Yet Paget was not done as he continued forward, caught up in the excitement. He grabbed hold of the driver's sword arm to control the fight in grappling, but it was in this moment he realised the grave mistake he had made. He was already celebrating having triumphed with one of his newly learned techniques when he suddenly found himself in a pitfall the Captain had warned him about. The driver was taller and stronger than he was. He grabbed hold of the Ensign's sword hand to save himself, and now had control over the smaller man. He was twisted around and caught a glimpse of Caffy coming to his aid.

"No, get the others!" Paget yelled, insistent that he would

overcome his opponent, especially after having foolishly blundered in despite Craven's advice. They each controlled one another's sword arm now, and Paget held onto both weapons for dear life, knowing if he released either he would be done for. In frustration, his opponent spun him about and slammed him against the spokes of a wheel to his cart. Paget gasped as the air was taken out of him, but as his head dipped, he saw the Frenchman's feet and an idea sprang to mind. He stamped down on one of them. His steel heel cap slammed down onto the toes of his opponent, and the man winced with pain, losing grip of Paget's sword. It allowed him to draw it back and thrust it deep into the man's body, causing him to slump forward onto the smaller man.

Paget brushed him off, letting him fall from his blade as he hit the ground to draw his last few breaths. It was a visceral experience that shocked Paget who couldn't stop thinking it could be him bleeding out on the ground.

"Are you okay, Sir?" Caffy asked in concern.

Paget was too stunned to reply as he saw a Bandido finish one of the enemies with the stock of his musket whilst another was shot on the ground with one of the French weapons.

"This is not…not honourable work," he muttered.

"War is not clean," replied Caffy.

Paget seemed to snap out of it in curiosity at his words.

"There are many awful things that may be done to a man, just pray they are not done unto you," he added.

The Bandidos were already rifling through the carts and the bodies to take anything of value they could find. Paget went to the back of the cart and pulled back a cover to find six barrels of powder and twenty muskets. His eyes widened in amazement at the cache.

"What do we do with this, Caffy?"

"They are rightfully ours now."

"We should take the powder and destroy the weapons. Deprive the enemy of them."

"Sir?" Pero asked.

"What is it?"

"These weapons. There are people who would fight the French if they just had the means."

"People?"

"The locals, they hate the French. These weapons could give them a chance to fight back, just like they have done so in Spain."

"Like Zaragoza? Do you know how many civilians were killed because of that?"

Paget had kept up to date with news and thought of the tens of thousands of Spanish civilians killed because they opposed French rule.

"People die in war. Who are we to stop them from fighting if they choose to?" replied Pero.

Paget didn't look confident and looked to Caffy for assistance as the only familiar face amongst them.

"Every man should have a chance to defend his home, his life, and his family," he replied sternly.

Paget could understand the sentiment and could also see the sincerity of Pero. He looked around at the scenery all around them as if expecting more trouble or for someone to pounce on them, and yet the scene was peaceful once more as the last of the powder smoke dissipated.

"All right, clear these bodies off the road, and let's get

these wagons moving!"

They quickly went to work, but it was not just French bodies they had to move. They carried one of their own dead onto a cart and another cradled his arm where a ball had struck near his shoulder. He was helped up onto the same cart that now carried the body of their comrade. Paget looked appalled, for it was the first man killed under his command.

"That shouldn't have happened," he growled angrily.

"Men die in war. Men die every day. So do women and children," replied Caffy as if he was well accustomed with death.

"Yes, but that man didn't need to die today. The enemy should never have seen us. How did they see us?"

Caffy looked down at the scarlet red tunics they were both wearing, and it suddenly dawned on Paget. They had been hiding amongst foliage, but their jackets stood out a mile away.

"You think they could see these jackets through the thicket?"

"Yes," replied Caffy confidently.

Paget shook his head in disbelief. "I suppose they weren't really designed for these kinds of actions," he sighed.

"Sir, we are ready," stated Pero, who had made quick work of their task.

"Lead the way, and stay out of trouble," he replied and climbed onto the last cart in the line. Caffy took up the reins whilst two of the Bandidos climbed into the back, sitting on the barrels of powder. They soon got underway, but Paget spotted some blood on the ground and was reminded of the man he had lost, and who would be in his thoughts for the rest of the day.

* * *

Nickle and Craven led their prospective units as they came together at a crossroads. Nickle looked far happier than the day before, though he was still on foot. They stopped at the crossroads and looked down into the valley below.

"Can we trust them?" Craven asked as his posse looked down on a small town. About two-dozen houses littered the road ahead in what was clearly a long-standing community. Nuno was on a horse beside him, though the rest of his men were still dismounted.

"I know some of the people here. They would not harbour the French nor aid them."

"You are sure?"

"If Napoleon invaded England, how many Englishmen would help the French?"

Craven nodded in agreement.

"Come on, and experience the hospitability of our people," he declared as he led the way forward.

The windows and doors to many of the homes were wide open as the families were at work nearby. The nearest soon spotted Craven and the others approaching. At first there was a look of dread on their faces until they realised how many wore British uniforms. Cries rang out across the town as excitement began to build, and as they drew nearer, he could hear Nuno's name being cried out.

"How well do you know these people?" Craven asked.

"I stole a horse from one of them last year," he replied unapologetically.

"And you expect them to welcome you with open arms?"

"A lot has changed in a year," he smiled.

Craven shook his head in disbelief; as to him that was one of the worst crimes one could commit and would be a death sentence in many places. Yet as they reached the edge of the community, many of the locals began to come out into the street. At first they looked at them with amazement, as if they had never seen a redcoat before, but excited cheers soon rang out as Craven and Nuno led the way down the narrow street. They came to a well that was clearly the main gathering point of the small community. The cheers soon grew louder as if they celebrated them as liberators. A woman rushed out from one residence and jumped onto Moxy, kissing him in joy.

"Well, I can get used to this," he said with a smile. He took her hand as they reached the well.

Several men rushed out with cups of water and wine and began to hand them out. Nuno leapt from his horse as a middle-aged woman rushed up to him. She slapped him hard across the face before embracing him lovingly.

"This your hometown?" Craven asked.

"No, but this woman is my aunt, Maria."

"Please, will you stay for a meal," she insisted.

She was about fifty years old and well built as a woman who worked the land, but full of life and with a beaming smile across her rosy cheeks. Craven could hardly say no to such a warm welcome.

"If you will have us," he replied gladly.

The woman clapped her hands in the air as she barked her orders to the others in her own tongue. The soldiers quickly took their rest wherever they could around the well and sat against walls, relieved to take such a break after a long day. But Charlie went straight for the Captain with a concerned

116

expression on her face.

"We should send a messenger back so that Paget knows we are safe."

"He'll be fine," Craven acknowledged her as he sipped back on wine.

"Someone returns to camp, that is the deal, or he might well come out at night looking for us. Same goes for Captain Ferreira."

Craven chuckled. "Nothing would keep him from his bed."

But she merely waited for a better response. Craven sighed, as he knew she was right, but he was just too caught up in the festivities to want to worry about it.

"He can take care of himself, you do know that by now?"

"Yes, he can, and he needs to know we can, too, so we may all rest so easily."

"I don't mind heading back. I am sure Paget will be glad to hear news," Nickle piped up, "If we leave now, we can be there before sundown."

It was clear he was keener to leave for his own reasons, as he felt entirely out of place amongst the Bandidos and Craven's comrades.

Craven sighed for they were ruining his party.

"All right, all right, but you take Matthys with you, and you return here in the morning before we head out. And take my horse," declared Craven, knowing Matthys would be the only one who would not protest at leaving the festivities.

"Yes, Sir," he replied enthusiastically and hurried off to gather Matthys and be on his way.

The populace showered down love on the troops and even

the Bandidos, as food and drink soon flowed in the most generous of ways. Craven smiled, sipping on his glass of wine as Moxy sat in a doorway. He was kissing the girl who'd greeted him on arrival as if she was the love of his life, and they had been reunited after several years. Nuno dropped down beside the Captain.

"They were expecting us?"

"No, although I was hoping we would come this way sometime."

"Where exactly are we?"

"On the border with Spain, though exactly where that border is can be a little vague in these parts."

"And they accept you, as Bandidos?"

"They didn't used to, but since we fight the French, we are now heroes to them," he laughed.

Craven looked about the smiling faces and enthusiastic conversation. It might be a poor town, but it was rich with energy and joy. He could imagine a lot of people would be happy for a lifetime in such a place as this, and yet for him it would only shine for a short stay. He needed more excitement in his life.

"Do you think you can win this war?" Craven asked.

"I don't know, but if not, I will die trying," he smiled again.

"I thought the goal was to keep on living?"

But Nuno spilled wine about his mouth as he shook his head in disagreement.

"No, no, there are worse things than death. We live like kings, and any time like this is better than a long life as nothing."

"As kings?" Craven asked curiously.

"We are free, and we fight for our people. We have wine

and Frenchmen to kill, is there a better life?" he asked seriously.

Craven smiled.

"To living like kings," toasted Craven as he held up his glass.

CHAPTER 9

Craven yawned as he awoke. He was sleeping on the floor of one of the local's home, but upon a pile of blankets that had been more than agreeable. Although his head was sore from all the wine, and he could see at least an hour had passed since sunrise. He got up, slipped on his boots and jacket, and stepped out into the road, just in time to see Nickle and Matthys return.

"You're late!" he croaked.

Though in all honesty he was glad of the rest, for it had been a tough few days, as when they were not fighting they were on the road. Or waiting anxiously in ambush amongst uncomfortable rocks and the beating sun. He was sore and yet glad to feel his leg was all but healed, and he hobbled no longer. He felt for the wound at his arm and found no such luck there. It was one of the worst injuries a swordsman could suffer, and that weighed heavily on his mind. He could fight without footwork, but not without the ability to hold a sword. He was skilled with his left, but he would never been as proficient as his primary hand. He'd get by for now, so long as he did not have to face off against one with mastery of the art.

"What news?"

"Sir. From Lieutenant Paget. One wounded and one killed, but he's captured three carts of equipment. Weapons, powder, and provisions."

Craven nodded in appreciation.

"And one more thing."

"What is it?"

"Paget says these red jackets won't do. He says they stand out a mile away and were the cause of his casualties."

"Oh, they won't do?" Craven asked in disbelief.

"He's not wrong," added Moxy who had barely peeled his lips from his new lover who he still had in his arms, as though he had not let go of her all night and morning.

"If we're caught without uniforms, we'll be shot on sight as spies," replied Matthys who had clearly given it some thought.

"Out here on this frontier, do you really believe our jackets would save our lives? You think the French would show mercy and take prisoners after the damage we have done them?"

Matthys shrugged at Craven.

"We should have kept our green jackets," replied Moxy.

"The jackets of a regiment which no longer exist, and couldn't have left England even if they wanted to?" replied Matthys.

"Well, then, there is nothing for it, unless anyone has any great ideas?"

"Make new ones." Ellis joined in the conversation. He was lurking in a nearby doorway. Craven looked to him and ushered for him to go on, and yet had to spell it out for him.

"Spit it out. Explain to us what you mean."

"If we may be shot jacket or not, why not wear whatever we choose? Whatever suits?"

"Oh, really? And so pray tell me what would that be?"

"Simple jackets in brown. We'd blend in with the scenery and the locals, too, if we needed to."

"And where would we get new jackets?"

Ellis picked up one of the blankets he had used in the night.

"Are you a tailor?"

"No, but I am," replied as she snatched the blanket from Ellis.

"You want jackets. I will make jackets," she declared, waiting for Craven's response. He looked to Matthys for his opinion, but the Sergeant merely shrugged in surprise that it was being laid out so easily for them, "Well?" Maria demanded.

"How long would it take you to make them?"

She sighed as if taking it as a challenge. Noon, and you will have your jackets."

"And two more, for one small man, and one large one, about the sizes of those two," he replied, pointing to Caffy and Charlie.

"Make yourselves comfortable and get some breakfast. You will need your strength," she replied in a motherly tone. She then yelled at several of the other women working nearby and left to get on with the task.

* * *

123

Paget carefully studied a map, as he pencilled in notes from the information he had gleaned from Nickle's visit overnight. Caffy sat admiring his newly acquired sword. Marvelling at it as if it were a jewel the likes of which he could never have imagined. All of a sudden a roar of angry voices rang out. An argument had erupted amongst the Bandidos. Paget leapt to his feet at the sound of the ruckus. He found a Bandido yelling at Pero and pushing him away. Finally, punches were thrown. The first landed on Pero's nose, and he nearly lost his footing as his nose was bloodied, but he gave back as good a blow. His attacker grabbed hold of him, but he struck him with a head butt, causing him to stagger back. Paget looked to Ferreira for help, but he and his Caçadores looked away as if wanting no part of the Bandido business. It forced Paget to handle it himself, for he could not stand aside and let it continue.

"What is the meaning of this?" Paget got between them. He was empty-handed but clearly expected them to respect his rank and authority.

"This man believes he should be in charge," Pero scowled.

"And what matter is that of his?" Paget asked as if insulted it should even be questioned.

"He led us once before Captain Craven arrived," admitted Pero.

But before Paget could get out another word, he heard a pistol being cocked and fired. He did not see from where, but the shot struck Pero's attacker in the forehead, and he went down dead. Beside Paget was Caffy holding his officer's smoking pistol. Paget was stunned, but not nearly as much as the Bandidos, who were well accustomed to violence.

"Captain Craven ordered this man to lead you," he said to the Bandidos as he pointed at Pero, "He leads you."

They didn't understand his words, but they entirely understood his meaning as Caffy handed the pistol to his officer, who was still stunned.

"Yes, yes, these are the Captain's orders. You will ensure they…they know them, and respect them."

The rest of the Bandidos soon sat back down now the excitement was over, not daring not raise another word against their Sergeant. Paget began to reload his pistol but was a little shaky from the adrenaline still pumping through his body.

"You killed that man, Caffy?"

"Yes."

"Why?"

"Better to deal with him now than in the face of the enemy. A man like that will shoot you in the back. Men like that you shoot in the front before they have their chance," he replied unapologetically.

Even Pero looked stunned as he struggled to relay Caffy's words in his own language.

"But was it absolutely necessary to kill him?"

"Do you want to know you can trust the men who fight with you, Sir?"

"Yes, yes of course."

"Then, yes, it was necessary."

Paget nodded in agreement. He clearly understood a difficult situation had been handled for good, but he couldn't help but feel sickened by it.

"You know, this place, this war, it isn't what I thought it would be," he muttered.

"What did you think it would be, Sir?" Caffy asked.

"Better, cleaner, more noble. The newspapers make it sound like a great adventure of great heroic deeds. One big adventure, that is what they say."

"It could be a lot worse, Sir."

"Worse? I doubt it."

"Life can always be worse. This life Captain Craven has given me is the best I have ever known."

"Even out here? With bloodthirsty Bandidos and the French hunting us?"

"Yes."

"How? How can that be?"

"Because I have friends, and I know who the enemy is," replied Caffy solemnly.

"You must someday tell me of your life, for it sounds you have led quite the colourful existence."

"I have lived, yes, Sir."

Paget nodded in agreement as he went back to his map.

"We shall head further North today. We must not allow ourselves to become complacent. We are still too few, and we need more horses," he said, looking at the eight tied up nearby.

"If we can just get everyone mounted, we can cover a lot more ground, and be infinitely safer, too," he added.

He watched as the Bandidos carried away the body of the one who had started the commotion. They were under the watchful eye of Pero, who was still wiping the blood from his nose.

Paget missed Craven. Life amongst the Bandidos was a far cry from the one he was used to. The Captain had been a shock to the system, but in the best of possible ways. Command had not been anything he could have expected, for the Bandidos made the common British soldier seem almost gentlemanly.

"Come on, get that body buried quickly. We have work to do!"

* * *

Craven was getting anxious as the sun was now high in the sky, and they had work to do. He paced back and forth in a frustrated fashion.

"Why the rush?" Moxy asked who was just eager to see his lady again, for she had been tasked with work with Maria.

"The rush? The sun is up and we are idle," replied Matthys.

"I fail to see how that is a bad thing. We've done plenty of work, made a good start, do we need to throw ourselves into battle every single day?"

"This is no battle. These are little more than skirmishes," replied Craven.

"Still, I don't see the rush to look for trouble."

"Because, Moxy, a battle is coming. A proper battle, and we'll be in it. How strong the French are opposing us is directly linked to what we do here."

"How did us making our fortune ever become this?" Birback asked.

"You know how," replied Moxy.

"Hey, nobody forced you to put on a uniform and draw pay," insisted Matthys.

"I'm just saying things are pretty sweet here, why the rush

to leave?"

Craven sighed. "What's her name?"

"Ana."

"And she will be here when we return, Moxy."

"Captain Craven!" a voice cried out.

It was Maria, which surprised them all, as her deep booming voice was akin to a sergeant on the drill square. She led out a party of women from one of the dwellings. Each carried a pile of jackets and began to distribute them to the redcoats, handing the first one to Craven. It was a simple short jacket made of very dark brown wool, of the kind worn by many of the local peasants. He took off his officer's tunic and placed it over the edge of the well before pulling on the new jacket. It was a loose and comfortable fit, but well suited to his frame. He looked impressed by the efficiency of the local women, and as he watched the rest of his comrades put on their jackets, he realised just how quickly they blended into their environment. For at a glance there was little to distinguish them from the Bandidos or even the local farmers.

"You'll need these."

Maria placed a black cocked hat into Craven's hands. It was soft but well formed, and not unlike a primitive version of the bicornes worn by most British officers, yet without any of the unique military adornments. Combined with the dark trousers his unit wore from their time in the Manchester and Salfords, they now blended in well with their surroundings. Their attire was generally drab and dull. It would work as a form of camouflage amongst the dusty towns and sun-drenched and water-starved countryside.

"He was right, wasn't he? Paget, I mean," said Craven as

he admired the rough and ready looking troops before him.

"Why, oh why, the light infantry continues to wear red eludes some of the greatest minds in the Army, for the rifle Corps knew from its beginning it was incorrect," replied Matthys.

"But it does look shiny." Craven smiled, looking down at his red tunic and realising quite what it meant to him. He'd not really noticed how much it had come to be his home and so much of his identity, something he had not felt since a young man, and he'd never truly appreciated it back then.

"All right, then." He marvelled at the ragtag looking bunch, and as he rolled up his redcoat, he thanked Maria sincerely.

"It is my pleasure," she replied with a beaming smile.

"Okay, Moxy, say your goodbyes to your lass. It's time to get to work."

Moxy still had his arm around the young woman he was besotted with. She looked as enthusiastic for him as he did for her, and disappointed as he kissed her goodbye. It was clear they could not communicate much with their words, and yet it seemed they didn't need to.

Charlie led Craven's horse to him. He packed his jacket and shako onto the saddle beneath a blanket and climbed onto the horse. His squad was now entirely mounted, but the Bandidos were still lacking enough horses, and he pointed to the five who were fortunate to be mounted.

"You're with us," he declared, knowing he needed to bolster his small squad of four, as he had lost Paget, Matthys, Nickle, and Caffy to the other squads. He knew they'd not be able to communicate easily, but they were all going to be busy with shot and steel this day.

"You know what you have to do. We'll bring back any spare horses we can find. It is of the utmost importance that we can move quickly. Let's ride!"

He kicked his heels in and soared out of the town to a hail of cheers as he parted ways with Nickle and Matthys once more, for they were forced to continue at the pace of those still dismounted. Craven couldn't help but feel good as he led the horsemen on. The wind rushed over his face as he took in the beautiful countryside, which showed no signs of war or hardship.

Farmers went about their daily work, and a line of carts ahead was being driven by oxen. The most docile and beautiful form of the creature he had ever seen, yet the carts they pulled looked so primitive it would appear they were unchanged since antiquity. The beds were made of simple planks nailed together and their wooden wheels completely solid. The entire axle revolved with the wheels, making the most incongruous of sounds as they bumped along the dry and rocky paths.

There was a simplicity and elegance to the primitive life in such rural parts that he imagined had gone relatively unchanged since the Romans. It was hard to imagine the people of such a peaceful and rural nation doing battle with the economic and industrial might of France, and yet it was a vivid reminder to not underestimate anyone. The driver of the oxen looked on at Craven with suspicion as he drew closer. He could tell he was not a local, and yet wore some of the local attire.

"Good afternoon!"

Craven tipped his hat. His strong English accent was all that was required to calm the man's nerves. All he wanted to know was that they were not French, and he soon saw the Bandidos who further calmed his nerves, despite fearing them just a year before. He thrust his staff into the air to spur Craven and his party on, knowing they were there to fight the invaders. It brought a smile to the Captain's face to know how welcome they were being made.

"Do you think we will see such a warm welcome in Spain?" Charlie asked who rode beside him.

"Perhaps even more so. Spain has had it far worse."

"You believe that? It's not just stories to harden our resolve and support back home?"

"Are you suggesting our leaders and newsmen would lie?" Craven smiled.

"I think they might report what is best for their ends, yes." Craven nodded in agreement.

"Yes, that much I am quite sure of. But the struggles in Spain are very real. Napoleon thought he could install a puppet and rule Spain without quibble, but I fear he is forgetting his history. The Spanish threw out their last invaders. It took hundreds of years for them to finally defeat the Moors. Hundreds. How many generations do you think that is? That is the resolve and determination you will find in this Peninsula. Don't be fooled by their agriculture, simplicity, and the manner of their dress. These are a tough people."

"You sound like you admire them?"

"Could you say you would be so strong in the face of what they have? England has not been invaded since William the Conqueror. I am not sure any of us can know what we might do, but many would not be so resilient as these people."

"What else would you do if your country was invaded?"

"Board a ship for the Americas," smiled Craven.

"And yet here you are, fighting."

"Not by choice."

"No?" she pressed as if she did not believe him, "I think you enjoy it more than you would admit."

"I said we would find our riches, and we made a start. What we took off the Marshals. There will be much more for the taking."

"You think Wellesley will let you keep the spoils?"

"Look at us. Who out here is going to stop us?"

* * *

Ferreira wiped his sweaty brow. He leaned back down on the stock of his rifle as he awaited the enemy. He could see them, and he knew he could strike them even from the four hundred yards they were at, but he dared not, as he waited and lured them in to ensure none escaped. He heard the crack of dried twigs under feet from behind and spun about quickly, taking aim with his rifle. To his surprise it was Major Thornhill scrambling up over a verge to their position. He looked as calm as could be and not in the least bit surprised to see them. He was not in his uniform jacket, but a dark green civilian jacket and black top hat. He looked most out of place amongst the soldiers, and yet blended in to their surroundings just as well.

"Afternoon, Captain," he declared.

Ferreira did not look impressed, for he was in the middle of a carefully planned and subtle operation. He took up his former position as the Major dropped down beside him.

"What can I do for you, Sir?"

Thorny smiled at the Portuguese officer's discomfort.

"You don't think I was going to walk away and let you boys at it without keeping one eye on the happenings?"

"How did you find us?" Ferreira asked, who'd been very careful in all of their movements.

"You know when you work in a country that is friendly and hostile towards the enemy, it is easy to find spies, and you need not even pay them," he smiled.

"The locals? They've been keeping an eye on us? Tracking our movements?"

"Of course. Some intentionally, and some merely because every man and woman takes an interest in what goes on outside their door."

"Not all report it to the authorities, though," replied Ferreira angrily.

Thorny didn't understand his hostility.

"You do realise these are our allies, Captain?"

"Yes, but recording such information, they could divulge it to the enemy under the right or wrong circumstances."

"Don't you worry about that."

Ferreira groaned. He didn't much like being checked up on. Especially being watched wherever he went.

"Any news from Craven?"

"He and Nickle's squad spent the night at a town several miles to the North. He sent Nickle back to report."

"Good, you've got to learn to use the people of this land to your advantage, Captain. They may not be soldiers nor wear the uniform of one, but it is their country, too, and they want to fight for it any way they can."

"Should fighting not be left to professionals?"

"In an ideal world, yes. But we have no such luxury. If this war had to be fought only with trained soldiers, it would already be lost."

Ferreira groaned once again. He was an officer of an elite unit, and for all his effort to appear as cool and collected as one could be, he had an immense pride in his abilities and his unit.

"What are you really doing here, Major?"

"I want you to press further to the East."

"East? Into Spain?"

Thorny nodded in agreement. Ferreira looked concerned, but soon refocused his attention on the enemy ahead. A twelve-man infantry patrol. More than capable of dealing with a ramshackle group of Bandidos, but not nearly prepared enough for trained and experienced riflemen. Thorny fell silent and let them go to work as Ferreira took aim. He need not say a single word of command to his men, as they all knew what to do. He squeezed the trigger, and the first shot rang out, striking the officer of the French troops. He ducked down for cover to reload as a hail of rifle shots struck the enemy. They ducked down and looked for targets. Sporadic fire came back at them, but they were firing blindly, and the Portuguese riflemen were set up behind a small natural trench so they could not be seen until the moment they got up to fire.

They could hear cries from the Frenchmen as they tried to spot the enemy and regain their composure, but soon enough Ferreira had loaded his second shot. He looked around to his comrades, waiting for them all to be ready before finally they rose up together. They fired almost simultaneously, killing most of the remaining Frenchmen. Three turned tail and began to run.

The Captain merely got up and watched as his compatriots reloaded to finish them, too.

"It is hard to feel bad about shooting a man in the back when he has invaded your country," declared Ferreira.

Thorny nodded in agreement. "Into Spain, then?"

"They will know we are here. We cannot hide our identity and pretend to be Bandidos if we cross over."

"I am sure the French are well aware of that. The Bandidos have had many successes, but they are far from professional soldiers. The losses they have suffered in these past days cannot go unnoticed. They will know we are aiding the Bandidos. Go East, and make them suffer. Let the French know there is nowhere they are safe."

Ferreira wearily sighed in agreement as several more rifles fired off around them.

"Into Spain it is."

CHAPTER 10

Several days had passed with little action as Craven led his squad to the crest of a hill where they could look out across the vast terrain before them. Though as it came into view, he found Paget already there for exactly the same reason. All of his squad were now mounted, and Craven looked impressed, as he knew that must have meant some successes, though he appeared a man or two short. Craven came to a stop at the top and took a deep breath of fresh air as he admired the view. Paget appeared to have aged a year in the time since they first met. He'd grown no larger, but his fresh-faced innocence seemed to be falling away.

"It's working, isn't it?"

Craven nodded in agreement.

"Less and less patrols each day. Scouts and messengers are routinely interrupted or killed. We have done precisely what we came here to do," he replied.

"And do you think it will make a difference?"

"Thorny seems to think so. Wellesley means to march through into Spain and perhaps even on Madrid. The Army needs all the help they can get."

"And that might end the war?" Paget asked as if he'd already seen enough of it for a lifetime.

"Napoleon put his brother on the throne. Perhaps if he is overthrown we might see an end to him in Spain, but even if that were to happen, there is a long way left in this war."

"It is not the noble pursuit I had expected."

Craven had no answers but looked to Matthys as the religious and steadfast one amongst them. He gestured for the Sergeant to go on.

"Sir, war is dirty work, but the goals which it may achieve, those are noble."

The group fell silent as they reflected on a week of arduous and dangerous work, but also the nature and beauty they enjoyed. In the silence they could hear the gallop of a horse approaching from the rear. Craven smiled to see it was Caffy, but the expression of horror and urgency on his face soon turned to concern for them all.

"Sir, it is the town. Maria," he exhaled.

Craven turned his horse about to see two black trails of smoke rising into the sky.

"Ana," Moxy gasped in horror.

He kicked his heels in and stormed back down the slope. No more words were needed, for Craven led the others after him. They rode like the wind, and it was not long before the smell of wood smoke filled their nostrils. It was so often an endearing scent as the sun went down, but in the light of day, and having seen the look of dread on Caffy's face, it now brought fear and despair. They raced on to the town without a single care or consideration for what trouble may lie in wait for them, as it was clear Moxy would not be slowed.

As the town came into view, they could see almost every single house was on fire. Hot embers brushed over them as they raced to the well, and Moxy leapt from his horse before it had even stopped. Bodies littered the road, and as Craven dismounted, he realised one of them was Maria, shot through the chest with a musket.

Moxy rushed from one building to the next in search of his beloved Ana, as the others looked in horror at one another, barely believing what they were seeing. A cry of sorrow rang out from one of the buildings, and they all knew what that meant, for Moxy did not reappear. His search and his hopes were dashed.

There was movement further up the road as Nickle took the bend. He was on foot and leading his horse. He was missing his hat, and a nasty sword cut along the side of his head above his ear bled profusely. His hands were bloody, too. He staggered, though more from despair than injury. Several of his Bandidos were with him, one limping and using his musket as a crutch. Several others were wounded.

"We couldn't stop them," said Nickle as he slumped down on a step and let go of his horse's reins, letting it roam without a care.

Paget rushed to his friend's side as Craven tried to find any words of comfort but found himself utterly redundant and powerless. He could hear Moxy's sobbing and went towards the sound of it, hoping he may help his friend. He stepped into one of the houses where he found Moxy cradling his new love's body. Her head had been struck, perhaps by a musket butt, and there was no saving her.

"We did this," sobbed Moxy.

Craven's expression turned from despair to anger at his words.

"No, Moxy! No we did not," he growled as he stormed out of the room, and Moxy kissed Ana before following him in curiosity. Craven went straight for his horse as he tore off his drab jacket, grabbed his redcoat, and pulled it on.

"We don't know what we're dealing with yet. We should think carefully before we act," insisted Matthys as the calming voice he always was, but Craven wasn't ready to hear it. A rider raced into the town as if to bring more news. It was Major Thornhill.

"The French are going town to town killing everyone!" he announced.

"Why? Why now?" Paget asked.

"Reprisals," replied Charlie.

"They cannot find or defeat us in open country, and so they come to destroy all those who lend us aid," replied Matthys.

Craven put on his shako and climbed onto his horse once more.

"What are you doing?" Thorny asked.

"What I am paid to do," he said, looking out to the trails of smoke that the enemy had left in their wake.

He kicked his heels in and stormed after them without another word, and his comrades were urged to follow.

"Come on!" Charlie yelled as she led Moxy's horse up beside him. He leapt on it and stormed on after the Captain. All those who could ride were soon caught up in the excitement, for even Nickle mounted up and raced after them. Thorny took one more look at the carnage, for only the wounded Bandidos remained now, sitting about the bodies of the murdered townsfolk. He growled as he turned his horse about and raced on after the group. The posse stormed through the countryside as a murderous mob.

They didn't just want to fight the enemy. They wanted revenge. Soon enough they passed several farmhouses that were burning and with bodies littering the road. Another few miles and they came up over a ridge where they could see French soldiers running amok as they murdered the locals. Craven drew his sword and charged without a word, and they all followed him.

It was not so much a town, but several homes loosely situated together with much open space in between. Oxen lay still in several fields still yoked by their horns, as was the local method of harnessing. Their drivers and teams lay dead about them. The French had all but finished their slaughter of the few families that lived between the houses when they spotted Craven at the head of what appeared to be a cavalry charge. Many of them hurried to reload their muskets, but they were disordered and too caught up in the killing to recognise the threat of danger before it was on top of them; though their bayonets were ready and already bloodied.

Craven stormed forward at the first man he could find. The man made a thrust at him with his bayonet, but he scooped it up with a hanging parry and threw the muzzle up, cutting under it in a large arc as though he wielded a cavalry sabre. His blade cut into both his arms as he passed on by, but hardly did enough damage to stop him for good. Unfortunately for him, Birback was next and slashed down at his head to finish him.

The British horsemen ran amok amongst the French as they cut and thrust relentlessly, exacting their revenge and fulfilling their bloodlust. No one showed mercy, and not one Frenchman begged for it. Yet as they cut and thrust their way through the enemy, a voice cried out, "Cavalry!"

A troop of light cavalry was now bearing down on them, and there was no time to flee, nor could the farmhouses be used for cover, as they were raging with fire. Moxy quickly sheathed his sabre and took aim with his rifle, and the others did the same. Six of the cavalrymen were dropped, but there was no time to reload, and cold steel was once more drawn as Craven held his sword high in the air, with his left hand circling it about his head.

"Charge!" he roared.

Nobody even doubted his decision, for they wanted payback, and the risk of charging at trained cavalrymen was not even a consideration. There were at least fifty of them soaring towards them with their deeply curved and heavy sabre blades held aloft. The huge plumes in their oversized cavalry shakos fluttered in the wind. It was a marvel to behold as the Hussars charged in all their finery, opposed to the ragtag group led by Craven, the only one wearing his red jacket. The two thunderous forces clashed together. Two of the Bandidos were run through in impact, and Nickle's horse was struck with such force they collapsed together, throwing him to the ground. Matthys was cut across the left arm but returned a thrust at his attacker. Craven was like a man on fire as he cut and thrust back and forth furiously.

He parried one thrust and returned a rapid cut across a

man's face. His blade could cut with only half the force of the brutish cavalry sabres, but twice the speed. As he spotted one attacking Charlie, he thrust it home into his chest and turned about to look for another. Blades were clashing all around, and he kicked his heels in to spur his mount on towards two more Hussars. Whilst in the face of such danger, his horse reared up just as one of the Hussars came up beside him and cut down with a powerful downright blow. Craven got his sword in place to parry, but the force of the blow caused his own sword to be knocked down onto his body. The force threw him out of the saddle, and he landed back first.

He was stunned from the impact as the wind was taken out of him, and yet he quickly got to his feet, eager to fight on even through a daze. The one who had struck him was now coming in for a killing blow, and the two he had meant to attack were closing in, too. He formed a broad guard, his left hand as far forward as his sword hand in readiness to grab at the horse's reins, yet a shot rang out and his attacker was slain. He looked up in time to see Thorny with a pistol in each hand, one smoking from the shot, whilst the other's pan lit up as another shot struck one of the Hussars. The other charged at him to avenge his comrades, yet Thorny dropped his pair of pistols into holsters in his saddles and drew out two more that were already cocked. He fired and killed the man before turning his other on one more who came for him. The second brace of pistols dropped into their holsters and the third were drawn. Craven smiled, as he now understood why the Major didn't carry a sword.

Two more shots rang out from the Major who holstered the third brace of pistols before taking out two small pocket pistols from inside his jacket, clearly being intended more for his own defence than a battle. Another of the Bandidos fell dead from his horse whilst Paget cried out as a sabre was thrust at him. The point narrowly grazed his slight figure, but the edge sliced into his arm. Many of them looked bloodied, and Craven knew they were in deep water.

"Retreat! Fall back!" he cried.

The French cavalry continued to stand their ground, but they were rocked by their own losses and not eager to pursue as they began to turn and run. Craven spotted Nickle. He was wandering about aimlessly with his sword in hand as if completely lost. As he rode past, he grabbed hold of him and hauled him back up onto his own horse. He took one last glance at the Frenchmen in disgust, but there was not an ounce of remorse for what they had done. Craven growled as he turned about and fled from the field. It was a bitter withdrawal, but the group's desire for blood had been smashed on the rocks as they licked their wounds and counted themselves lucky to not have fallen to the same fate as the local peasants. Craven stopped one last time as he reached a treeline to look back at the enemy, just in time to see Major Claveria join the cavalry with several of his officers. He lifted his hat in salute as an insulting gesture. It worked, but Craven was not foolish enough to look for another fight as he turned about and left.

Their return to camp was a solemn affair. Ferreira spotted them approaching from afar and looked in disbelief at the state in which they returned. They had five riderless horses in tow, and few had escaped without wounds. As Craven came to a stop before him, his face was black with powder residue mixed with sweat and wood smoke. He was at a loss, but before he could say a word, Nickle toppled off the horse and crashed to the ground. Craven leapt down in concern as Paget rushed to his aid. They turned him over to find he was pale and weak. Craven touched a dark patch on his brown jacket and found it was wet with blood. He opened it to find a piercing wound in the chest. Matthys rushed to help them, but he needed just one quick glance to know the young man's fate was sealed. He shook his head solemnly.

"Sorry," the dying man muttered.

"No, this was not your fault. It was mine," replied Craven.

"Jonnie?" Paget took his hand and looked into his eyes, but the life faded from him before he could say another word.

"No, you can't die!" Paget looked to Craven to do something. Yet the Captain got up and walked away in anger. He stopped and looked up at the sky, trying to understand how it had come to this.

"He's gone," Matthys said to Paget, who struggled to accept it and began to weep. Even Major Thornhill looked stunned as he dismounted to see the dead officer in Paget's arms.

"What the hell happened out there?" Ferreira demanded.

"Total slaughter," replied Thornhill.

* * *

The last shovels of dirt were laid down over the graves of the town just a few hundred yards from the sight of the slaughter. Moxy knelt at the feet of one with a cross he had engraved simply with the name Ana, for he knew nothing else of her name. Pero pushed a cross into another grave of his aunt as his younger brother watched on. Nickle was buried beside them, too. They were all were gathered around in a circle, mustering the best service they could. The Caçadores lined up and to attention with their rifles ready for a final salute to the fallen officer.

"Would you like to say a few words?" Matthys asked Craven.

He could not muster any, and so the Sergeant went on as the closest thing they had to a priest.

"The people of this place embraced us as family. They welcomed us into their homes and into their hearts. They fed and clothed us. They worked to win this war in all the ways they could. Our Bandido brothers fought like lions and will be remembered as heroes. Lieutenant Jonnie Nickle gave his life for this land and these people, and he shall not be forgotten. May their souls rest in piece and be remembered for an eternity."

Matthys nodded towards Ferreira who called out his orders in English so they would all understand.

"Present arms! Fire!"

The volley echoed about the whole valley and was the moment they had all been dreading. The moment they had to decide what to do next. Craven finally stepped up to Matthys knowing they needed some words from him, and yet still could not find them, and so it was Thorny who stepped up.

"I know you are hurting; we all are. But this is war. People die, sometimes those who should never have been in harm's way. But what happened here tells me one thing, the work you have done these past weeks is working. The enemy is desperate. A desperate enemy is a very dangerous one, but we must not lose sight of what we have to do. Now is not the time to stop. I must return to the army, but I will be back. Do not despair. This is a foul day, but many better ones are yet to come. Keep your resolve, and trust in one another."

He walked away to his horse, leaving Craven once again as the senior officer. All eyes were on him now, as they needed hope, or something to hold on to. He coughed to clear his throat, trying to set aside his own emotions.

"We've been through a lot together, and we will go through a lot more. This is not the end. For that is what the enemy wants. We will not submit to them, but we must take stock and lick our wounds. See to one another, and take two day's rest. Let us heal wounds and hearts, and let's have a great feast this night in honour of those we have lost."

Moxy sighed as he walked away in anger, heading for his horse tied up nearby.

"Back to the camp, get some rest!"

Craven went after his Welsh friend, reaching him just as he began to untie the reins from a post.

"What are you doing?"

"I'm going home."

"What? Why are you doing that?"

"You know why."

Craven grabbed him and shook him strongly in frustration.

"So, you would leave us? You would leave your brothers?"

"You are not my brothers."

"You're wrong there, Moxy. We're the only brothers you've got. Can't you see that?"

He didn't look convinced as Craven laid his hands on Moxy's shoulders in a friendlier tone.

"Look, I know it is an awful time. I get it, I really do, but this is no time to walk away from each other. Ana and Maria, and all the people of this town fought for their freedom in the only ways they knew how. How many more people like them are out there at the mercy of the French? You've seen what they are willing to do. They rule through fear. And still these people resisted, would you leave their country folk to the mercy of the French?"

Moxy was inflamed by his sentiment.

"What would you care? You didn't come here to fight for anyone but yourself," he spat back.

Craven nodded in agreement.

"Yes, I did, but people change. You didn't come here looking for love, did you? And yet you found it. Maybe we all found something here. Something we didn't know we were even looking for," replied Craven sincerely.

"So what would you have me do?"

"Mourn those we have lost, but fight for those who remain."

Moxy sighed and finally nodded in agreement.

"Good, now find us something to eat, and do what you do best, shoot."

He nodded again, and Craven tapped him on the shoulder in a friendly gesture. He then went to find Thorny before he left. He found him standing beside his horse reloading his pistols before he set out.

"You know you can carry as many pistols you like, but eventually you run out of shot."

"Captain, if you get yourself into such trouble where eight shots is not enough, then you have larger problems than may be resolved with a sword."

"I beg to differ, but thanks."

"What happened here is a tragedy, and Wellesley will hear of it, but it is far from the first atrocity in this war. The French are encouraged to terrorise the people in the lands they conquer. A simple means to suppress a populace. There are those in England who would follow the same methods, were it not for men like Wellesley."

"What would you have us do?"

"You know what you must do, for you have already been doing it, and that message you intercepted?"

"What of it?"

"It confirms all we had thought. The French still believe we will enter Spain to the North, following up on our victory at Porto. The enemy is much in the dark, and that is where we must keep them." He finished loading the last of his pistols and dropped it into the holster before climbing onto his horse.

"Good luck, Captain," he declared and led his horse away.

CHAPTER 11

The clash of singlesticks echoed through the clearing as conversation went on. Craven was sharpening his sword when he stopped at the sound of laughter. It was the first time he had heard such joy in several days. Since that fateful day when they had all lost so much, though some more than others. Moxy was sitting alone and still wanted little interaction with anyone, but it was remarkable to see some good returning to their lives. Though Paget felt the loss as heavily as Moxy, his youthfulness seemingly taken away in one swift and cruel day.

"Captain?" Nuno asked. Craven looked up to see the Bandido looming over him.

"What is it?"

"It has been long enough. You saw what they did to us. We must find them and make them pay!" he roared passionately.

Craven didn't have the heart to shoot him down and so got to his feet. Those training with sticks came to a stop as they heard the commotion. The Captain studied all of their faces. They were looking to him for answers, and yet he had none for them. Before he could say a word, a rider galloped into the camp. It was Ellis.

"There's a carriage and several horsemen on the road."

"A carriage?" Craven asked in amazement, for no one so wealthy would choose to travel on such dangerous roads filled with soldiers and Bandidos. He rushed to his horse and climbed up into the saddle.

"What are your orders?" Matthys asked.

Craven shrugged as he tore off down the track back to the road where he could intercept the carriage, more out of curiosity than anything else.

"Go with him!" Matthys shouted across to Ellis, infuriated that the Captain would rush off alone.

Craven reached the road just in time to see several of the horsemen come into view. They wore British uniforms; which was a relief, but their attire was most surprising. There were eight cavalrymen dressed in that of the British light cavalry, with their ubiquitous fur mohawk rising up and over their peaked Tarleton helmets. They wore the Hussars dolman, short cut, and well fitted with a decadent amount of buttons and lace, and yet it was not blue as was the uniform of the British light cavalry. Their jackets were crimson red. Craven had only seen such cavalry operating as Yeomanry back home. Behind them was a carriage, which they were escorting, but he soon recognised another face of one other rider between the cavalry and the carriage, for it was Major Thornhill.

The Captain of the cavalry drew them to a halt as they reached Craven. They didn't even look surprised to see him or wary in any way, but they did have an air of confidence and arrogance about them, as if they had wholeheartedly committed to the Hussar reputation.

"Good afternoon, Captain," Thorny greeted him.

He seemed to be in good spirits, but also had a mysterious and perhaps even mischievous look about him. Craven could not help but give in to his curiosity and urged his horse on so he may get a look inside the carriage. As he got closer, his eyes widened. He was astonished at the sight of the lady looking back at him.

"Hello, James," said the Lady Sarmento.

"If we may have a few moments of your time, Captain, I bring news," added Thorny.

Soon enough they were back at the clearing, and the Bandidos looked on in amazement at the finely dressed lady. She couldn't look more out of place amongst such a simple place they called home, and a canvas tent was considered a luxury. They watched her with awe from a distance as she caught up with Paget. He seemed to perk up at her presence and forget many of his woes, whilst Major Thornhill conversed in private with Craven and Ferreira.

"Before we begin, what is she doing here? Do you know how dangerous these parts are?" Craven pointed to the lady, remembering how much trouble she had gotten them into last time.

"The Lady Sarmento is on her way into Spain where she will meet with General Gregorio García de la Cuesta," replied Thorny, as if that should mean something to Craven, but he looked none the wiser, causing Thorny to sigh with frustration as he went on, "General Cuesta who commands the Spanish

Army in the South. I know Wellesley discussed this with you."

"We discussed a lot, but a Spanish General hundreds of miles away is of little concern to me."

"Well, it should be. If we are to engage the French in open battle, we will need Cuesta's army, and at present he is unwilling to move or agree to any plans with which Wellesley proposes."

He got out his map and pointed to a town named Abrantes.

"Wellesley is here, on the River Tagus, a river which runs all the way to Madrid, but it is a long river indeed. Our army remains forty miles inside of Portugal when it should be well on its way through Spain whilst we still maintain the element of surprise."

"Why isn't it, Sir?" Craven asked impatiently.

"General Cuesta," groaned Thorny, "Cuesta will not agree to a plan, and moreover he promises to maintain supplies to Wellesley, and yet is barely able to do so for his own troops. For whatever reason, Cuesta will not be moved, and any attempt to do so had failed. That is where the Lady Sarmento comes in. She is an old friend to Cuesta, and she may be able to change his mood in ways others have failed."

"You are sending her all the way to this Cuesta, across the border and through French occupied territory, with nothing more than this handful of jumped up parade ponies?" He looked across at the cavalrymen and their beautifully kept uniforms.

"Do not be fooled. They may be a new outfit, but they are formed from the very best of bilingual Portuguese soldiers. That is Captain Suarez of the Corps of Mounted Guides."

"Never heard of them."

"That is rather the point. The Guides are many things;

they are in fact whatever they need to be. Soldiers, spies, provosts. They are most capable men, and they have been tasked with this mission which is of vital importance."

"I don't give a damn who they are. They aren't near enough protection for the lady to cross the border. They shouldn't have even brought her this far. You know how dangerous these lands are. You have seen it yourself."

"Yes, all the more need for this mission to be a success. We must break this stalemate and whatever it is that is holding the General back. Wellesley cannot advance into Spain until he has the reassurance of the support of Cuesta."

"If it is of the utmost importance, you will need more than them to keep the lady safe," insisted Craven.

The Major shrugged as if didn't know what to say.

"I will join the escort, and you and your men are coming with me. Have your men ready and mounted," Craven pointed across to Ferreira.

"You have work to do here," replied Thorny.

"Yes, there is work to be done, and more than capable men shall remain to do it. We will make sure the lady reaches the General and back. I will not have a repeat of last time, not in my care or anyone else's," Craven said firmly as he went over to the lady to announce his decision.

"You didn't just come here to bring news, did you?" Ferreira asked the Major, yet he had nothing to say, despite a smug expression.

"And the road the lady must take is far to the South. She needn't not have come this way," he went on.

Still there was nothing from Thorny.

"You knew Craven would go with her?" Ferreira smiled.

"Sometimes men need to be given the opportunity to make the best decisions for them and others. Nobody forced the Captain to do anything here."

It amused Ferreira to see Thorny's plan unfold precisely as he'd planned it whilst Craven saw himself as a rebel for seemingly going against orders.

"Captain, interesting company you keep here," marvelled the lady as Craven approached.

"They might not look like much, but they'll do in a fight," he replied in their defence, having already begun to respect them for their willingness to fight.

"What can I do for you, Captain?"

"It is more what I can do for you. You are crossing dangerous territory with these eight men, can they even fight?"

Captain Suarez clearly heard him, and Craven made no attempt to be subtle. The Portuguese officer stiffened up as he took the insult for what it was, his hand slowly reaching for his sword as if to defend his own honour.

"I wouldn't," declared Thorny.

The officer froze.

"I have no doubt you are a fine swordsman, but that is James Craven, celebrated prizefighter."

"I know who he is. The same Craven who lost the Lady Sarmento when under his care," seethed Suarez.

"And got her back," replied Craven with a smile.

"You are no soldier. You are a fool playing at war."

Craven looked up in surprise. The scene was tense, and several casually reached for weapons as if it could explode at any moment, but instead Craven burst into laughter. They soon relaxed as he went to the Captain and put a friendly arm on his shoulder.

"My friend, if this is a game, then I shall play to win."

"You would have this man join us?" Suarez asked Thorny furiously.

"Captain, this is the Army, and we are in it together. Be grateful of help when it is offered, for the day you need it, and it is not you will regret your pride."

"And Wellesley's orders, are you not to lead us?" Paget asked, as if fearful of losing him.

"Our work here will continue as ordered, and you will lead it."

Paget looked stunned.

"Our work here is important, but the safety of the lady is also of the utmost importance to the war, and I will see her to the General and back."

Paget didn't argue with him, but he didn't look confident about his newfound responsibilities either, especially as it dawned on him he would be the only officer remaining.

"Lean on Sergeant Keck." Craven gestured towards Matthys, as they all knew him.

"We'll be just fine," insisted Matthys.

"The enemy has changed strategy, and so must we. Don't make the same mistake I did. I let my emotions get the better of me, and we paid dearly for it."

"We were all of one mind," admitted Matthys, and the others were firmly in agreement. There was not one amongst them who did not want to go after the enemy and exact their revenge, and despite their losses they still found some satisfaction in the toll they had exacted on the enemy.

"Still, it was my decision to make. You have to be smarter

than that. We all do. We've all rested enough, so let us be on our way," he ordered as he went to gather his things, taking only what he could carry on his saddle. Thorny approached as he began to tie down his equipment.

"Believe me when I say this. The importance of a positive outcome from General Cuesta cannot be stated more highly."

"And yet you send Lady Sarmento of all people?"

"Only because all before her have failed. Cuesta doesn't like Wellesley and seems set to refuse any agreement he might suggest. The reasons why are his own, but one can guess."

"Wellesley rules the armies of Portugal, and this Cuesta doesn't want the same for Spain?"

Thorny looked impressed.

"It's not hard to imagine."

"Be wary of this Cuesta. He is a noble man and no coward, but he does not appreciate being told what to do or how to think."

"You have met him?"

"Of course. I tried my hand and failed. Somehow, you and the Lady Sarmento must succeed where others have failed. You are the last negotiators I would ever send, and so perhaps now you understand our position. Wellesley gathers his supplies, he has reorganised the army into the four divisions who led us across the Douro. But in all honesty, Wellesley cannot march on to Spain without reassurances from Cuesta, or I fear another retreat the likes of which would even overshadow the retreat to Corunna."

"Then we must not fail," smiled Craven.

"Many a gentleman has before you."

"Then perhaps it is time for something different," he

replied as he climbed onto his horse.

"Can I give you a little advice?"

"Sure."

"Get yourself a pistol, at least one for the love of God."

"My sword does just fine."

"Yeah? And without my pistols, you'd be a dead man."

Craven nodded in appreciation.

Suarez led the Captain back the carriage before climbing onto his horse. He sat bolt upright in his saddle, puffing his chest out as if he were on parade and looking down on Craven and his green-jacketed compatriots.

"Captain Ferreira, take up position at the head of the column if you would!" Craven ordered.

Suarez was immediately incensed.

"Captain, you may tag along for this ride, but I am in charge of this mission!"

"You are in charge of the defence of Lady Sarmento. Ferreira's Caçadores are expert marksmen who would blow your head off before you knew you were even in a fight. You keep the lady safe, and we will keep you out of trouble."

Suarez looked to Thorny to intervene, but he would not.

"Good luck to you all," he replied, saluting the three Captains as they departed.

"What have you got us into?" Ferreira questioned.

Craven merely smiled in response.

"For a man who didn't come to Portugal to fight, you sure are picking a lot of fights."

"Who said anything about fighting? This is an escort duty. We get in and out quickly, and without incident."

"When is anything you do without incident?" Ferreira

laughed.

CHAPTER 12

"You see that, Sir?" Matthys peaked out through the narrow gaps of the closed window shutters on the second floor of a farmhouse. He was pointing to movement on the road ahead where French infantrymen came up over the crest.

"You are sure this is a good idea?" Paget replied.

"Captain Craven said we needed to change strategy, and that is just what we're going to do. The enemy is having to move further into the country as they look for homes to burn. They have had to spread themselves thin. Their cavalry are many miles away according to the Major.

"And if there are too many of them?"

"These walls are thick." Matthys slammed his fist down onto the stone windowsill.

Paget still looked anxious, though more so for having been left in charge than having to face the enemy, and the Sergeant could see it.

"Sir, if I may say so, the Captain would not have left you in charge should he not have absolute confidence in you."

"Or maybe he had no other choice."

"Craven is a rogue, not a fool. You may think he lives free and easy, but he cares about his friends more than he lets on."

"Thank you," replied Paget sincerely, knowing precisely what the Sergeant was doing. He looked out to the hedgerow stretching out in parallel with the road leading up to and beside the house. It looked like any other, but he knew what lay in wait behind it, and the same for a similarly empty looking barn, the doors of which had been left open as if the owners had fled in a hurry. It was a tranquil sight, were it not for the French infantrymen advancing on them.

"The cavalry, they will come for us again, won't they?"

"Yes, but they can't be in all places. We will not fight them on their ground again."

They both remembered the bloody brawl that had left both sides reeling. The enemy was still far into the distance, and there was nothing to do but wait for them now, until they could see the whites of their eyes as one American officer had once ordered. All preparations had been made.

"Do you believe the Captain will succeed?"

"I do. He is a resourceful man and has pulled victory from the jaws of death more than once."

"But he does not go to fight, but to talk, to mediate and change the mind of a stubborn man. Is he up to the task?"

"That is Lady Sarmento's job. The Captain only has to keep her safe, for which we know he is most capable."

"I fear the Captain is unable to remain silent."

Matthys chuckled in agreement.

"Don't you worry about Craven. If he cannot bend the will of heaven, he would simply move hell."

"I'm not sure that is an encouraging thought," sniffed Paget.

The room fell silent as they waited and watched the French amble into their ambush. It was a satisfying sight. They knew what the soldiers had in mind as they torched homes wherever they found them. Moxy had his rifle resting at the corner of another windowsill nearby, watching the enemy like a hawk and desperately wanting to take his shot, for he could have ended any one of them in the last few minutes.

"This is it, one hundred yards," declared Matthys as he watched the first Frenchman pass a tree with a white marker they had painted on it.

"Just a little further," insisted Paget, "Come on, come on," he whispered to himself, tapping his pistol up and down in his left hand. He finally looked to Matthys to confirm the distance, and the Sergeant merely nodded in agreement.

"When you're ready, Moxham," he ordered.

The Welshman couldn't be more pleased to exact some revenge and had already picked out his target, a sergeant, marked out by the single yellow stripe on the cuff of his uniform. Moxy squeezed the trigger, and the tranquil scene was in one second changed as the Frenchman went down. His compatriots looked around in shock, unsure what had happened or even where the shot had come from. They had been too busy in conversation to see the muzzle flash. Yet before they could recover, a line of Bandidos rose up from the hedgerow where they had been concealed and opened fire on the French. They were completely exposed to their fire at close range.

Six of the infantrymen fell from the first volley, and shots from the house and barn followed as more were picked off, but catching the attention of one of the enemy officers. He drew his sword and called out to rally his men and lead them forward in a charge against the house.

Sporadic fire continued to ring out, but the Frenchmen stormed towards the house fearlessly. It had been what Paget feared the most, for they were too few to resist such a sizeable force in hand-to-hand combat. He placed his pistol in his left hand and drew out his sword, readying himself for the worst. As the officer led the charge forward, he was shot down by Moxy's second shot. He showed no mercy or hesitation in gunning down the enemy leader. A junior officer continued on, but their pace had slowed at the loss of their leader, and another volley from the Bandidos ripped through their ranks. Paget took his shot now and hit one of the men in the shoulder, causing him to lose his musket and retreat to the rear, yet they were just ten yards from the house now.

"Cavalerie!" yelled one of the Frenchmen in horror as he pointed up to the top of the field.

The troops came to a standstill as they took heed of the warning. The assault came to a standstill, and the troops quickly began to run, soon struck by yet another volley from the Bandidos. Little more than thirty were still on their feet and able to run when the thunderous sound of hooves echoed through the building. Paget rushed to the door in amazement at their luck, yet it was not what he had expected or hoped for. Timmerman charged down the hill at the head of his own Bandidos and the few red-coated entourage he had brought to Portugal with him. He had his sabre in hand and cried out in

French enthusiastically to insult the enemy further as he ran them down. Pero and Nuno yelled with excitement as the horsemen rushed after the fleeing French troops. They had no scruples about Timmerman and his methods. They only wanted to see the enemy pay for what they had done to the locals.

Matthys and the others began to step out of the two buildings as they watched the pursuit unfold. What remained of Craven's unit was barely distinguishable from the Bandidos. They wore the locally sourced jackets that had resulted from Paget's own recommendations. Yet as he watched the mounted Bandidos run down the fleeing enemy, he couldn't help but feel sick. He unbuttoned the jacket, revealing his redcoat beneath, for he had never removed it, having too much pride to serve without it. Cheers continued to ring out as Timmerman put the Frenchmen to the sabre. He cackled as he ran amongst the enemy, hacking at them wildly.

"Let's move out," he ordered with no enthusiasm at all as he went to collect his horse from behind the house.

"We won," declared Birback excitedly.

"There is no honour in a butchering," replied Paget.

"I'll take my life over honour," replied Charlie.

But Paget was not convinced as he mounted and led them away. They were heading back down the same road the French had come up. It was lined with bodies, which he had to navigate. They didn't bother to clear up. The locals would sort it out if the French did not. They had only gotten half a mile when they found Timmerman and his men gathered around three carts carrying families and handing over foodstuffs to the Major. He was on foot with several of his men whilst the horses were held nearby. The families looked terrified.

"What is the meaning of this?" Paget demanded.

"It is hot and heavy work out there, but the spoils go to the victor!" Timmerman roared as he slicked back his sweaty hair and wiped his face with his sleeve before biting into an apple taken from the locals. He was sitting against a large rock relaxing after the heavy work they had just witnessed.

"We do not take from these people," insisted Paget.

When he got no response, he leapt from his horse and stormed towards the Major who continued on as he pleased.

"Give them back what is theirs," demanded Paget quietly as if to not cause embarrassment amongst the men.

"Why? We fight for these people. The least they can do is feed us," replied Timmerman casually.

Paget was in no mood to be toyed with as he had reached boiling point.

"Give it back!" he roared boldly for all to hear.

The playful look on Timmerman's face was quickly wiped away as he scowled at Paget.

"These peasants?" He tossed the apple at one of the men, striking him in the face and drawing laughter from the Bandidos following him.

"Shame on you, Sir. You may choose to act like an animal, but you have no right to treat these people as such!"

It was clear he had been pushed over the edge, and Matthys could see him reaching for his sword as he went forward. Timmerman closed the distance to meet him. The Sergeant leapt in between them and held them at bay.

"Enough of this!"

Timmerman shrugged him off and struck him a hard punch to the temple that dropped him in one. The Sergeant looked dazed as he lay on his knees. Yet Timmerman was not done and brutally kicked him to the face whilst he was down. Paget reached for his sword, but was yanked out of the way by Birback, who to the amazement of the stunned Sergeant went right for the Major. He grabbed him by the collar and smashed him in the face with a brutal head butt before throwing him back down against the rock where he had been resting moments before.

His comrades quickly drew weapons, but Paget's squad did the same, with rifles trained on Timmerman and his closest allies before they could draw blades. Timmerman wiped blood from his nose as he got back to his feet and looked at them with furious contempt. He reached for his sword, but Moxy cried out, "Don't!"

Timmerman looked into the Welshman's eyes and could see this was no bluff. He was quite ready to shoot an officer. He let go of his sword, not wanting to test Moxy further before scowling at Birback.

"You have struck an officer. You know what that means, you'll hang for this!"

"He will not!" Paget cried.

"Who do you think you are talking to?"

"A scoundrel not fit to wear your uniform, and one who is not in favour with Sir Arthur Wellesley, and yet I have his ear."

Timmerman laughed at him.

"One man fought in my defence, and should you raise issue, I will be sure to make Wellesley aware that you attacked me."

"You make the excuses of a woman," Timmerman blurted out.

"And you have none of the grace of one, nor the honour of a gentleman."

Timmerman finally smiled, knowing he was between a rock and a hard place. He went back to his horse and mounted up, signalling for his associates to back down.

"This is no place for weakness. The weak never survive."

Timmerman sought to insult Paget with one final pass, but the young man would not rise to the occasion, for he knew he must enjoy the small victory Birback had achieved. Timmerman spat on the floor before them and then led his troop away. Finally, when they were a good distance away, Paget breathed a sigh of relief.

Birback helped Matthys back to his feet. He looked just as surprised by his help as he was to see him fighting in their defence.

"You took a hell of a chance there."

"He had it coming."

Matthys still looked astonished, as he'd never thought of Birback as anything more than a selfish brute, and now found himself with a newfound respect for the man who he thought he had already figured out.

"We should move on before any more trouble comes our way," insisted Charlie.

CHAPTER 13

"He doesn't much like me, does he?" Craven asked Ferreira as they rode on through the peaceful countryside.

"Who?"

"The Captain of those Hussar imposters," grumbled Craven.

"I don't think he likes many people, but he sure does like that uniform."

"We have their sort back in England, the Yeomanry, civilians who don uniforms, and gallop about as they play war. Some are genuinely as good as any cavalryman you will find on the continent, but those are few and far between. Many enjoy playing at being a solider than actually being one."

"And you think he is one of those?"

"I don't know yet, but watch yourself. Just because a man has the finest of military equipment, that is no indicator of his skill or knowledge of any of it."

"Well, I guess we are about to find out."

Ferreira came to a stop and pointed forward. Through the trees they could see movement ahead where a troop of French cavalry watered their horses at a stream. The column came to a halt behind them, but they soon heard the gallop of Captain Suarez as he came to see what the hold up was for. Craven signalled for him to slow down and be quiet, and yet the Captain did as he pleased as he strode right up to them.

"What is the meaning of this?"

"Enemy cavalry ahead," replied Craven angrily.

"How many?" he demanded, as he spurred his horse forward for a better look.

"Enough to cause us trouble."

"I see eleven horses, nothing we cannot handle," he insisted.

"You can go right at them if you want, but you will get men killed."

"And I suppose you think you could do it better?"

"Smarter, and with less risk, yes."

"This is what we are trained for," Ferreira added.

"All right, Captain, do it your way, but on your head be it should you put us in more danger than we already are. What would you have us do?"

"Get the lady's carriage well back for a start, and then have your men take up position beyond that bank," he ordered and pointed to a drop on the other side of the road.

"And then?"

"Wait for a volley, and then you come out for your moment of glory."

Suarez imagined the opportunity before turning back to

see to the lady's safety.

"You think you can trust him not to mess this up?" Ferreira asked.

"It is a simple plan, what could go wrong?" he replied with a mischievous smile.

"What plan?"

"Set your men up along that treeline and wait."

"Wait for what?"

"The French think they came here to hunt us, so let them think the hunt is on."

Ferreira looked confused.

"Paget had us cover these tunics to not be seen, but sometimes that is precisely what you want," he replied mysteriously.

Ferreira shook his head but did as ordered. Craven continued to watch the enemy for any sign they had caught on to their presence as the horses were moved and the carriage rattled along the road. They seemed completely oblivious to the noise, and Craven could see why. There was a fast flowing section of water caused by a small shelf. He licked his lips as he could imagine the taste of the fresh water that was always welcome after a long march, but especially in such heat. He looked back to see the carriage had already gone out of sight, and the Portuguese Guides had vanished from view as he had asked. Ferreira's riflemen were in positions amongst the trees where they could only be seen if you knew to look for them. They clung to the foliage and tree trunks, their brown uniforms blending in seamlessly.

Craven rubbed his chin as he readied himself for what he must do. He looked down at his red tunic and smiled.

"Like a cloak to the bull," he smirked.

He kicked in his heels and spurred his horse forward, rushing out into the open along the road leading directly towards the stream. It didn't take long to catch the attention of the Frenchmen. He quickly brought his horse to an abrupt stop, kicking up a cloud of dust as if panicked by their presence. Several of the enemy cried out as they leapt onto their horses, seeing the opportunity for what it was. For like their attacks on French messengers, this appeared the perfect opportunity to turn the tables.

Turning his horse about, Craven appeared to flee from the cavalry with all haste as they rushed on after him, eager to catch their unexpected prize. Craven stormed across the open ground and could hear the gallop of horses in the distance, yet he soon slowed and came about. The first Frenchman who came into view stopped thirty yards short. He was suspicious as to why their prey had turned to face them. The rest came to a standstill and looked about as if suspecting a trap, but it was too late.

Rifles rang out, and several of the Frenchmen were killed instantly whilst the same number were wounded. An excited cheer rang out from over the ridge, and the men of the Corps of Guides stormed over the crest, their Hussar uniforms unmistakeable. They waved huge sabres about their heads, the famed 1796 light cavalry sabre which the French had come to fear for its tremendous cutting power. The eight cavalrymen charged with grace and all the vigour they could muster as if they were at the head of an entire brigade.

Craven drew his sword and placed it into his left hand once more and raced on to join them as they clashed with the Frenchmen. They had barely managed to gain any pace as the

Portuguese rushed into their position. Suarez was still bolt upright in his saddle as if on parade as he fought one of the Frenchmen. He looked fearless as he dealt with his adversary just as Craven reached the melee. Yet the work was all but done as he made his first attack, only to find the Frenchman cut down by one of the Guides. Suarez passed another and gave a strong back stroke, and the fighting was over just as quickly as it had begun. Suarez looked pleased with himself and his men, and he surveyed the scene and their complete victory, with just a single light cut on the bridle hand of one of his men. Ferreira soon came to join them, mounted once again as his riflemen followed him out from the treeline.

"Outstanding, Craven, that was a fine plan, nice work."

"Nice work? It was we who did the work, your riflemen and my Hussars. This was the work of our countrymen, not his," growled Suarez as he wiped his blade down with a small cloth. He sheathed it once more and went back to find the Lady Sarmento and her carriage.

"And you thought I was salty?" Ferreira asked Craven.

"He knows we're on the same side, right?"

"He's clearly got a lot to prove."

"That is what worries me."

"Really?" Ferreira asked in an accusing tone.

Craven did not get his meaning.

"You're just like him," laughed Ferreira.

"What?" Craven did not look impressed.

"Stubborn, proud, fearless, and a braggart, it must be like looking in a mirror."

Craven initially looked angry but tried to wrap his head around it, for he hadn't seen it himself. He saw nothing similar in the arrogant Portuguese officer.

"Get moving, we cannot lose time," insisted Suarez as he returned with the carriage and pointed for them to go on, leading the way.

* * *

"Where the hell is Birback?" Matthys asked as he carried a stack of firewood to the camp, "Anyone seen Birback?"

Grumbles followed as nobody had any news for him whilst he stacked the wood near the fire. Paget was looking after it and throwing more logs on as it got going.

"Have you seen Birback?" Matthys asked him.

"Not for a while. He's probably foraging."

"For food?"

Paget shrugged.

"It's getting a bit late. He'll want to be back soon."

"Thank you for today," declared Paget.

"For what, Sir?"

"For putting yourself between me and Timmerman. You didn't have to do that, and it could have cost you everything."

"It is my job to look after everyone here, and that is what I will do."

"But Timmerman, you know what he's like, you know what he's capable of."

"Yes, I do." Matthys pawed at his swollen head from where he had been struck down.

"He must be dealt with, mustn't he?"

"Who?" Matthys looked to the Ensign with concern.

"Timmerman. He's already tried to kill the Captain several times, and I fear he would gladly kill any one of us should he expect to get away with it."

"Don't you worry about him. Craven will see to him."

"Captain Craven isn't here. We are," fretted Paget.

"We've made a difference here, you know that, Sir?"

Paget did not respond.

"This was never going to be an easy mission. It is no field battle with a clear winner and loser. This is a grind. Wellesley wanted us to raise hell, and that's just what we've done, and continue to do."

The last rays of light were fading when Birback finally rode into camp.

"I hope you brought a feast!" Charlie yelled at him.

"I wish."

"Nothing?" Ellis asked.

"The hills are empty. The French have taken everything."

"You're the worst hunter ever," laughed Charlie.

"Too big and loud to be a hunter," joked Moxy.

Birback smiled as he took it in his stride, which struck Matthys as strange. It was the second time he had been surprised by him that day. He wondered if the ruffian was at a turning point, but nonetheless he was glad to see him back as they all sat down to enjoy a meal beneath the stars.

* * *

Craven marvelled at the sight of the Spanish army as they were escorted along a road through the camp. The British Army in the Peninsula was so often spread out over large areas when in camp, so as to not drain the resources of one area and be too large a burden on the locals, but Cuesta had gathered his force together in a powerful display of strength. Leading them on was an older officer who was an aide de camp to the General, being one of his closest advisors. Craven had never seen a uniform the likes of which the man wore, for it was a bright lime green with pale blue facings. He wore a huge bicorne hat with an equally large black plume and carried his sword in a well polished and gleaming solid brass scabbard, the likes of which would usually only be seen in full dress, if at all. It was like nothing he would ever expect to see a military man wearing, especially in the field. Though as they passed through the camp, they found it equally as colourful. Tunics of white, red, green, and blue all mingled together. There was not the uniformity he had come to expect, and yet they had the numbers and wore their uniforms with as much pride as any man. Ferreira didn't look impressed, for his countrymen wore far more reserved attire.

"A fine sight, are they not?" Craven asked him.

"Peacocks," replied Ferreira.

"What?"

"That is how they dress, not for war."

"And a red tunic is any better?"

"Not particularly, but at least it is consistent," scowled Ferreira.

"Listen, I don't care if they go into battle bare buttocked, we need them. Wellesley needs them, and if we can't get them, we might all be in a world of trouble."

"And you believe they will defeat Napoleon's armies?"

"What do you know of Cuesta?"

"He is hot headed, but also brave. He has marched several armies into battle with no chance of victory, but he had some success, too."

"Not a man to rely on, then?"

"He is a patriot and would give everything for his country, but he is no military genius."

"Have you met him?"

Ferreira laughed.

"How would I have met him? I am a Captain in Portugal, and he is a General in Spain. Do you know many generals outside of England?"

Craven shrugged in admittance of his silly question.

"But you know these things about him?"

"I know the news, and I know what soldiers say."

"What soldiers say? And you trust that?"

"It has some value. I will take what news I can get."

They soon reached a tree-lined road leading to a large palace. Cavalry exercised on the gardens leading up the grand structure whose tall towers dominated the landscape. Lavish and exotic columns around it were an instant reminder of the nation's Moorish past, decadence that had been embraced by the triumphant populace who now treasured the architecture they had conquered. Everywhere they looked there were soldiers, more than Craven had ever seen in one place.

"Cuesta says he has thirty thousand, you think that is accurate?"

"I'd say so," gasped Ferreira as he thought of the seemingly endless camp they had passed through, and he marvelled at the huge force all around them.

"If that were true, this Cuesta could field a larger army

than Wellesley."

"Which is why his help is so important, but the General must be desperate to resort to this."

"Desperate?"

"The Lady Sarmento is an incredible woman, but sending her to negotiate for an alliance? How many officers must have tried before us?"

"Wellesley sent the lady, not us. We are merely here to keep her safe. I am no diplomat, and you are probably worse still."

Ferreira smiled and nodded in agreement, for he didn't like many people and was not good at being tactful. They reached the entrance to the grand home and came to a stop. Craven leapt down and looked back. Suarez was already at the Lady Sarmento's carriage and opening her door to help her down.

"You will be seen to your accommodation," declared the Aide-de-Camp.

"Thank you," replied Craven.

"Good luck," Ferreira gloated, for he knew it was not going to be an easy job, nor would an English officer be likely made welcome by a General who clearly had some issue with Wellesley.

"Oh, no, you are coming with me."

"You think I can make any difference in there?" Ferreira questioned.

"No, but you can back me up."

Ferreira sighed in frustration, but passed on his orders to his men. He then dismounted, passing the reins of his horse to one of them.

"You don't ever make my life easy," he groaned.

"No, but I save it from being boring."

"That is certainly true."

Suarez led the Lady Sarmento inside with the two other Captains following. They passed several cavalry officers who were in a heated debate. Craven understood little of their language, yet Ferreira smirked as they went past.

"Did you understand what that was about?"

"I can't speak the language, but it is close enough to my own for me to get their meaning. They're not happy."

"Regarding what?"

"Everything."

"They worry about facing he French alone, just like Wellesley, don't they?" he pressed.

"It would seem so."

They were led through the decadent property as Craven studied each and every item of gold and silver and everything of value. It was a palace of which he had always dreamed of, and Ferreira noticed him eyeing everything up.

"Don't you dare! This is no place for games."

"I wouldn't dream of it," smirked Craven.

Eventually, they stepped out into a closed inner garden. Large columns supported the terrace. It was a classical Roman closed garden, allowing privacy and security, shade, and yet sunlight. Water features and flowers made for a beautiful sight, and at the far end was General Cuesta. He was pushing seventy years old and really looked it, for as he turned to greet them, he was stiff and pained as if by both age and injury. His fine long hair had long faded to grey. He appeared as a man well past his best days. Craven began to wonder why he was the man in charge. Whether he was an expert politician to have secured the position, or merely the nation was desperate, and he was the best they had. The closed gardens were vast, almost large enough to conduct a parade, and Craven could only imagine how exceptional a fencing salle they would make.

"Welcome, My Lady," declared Cuesta with a smile. He bowed a little before her, and she returned the gesture.

Cuesta was not just very old for a soldier; he was also rather portly. He had the look of a soldier long retired and expecting to live out his days in peace and opulence.

"May I introduce Captains Suarez, Craven, and Ferreira," declared the lady with a smile.

"Wellesley sent captains to negotiate the future of our armies?" Cuesta asked as if insulted.

"Sir, Sir Arthur Wellesley sent the Lady Sarmento. We are merely here to ensure her safety on a dangerous road," insisted Suarez.

"And it was left to captains?"

"It was left to fighting men," Craven interrupted.

Cuesta looked curious as Craven spoke out against him and took an interest in the only Englishman amongst them.

"And you are a fighting man, Captain?" Cuesta stepped up before him.

"Sir, it was Captain Craven who led our forces to victory over the Douro." Ferreira quickly came to his aid.

Cuesta did not take his eyes from Craven as he continued unconvinced. "A stroke of luck, I hear. You caught the French napping, but can you fight a real battle? When thousands of French march at you with the intent to run over you like a wild stampede, then are you a fighting man? Because I have seen them, I have seen the Emperor's armies in all their might. They knock down all who is before them. They are merciless and brave. When you see this, will you still be a fighting man?"

Craven wasn't one to back down from a fight, and he had seen the field of battle before, but he was acutely aware he had never faced an organised and determined army of Napoleon's in open battle. It was something that weighed on his mind as much as General Cuesta, for he knew they stepped ever closer to such an experience. He did not reply as he dwelled upon it.

"No answer? At least that is honest. For many an officer would jump to say he would without knowing the first thing of battle or how he may act."

"We must all face tests when it is our time." The Lady Sarmento tried to lighten the mood and soften the General up, yet he remained fascinated by Captain Craven.

"Tell me, Captain, will your Englishmen stay and fight this battle and this war? Or will they flee to the sea once more?" he asked, recalling the retreat to Corunna. It was ever a sore point to all in the Peninsula. Yet Cuesta went on, not giving him a chance to defend himself or his countrymen, "You see there is no retreat for us. This is our country, and we have nowhere else to go. We win, or we die."

"I didn't come here to lose," replied Craven confidently. That much was certainly true, and it clearly showed to the General, who went back to the Lady Sarmento.

"You have travelled far. Would you take some rest before we speak?"

"As much as I would like to, General Wellesley would not have me waste a moment in talking with you. For that is my purpose here."

"Very well, then say what you have to say."

"My dear General, Sir Arthur would have me extend his deepest respects to you. He is fully aware of the difficult position in which you find yourself, and he too understands the importance of avoiding another Corunna. Wellesley appreciates your offers to supply his army, and yet also understands the difficult logistics in fulfilling such an offer. The General is currently amassing supplies so that he may enter Spain without putting further burden on you and your people. He wishes to stand beside you on the field of battle as an equal, and to conquer the French together."

Cuesta's serious tone seemed to melt away at the Lady's soft words, and it was clear he was more malleable to her than any officer who had been sent to him thus far, although he still remained suspicious.

"Tell me, are these your words, or the words Wellesley has put into that beautiful mouth of yours?"

"I am no mouthpiece to any man. I would have both our great countries rid of Napoleon's scourge. My late husband's brother even fights for the French and is a traitor to his people. I would do anything to see us to victory, and to see our two countries free from this plight."

"Then what would you have me do?" he asked as if he were at the lady's mercy.

"Advance on the enemy, up the Tagus, and have General Venegas threaten from the East. Force the French armies to divide themselves as Sir Arthur advances, and then have your two armies crush the French grand army in one."

Cuesta looked impressed.

"Wellesley discussed these plans with you?"

"He did, for he did not only send me here as a pretty face,

but he did indeed believe that a man might be more amenable to hearing plans from softer lips."

Cuesta smiled. "I must concede he is of course correct," he admitted.

"Sir, if I may?" Craven asked.

Cuesta gestured for him to go on.

"Sir, the French lack information. Guerrilla forces on both sides of the border continue to harass the French scouts and messengers. I know this because I was tasked with assisting the Bandidos. Right now, the enemy has no idea where Wellesley is, nor his strength. We have the element of surprise, and together we have the numbers. Now is the time to move whilst the enemy is in the dark."

The General looked deep in thought before he gave his answer.

"Do you know what it cost me to advance on the French?"

"No, Sir."

"More lives than I can live with, the lives of my countrymen. Lives must be lost in war, but never should they be lost needlessly. I will advance on the French so long as I have absolute assurances the English army will be by my side every step of the way, and yet I find it hard to trust any such word. For how can you give it to me? A Captain. What is your word worth?"

Craven stumbled, knowing he could not speak for Wellesley.

"Lady, if you would dine with me, for I have much to think about," insisted Cuesta.

"It would be my pleasure, General."

She took his arm and was led away. Captain Suarez followed as her personal guard, but scowled at the other two Captains as if demanding they not follow. Craven had had his fill of negotiating for one day, for it was never his strength, and so he was happy to stay out of further discussions.

"How long do we have to stay here?" Ferreira asked.

Craven shrugged.

"As long as the lady requires in order to get what we need from Cuesta."

"And if she cannot?"

"Have a little faith. I suspect that woman could talk a man out of anything, perhaps even a king from his crown," he smiled.

"So what now for us?"

"We wait. Our job is to protect the lady. I would not leave it to that jumped up fool."

Craven thought of the pompous Captain by her side. They took a seat on a bench and marvelled at the luxurious gardens. A number of officers of the infantry and cavalry were gathered and in discussion, as well as some of Cuesta's staff. Two hours had passed slowly when a group of four ladies came into the courtyard. They instantly piqued Craven's interest as the first welcome sight since the Lady Sarmento had left them. He had been leaning against a column looking weary until the women arrived and soon perked up. Yet as he admired their beauty, Ferreira's attention was drawn to a Spanish officer who appeared in a trance as the women passed him. Craven jumped into action. Ferreira merely shook his head, knowing trouble was heading their way, but didn't have enough energy to try and interfere with Craven who went right for the group of ladies.

"My Lady, Captain Craven at your service," he declared

politely and gracefully.

Two of them giggled whilst another blushed at his bold forwardness.

"Señor!" yelled the officer who'd not been able to take his eyes from the ladies until Craven's interruption.

Craven ignored the cry, fully knowing it was meant for him, and merely smiled at the ladies. Yet he heard the click of heels and stamp of boots as the officer raced to confront him. He turned just in time to see the Spaniard stop before him, the officer's huge black and red bicorne almost stabbing him in the face, and worn tilted at an angle and trimmed in gold. He was not much younger than Craven, and yet could not match his cool composure, for he was almost boiling over with rage. His chest puffed up and down beneath the large red facings of his navy-blue uniform, trimmed in gold lace. He was well tanned and with a narrow pencil like moustache and long large sideburns, striking quite the figure. The Lady Sarmento had returned and stepped up beside Ferreira as they both enjoyed the show, listening to the angry Spanish officer.

"Señor, is it not enough you would come to take our army, and now you must take our women!"

Craven looked flummoxed by the accusations.

"Take your army? We are all allies here, are we not?"

"Sir, you insult our General and our women with your actions."

Craven looked confused, but Lady Sarmento was way ahead of him as she whispered to Ferreira.

"There is a man shy with the ladies and quickly angered by those who are not."

Ferreira chuckled as he watched on. The Spaniard placed

an angry finger onto Craven's uniform.

"You do not belong here!"

Craven's amusement at the scene turned to anger, and he scowled at the officer.

"Take your hands off me," he hissed.

But the Spaniard did not back down and kept his finger in place. Before he could speak another word, Craven violently shoved him away to gasps of the crowd who were now watching them. The Spanish officer looked appalled and stunned, and yet as he looked to the women, he clearly felt compelled to respond in kind to save face and protect his honour. He ripped his sword from its scabbard. It was much the same sort as the regulation British infantry officer's sword, of which Craven carried a very unique and special example. The Spaniard rushed furiously towards him to cause him harm, not caring to do him the honour of letting him draw his own sword. Craven reached for it and drew it just in time as it went straight from the scabbard and into a parry, stopping a cut coming down to his head. He had no time to change to his left hand as he was forced to defend himself, and in that moment forgot his wounded arm.

Echoes rang out amongst the gardens as steel clashed with steel. Nobody made any attempt to stop it whilst they watched on with intrigue, none more so than the ladies who had been the catalyst for the combat.

"Barely said a word and he's already got them," sighed Ferreira.

"Are not all moths drawn to flame?" she opined.

Ferreira chuckled once again, as it amused him to think of Craven in that way.

Cold steel continued to clash as cut and thrust followed

parry after parry. Craven made no attempt to appease the man, as he could not see how he could have insulted him, although the Spaniard attacked as though years of pent up anger were being released like a volcano upon the Englishman. The Spaniard was clearly well trained but was letting his anger get the better of him. Though Craven fought to protect his own skin, he dared not risk slaying a Spanish officer when surrounded by thousands of his comrades, and on a diplomatic mission for Wellesley.

When the Spaniard was not swinging a cut, he kept an extended guard, his arm stretched forward and hand kept well behind the shells of his guard, his blade pointing forward to always threaten whilst maintaining pressure on Craven's blade. It was an aggressive way to control the centre line, though as he lifted for cuts, he presented large targets for timed thrusts. Craven dared not take them, though he was smiling the whole time, as it was an unexpected and welcome break from the boredom of waiting. However, his incessant smile only fuelled the Spaniard's rage further.

Craven backed away a few paces, and his opponent's sword cut past, taking the top off of a narrow tree. Yet with another step back he found himself backed up against a large pot. His attacker lunged forward with the point, and Craven displaced it before closing in and taking hold of the man's sword hand, locking him in place.

"You want to kill me over those women?"

"That would be reason enough, but you do more offense."

He shoved Craven away. It was enough to apply pressure onto Craven's healing arm, and he lost hold of the officer, who swung his blade as they separated. It sliced a button from his tunic as he leapt back to avoid the cut. This was serious now, and he knew he could not toy around any further. He made several feints and baited his man into plunging a thrust into his chest, which the Spaniard kindly obliged. Craven disengaged the blade as it came forward, stopped it with a parry and stepped in. He then encircled the sword with his hand, applying leverage so that it was ripped from his opponent's hands, and the man staggered back in disbelief. Gasps rang out, and the courtyard fell silent until the sound of boots could be heard as General Cuesta stepped back onto the scene. The Spaniard went on in his mother tongue as he began to plead forgiveness from the General, but Cuesta merely held up his hand to call for silence, and he got it.

"We are all passionate men who have come here to fight. Sometimes passions get the better of us, though I am thankful no blood has been spilled here, for there will be time enough for that in the coming weeks. We will consider this a friendly contest and be done with it. But there will be no more violence here, am I clear?"

Craven welcomed the outcome and held out the officer's sword to return it to him, but he did not look happy about it as the General continued speaking.

"I have heard the arguments presented, and I will think on these matters overnight, and I shall hear no more of it, is that clear?"

"Yes, Sir," replied Craven.

The Spanish officer who had so desperately tried to kill Craven now took hold of his sword, but Craven kept a firm grip, unwilling to release until he looked him in the eyes. Finally, the man obliged, and Craven had his attention.

"What is your problem with me, with us? This is about more than those women."

"Your Wellesley wants it all," he jeered.

"What are you talking about?"

"He doesn't just want to be our ally. He wants to be the Commander in Chief of the Spanish Army, just like he has for Portugal. Napoleon installed his own brother on our throne, and your King would place his man at the head of our army," spat the man.

Craven didn't know how to respond, as he knew little of the politics.

"You don't deny it?" the Spaniard asked when he hesitated.

"I know nothing of this, but I can tell you the only thing Wellesley wants is an end to this war so he may go home. He isn't here because he wants to be, but because he has a sense of duty to, which is a hell of a lot more than I can say for myself."

"Then why are you here?"

Craven pondered it as he looked over to Ferreira and the Lady Sarmento beside him.

"Mostly for the people I care for."

The Spanish officer looked surprised.

"What is your name?" Craven asked him.

"Manuel Moraga."

"Captain Craven," he replied, releasing his grip on the sword, "Listen to me. The only reason we are here is because we need one another, and Wellesley knows it. We have to bring our forces together to fight the French. We aren't asking you to serve us. We are asking you to fight beside us as brothers. A big battle is coming, and if we cannot stand together, I fear neither of us will succeed, and your country will be at the hands of that puppet Joseph Bonaparte for as long as he lives."

"Why are you telling me this?" Moraga demanded.

"Because I think you are a man of honour. Not many would say as much for myself. Your General is suspicious of us, and he need not be. We want the same thing. Bringing the Lady Sarmento here is a desperate last attempt to move things forward, that much must be obvious, but it is also testament to how important this is to Wellesley and to the entire war. I ask nothing of you. I only want you to know the truth."

The Spanish officer was intrigued as he took a closer look at Craven; clearly realising he had underestimated him the first time.

"Sir, I trained with the finest swordsman in Madrid for three years, and yet I could not land a touch, how is that?"

Craven smiled.

"We all must be good at something, and this," he said, resting his hand on the pommel of his sheathed sword, "This is me," he replied mysteriously.

The Spaniard was still infuriated by Craven, and yet he knew he must curb his emotions and tolerate him.

"Will you join me in a glass of wine?" he sighed.

"Now that is an offer I must always accept."

CHAPTER 14

Craven laughed incessantly as he patted an officer on the back who he didn't even know. The others laughed along, too, as he carried on and slumped down at a table where the Lady Sarmento was enjoying as quiet a drink as could be achieved. It was a lavish reception room, one of a great many about the grandiose palace. As Craven crashed down like an elephant, the table was rocked, and the lady snatched up her glass of wine just in time to save it. Ferreira was beside her, keeping her company as the only one of her country folk in the area. He clearly didn't much like being around the Spanish, though that was nothing new, as he didn't seem to like many people at all.

"A good night?" Lady Sarmento asked.

Craven lifted up a full glass of claret with a smile.

"Good wine always makes for a good night," he jested.

Ferreira nodded in agreement.

"Captain, tell me more about yourself, your family. Have

they long served the army?" Lady Sarmento asked of Ferreira.

He sighed as he thought back on it. "No, no. My father is a fisherman. Quite a successful one, though."

Craven looked curious, as he'd never thought to ask such questions of his Portuguese friend. "How does the son of a fisherman become an officer in the rifles?"

"Are you not the son of a merchant?"

"Yes, though you'd think he was a vicar if you didn't know better."

Sarmento laughed.

"Yes, as you can imagine I am not exactly made welcome at his table," growled Craven.

"And your parents, what do they think of you in this uniform?" she asked Ferreira.

"They don't understand why any man would want to go and fight. They don't care who rules the country. As far as they are concerned, it wouldn't matter. All leaders are the same."

"There is probably some truth to that," replied Craven.

"A half truth at best. A leader can always be worse," insisted Lady Sarmento.

Craven wondered from what experience she spoke, and yet remembering Mardel's attempt to take control of her estates he needed not press further.

"Then why did you join up?"

"The uniforms," he replied dryly.

Craven began to laugh, stopping himself after the Portuguese Captain maintained a straight face.

"You've risked your life for wine, and yet you find it amusing he does so for fashion?"

Craven was silenced. She had a point.

"Okay, but of all the uniforms you could wear, why this one?" Craven touched the drab brown uniform he wore.

"I am proud to wear this uniform. There is more to fashion than bright colours, gold lace, and gleaming metals," rebutted Ferreira loudly so that several Spaniards nearby heard. They turned their noses up at the jibe but went on with their business.

"I'm done," Ferreira said.

"Good night, Captain," replied Lady Sarmento.

"With any luck, we'll be back on the road tomorrow," Craven said.

Ferreira nodded appreciatively before taking his leave. When Craven turned to the lady with an unsubtle look of amorous desire, she only smiled back and took another drink.

"I am only here to share a drink with you, Captain." He looked disappointed, but she pointed to the far side of the room, "But that lady has been watching you since the moment you arrived."

One of the ladies whose presence had led to the fight earlier that day was standing beside a column and glancing over at him. He looked back to Lady Sarmento as if to ask permission, as he didn't want to leave her alone.

"Go, for that one knew what she wanted even before you did."

Craven downed his wine as got to his feet. He was a little shaky and looked surprised at the strength of the wine before finding his feet and finally going in a straight line.

"May we all be in better spirits come first light," Lady Sarmento said to herself. She continued to sip from her glass and considered her strategies as she manipulated and moulded those around her, all under the pretence of merely being a soft-spoken messenger.

* * *

Craven crawled out of bed, leaving the sleeping lady beneath the sheets. He staggered about looking for his uniform, which was spread across the room of one of the many lavish bedrooms of the palace. As he reached his tunic, he spotted a wine glass half empty and downed it with a smile. He pulled on his tunic and fixed his sword belt. He took one glance about the room that was decadently decorated with gold and silk. The room, the wine, and the lady were a hard thing to part with, and he sighed at the prospect before finally going on his way. He had no idea how to navigate the vast structure, but as he wandered about, he soon came to a balcony overlooking the inner courtyards, where he could see General Cuesta gathered beside Lady Sarmento.

Suarez was several steps behind her and immediately spotted Craven, looking at him with disgust for his seemingly unprofessional conduct. Craven wandered on and soon found some steps. He headed down to greet them, taking up position beside the Portuguese Captain of the Guides.

"Does the safety of the lady mean nothing to you?" he scathed.

"It absolutely does, but protecting her is your job. It was my job to protect you on the road," he shot back.

It was then General Cuestas noticed him and turned to face the Captain.

"You can tell Wellesley I agree to this plan. We will march together, and we will fight together."

"I am sure he will be most pleased to hear it," insisted Lady Sarmento.

"And you, Sir, will you deliver this news to your General?"

"That duty belongs to the lady, Sir, for I only came to ensure her safe passage."

"You will not be reporting back to Wellesley?"

"I have my own duties. The lady's path and my own crossed on her journey here."

"But you will advance into Spain with Wellesley?"

"I surely will."

"Then I will see you on the field of battle, Captain. Good luck to you."

"Thank you, Sir."

He left with a huge smile. "We did it, didn't we?"

"Yes, I had Cuesta close, but words by Moraga tipped the balance. Whatever you said to him was worth it. What did you tell him?" Lady Sarmento asked.

"What he wanted to hear."

"Then you don't know Wellesley's mind as to taking charge of the Spanish Army? For the General seemed most concerned by it."

"The only man who knows Wellesley's mind is Wellesley."

"Then you what, lied?"

"I explained my understanding of our General based on my experience, nothing more."

She shook her head in amazement.

"You didn't just come here to chaperone, did you?" she asked inquisitively.

Craven shrugged.

"Honestly, that was my purpose, but I'll admit I was more

than a little curious about our new allies. It wasn't so long ago they were our enemy."

"And? What do you make of them?"

"There sure are a lot of them, just as Cuesta made out, but I'm not so sure they are up to a fight."

"It is a powerful motivator, to have one's own country and freedom at stake."

"Maybe when you have a lot to lose, but you heard Ferreira, his family wouldn't care whether we won or lost."

They passed through the house and outside to find the lady's carriage awaiting her, with Ferreira and the others waiting for them. Craven helped the lady into her carriage, much to the chagrin of Captain Suarez who merely huffed in frustration as he mounted his horse. The lady took her seat but marvelled at Craven for a moment as he stood at the open door.

"I couldn't have done it without you."

"And Wellesley couldn't have done this without you. Battles can be won or lost in their preparation, and you might well have just won a battle without ever having to lift a sword."

He closed the carriage door and climbed atop his horse, letting out a contented sigh, for it had been a successful mission. The lady from the night before waved at him from a balcony, and it did not go unnoticed by Moraga who scowled back at Craven. He was fuming, and that caused Ferreira to laugh as they went forward.

"What?"

"Just the fires you leave behind," he smiled.

CHAPTER 15

"It was a successful venture then, Sir?" Paget asked Craven as they watched the lady's carriage continue on to return to Wellesley. The Portuguese officer escorting her stopped beside him as his cavalrymen remained with the carriage. Ferreira had long gone on his way to continue with his duties, and it was just Craven's Blades and a dozen Bandidos left on the bleak rolling hilltop.

"Thank you for your assistance," he declared in final admittance and appreciation of the Captain's efforts, though it pained him to do so.

"My pleasure," replied Craven before the officer rode on to join his troop.

"Tell me everything, Sir, what of this General Cuesta? Will he join us?" Paget pressed.

"We did what we needed to do."

The carriage had barely vanished from view when a rider galloped up to them. It was Birback, kicking up a cloud of dust as he came to a halt.

"It's Mardel. He's here!"

"Not again," Craven growled.

"Where?" Matthys demanded, as he leapt onto his horse in readiness.

Birback pointed down one fork in a cart track that converged with the one they'd just returned on. Craven looked back to where the lady had just vanished from view, knowing the carriage would not outrun any cavalry.

"How many are they?"

"I'm not sure. I only saw Mardel and five riders with him."

"Are they coming this way?" Matthys asked.

"I don't know."

Craven looked conflicted as he looked back and forth.

"We could set up and wait for them here?"

"And if they take another path, Matthys? They could travel well wide of us, and there are many more miles before Lady Sarmento reaches the safety of our lines. I want him, now!"

Craven wheeled his horse about and charged on down the fork in the road, with only Moxy beside him.

"Damn it." Matthys jumped onto his own horse and followed on after the Captain.

The others knew they had no choice now and quickly mounted, galloping on after their leader. The excitement was building, for despite charging towards the unknown, they were all eager to get their hands on Mardel, but none more so than Craven who had narrowly missed his opportunity at Porto. He still felt robbed by it and knew however long Mardel was out there the Lady Sarmento would not be safe. He dug his heels in again and again as he spurred on his horse to even greater speeds, desperate to get his chance at the traitorous Portuguese Bonapartist.

It was not long before Craven took a bend past a rock outcrop, and there he was. Colonel Juan Mardel, the brother of Lady Sarmento's late husband and rampant Francophile. Beside him were four French cavalrymen, as he appeared to be studying a map. Craven drew his sword and charged without checking to see if he had any support. His friends and Bandidos were desperately trying to catch up, but most were trailing far behind, except for Moxy. He took aim with his rifle and shot one cavalryman dead with an incredible shot, considering the speed at which they galloped.

He, too, drew his sabre as they closed the distance, but Mardel turned and fled. Craven cursed furiously as he continued in pursuit. They had barely made two hundred yards when Craven spotted a French Voltigeur amongst some trees ahead, and his heart almost stopped as he realised what was happening. They were the French skirmishers who so often plagued British troops.

He pulled on his reins and brought his horse to an abrupt halt. Moxy followed suit, the rest of their companions drew up behind them. Craven opened his mouth to yell a warning, but it was too late. Musket fire rang out all around them, for they had been led into a trap with ease. Moxy was struck by a musket ball and knocked from his horse. The volley caused Craven's horse to rear up in panic, inadvertently saving his life as two musket balls struck the animal, and they both collapsed together. The weight of the dead animal trapped his wounded leg, and he cried out in pain. Yet from where he lay on his back, he could see Moxy was flat out. He was still breathing but unable to move, and several of the Bandidos lay dead behind them. Three more horses had been killed in the salvo. Several of the others had taken cover behind the horses, both dead and alive, as they returned fire.

The gunfire was sporadic now, as both sides loaded and fired at will. The Frenchmen were spread out amongst the cover of the trees around them in a shallow valley. Mardel was nowhere to be seen as he had taken shelter. The Frenchmen were dug in amongst thick foliage for cover, not just from musket and rifle fire, but making the ground seemingly unreachable to their horses even if they could make it through the whittling fire.

Paget crawled forward to Craven and fired his pistol towards the enemy. He took Moxy's rifle and his cartridge box to reload and keep up the fight, taking shelter beside Craven's dead horse.

"What do we do, Sir?"

Craven was at a loss, for he had not seen the ambush coming, not even the slightest sign. He'd let his emotions get the better of him, and he was already regretting it, yet he knew he could do nothing whilst he lay trapped.

"Help me get free."

Paget finished loading and rested the rifle against the haunches of the dead animal. He took aim as one of the Voltigeurs leaned out from the cover of a tree to take his shot. He took stock of the yellow collars of distinction and yellow tipped green plume upon the soldier's shako, the marks of their elite status they wore as proudly as the Caçadore brown jackets. He squeezed the trigger, and Moxy's rifle flashed before his eyes. The ball struck the Frenchman at the shoulder, and he dropped his musket before retreating from the fight. Paget turned his attentions back to his Captain as he lay the rifle down.

The peaceful sunny valley was now already fogged over with powder smoke, but it was at least giving them some cover from the enemy. He pushed with all his strength to get Craven free, but even together they could not move it, and the Captain could get no leverage where he lay trapped. Matthys could see them struggling and scrambled over to help.

"We really got ourselves into this time, didn't we?" Matthys asked as he checked Craven over.

"This was no accident. A trap was set, and I ran straight into it," Craven cursed.

"Let's worry about that when we're well clear, shall we?" Matthys replied calmly.

Paget couldn't believe how measured the Sergeant was as musket balls struck the ground and the dead horses around them. He was an inspiration to the young officer, and a perfect example of how a leader should act under fire.

"If you would, Sir, on three." Matthys braced himself against the dead animal in readiness to lift as one.

"Three, two, one, lift!"

The three men heaved with all their strength. They barely managed to lift the body at all, but thankfully it was enough. Finally, Craven was able to free his leg before they all gasped and let the weight back down. Blood had already soaked the Captain's trousers where the leg had been crushed, and his wound opened once again, yet it was the least of their problems in this moment.

"What are your orders?" Matthys asked.

"We cannot advance on them. The only way is back."

Craven winced as he got up to one knee.

"Can you walk?"

"I can run if it means getting out of this, Matthys." He picked up the sword he had dropped as he fell, and took out his sabre from beneath his saddle, not wanting to leave it to the enemy.

"Withdraw, back, everyone!" he ordered.

Matthys then noticed Moxy who had been forgotten amongst the hail of fire and powder smoke. The Sergeant slung his own rifle over his back and went to his aid. He was still alive but weak, and he had no chance of getting him on his feet.

"They shot me," he protested.

"Yes, they did."

Matthys pulled the wounded Welshman onto his shoulder and hauled him up off the ground. Shots continued to ring out from both sides as they began to pull back. Paget took another shot with Moxy's rifle as he covered their retreat. The powder smoke was intoxicating now. There was no wind to sweep it away, and it clung to everything around them. The group had lost half their horses in the action. Some helped others up onto the croup of their horses, but a few were wounded and barely able to bear their riders let alone any more weight. Craven shrugged off Charlie's offer to climb onto her horse and instead gestured for her to take Moxy. He was loaded on in front of her saddle for her to hold him in place.

"Go!" Craven slapped the posterior of her horse, causing it to spur forward as those able to galloped away to safety.

"Where is Birback?" Matthys demanded in frustration, expecting to see the brawler there and most willing to fight when it was needed, but Paget shrugged for he had no idea of his location.

Paget's beloved Augustus was nowhere to be seen as he reloaded his rifle and fled on foot with Craven, Matthys, and three of the Bandidos. Musket fire rang out as the French gave chase, the Voltigeurs coming out from their cover. Craven limped but managed a jogging pace as they got about the bend that had led them into the trap. He could hear horses at their backs. He stopped and drew out his sabre, leaving his spadroon sheathed on his side.

"What are you doing?" Paget asked in horror, realising Craven had stopped.

"There is no outrunning cavalry on foot. If I am going to die, it will be facing my enemy."

Craven buried his feet in the dirt to defiantly stand his ground. Paget hurried to reload Moxy's rifle, as Charlie and Caffy returned to them to make their stand. The others continued to flee with the wounded. Just five redcoats now held out as the Frenchmen closed in on them. Paget got his rifle reloaded just in time as the first Frenchmen took the bend ahead. He fired and shot the horse out from under him, whilst Caffy and Charlie fired, killing the downed rider and the next cavalryman to follow. They drew their swords as more followed in their footsteps. More than a dozen cavalrymen lined up before them, coming to a stop as they made way for Mardel to move up between them, and Voltigeurs soon rushed up to the flanks of the cavalrymen.

"Surrender!" cried the Portuguese traitor.

Craven clung to his sabre ready to fight.

"This is over, Captain. You and your men are now my prisoners," insisted Mardel.

"Not yet."

"Don't be a fool, Captain. You are either my prisoner, or you are a dead man!"

Craven said nothing as he lifted his sword into a guard ready to fight. Mardel shook his head in disbelief. He pointed his finger for his dragoons to go forward and finish the job the Voltigeurs had started. They got just a few paces when a volley of fire rang out, and three of them were felled from their saddle, whilst one musket ball clipped Mardel's left arm and caused him to cry out with pain. Craven turned in disbelief to see Timmerman at the head of their saviours, leading his Bandidos in a charge towards the Frenchmen.

Mardel looked in horror as the Major led a charge at him with his sword raised over his head. The traitor turned and fled in a panic as he cried out panicked orders to his men, falling back to the defensive positions where they had launched their ambush. The French skirmishers fired off several desperate shots but quickly turned and fled in the face of a cavalry charge that would decimate them.

Timmerman's posse rushed on after the enemy as he came to a stop beside Craven. Two of his men brought up fresh horses for them. Craven could barely believe his eyes to have been saved by the man who hated him most in the world, and yet Timmerman looked amused by the entire experience.

"Why?" Craven asked in disbelief.

"You think I would let a damn dirty Frenchman have your head? You will die when I say you die," he smiled.

Timmerman's troop soon came to a stop, not wanting to fall into the same trap Craven had befallen. Craven took one of the horses and hauled himself onto it, wincing as he put weight on his injured leg.

"You would do this, just so you could kill me on a different day?"

"I say what happens to you, remember that. There will be time enough for me to settle personal matters, for now I serve the King and England, and if there is anyone I hate more than you, it is that traitorous dog Mardel."

"He's no Frenchman," replied Craven.

"No, he's far worse. For all you have done, at least you still remain loyal to England. I would see Mardel strung up for what he has done, and I imagine in this we are of one mind."

Craven nodded in agreement, though he could still hardly believe what he was hearing, half expecting the villainous Timmerman to turn on him at any moment.

"Go. Mardel has Major Claveria aiding him. We do not need that fight now."

Craven nodded in appreciation though still looked suspiciously on at the man who had tried to kill him more than once, realising there was just one thing which they shared, the red jackets they wore.

"Thanks," he replied reservedly, stuffing his sheathed sabre into the saddle and leading his new horse on.

* * *

Moxy cried out in pain, his shrieks echoing about the clearing, and he was not the only one as the wounded were seen to. One Bandido followed him as his wound was cauterised. Yet even as the wounded were seen to, wine was passed about as they celebrated victory. They had to imagine that is what they had achieved, for they had all flown in the face of death. Timmerman and his troops kept to themselves around their own fires. It was the first time he and Craven had been in the same area without Major Thornhill to ensure they were not at one another's throats, and yet despite suspicious glances, neither officer made any attempt to instigate another fight. They were all weary from the action that day and the weeks they had faced together.

Craven's attention was then drawn to Birback as he noticed him sitting alone. He was unscathed, which was an unusual sight for the one who seemed to attack musket balls and blades as much as a target and pell. Craven went to him, towering over him as he sat on a fallen tree trunk.

"Where were you today?"

"In the middle of it all, same as the rest of you."

"But not at the front? Not getting stuck in?"

"Until the wounded needed help."

"You went to the rear with the wounded when there was a fight to be had?"

"It was chaos out there. We just had to get out as best we were able and save whoever we could."

Craven only looked half convinced when he noticed a gold ring on one of Birback's fingers. The Captain had never seen it before, and it had to be worth more than everything else Birback owned.

"Captain!" Matthys yelled.

He knew the Sergeant had been seeing to Moxy's wounds and turned his attention to their wounded friend as he rushed to his side. He lay in an officer's cot, kindly donated by Paget. He was conscious but looked weak.

"That ball was meant for you," he joked as he looked to

Craven.

"What were you doing at the front? Your place is behind a rifle."

"I was following you," he smiled.

Craven nodded in appreciation.

"Thank you, all of you. That was my mistake, but when it came down to it, you were all there to back me up." He looked around at them all and finally to Birback who looked down and away from him. Craven turned his attention to Matthys who was the closest thing they had to a surgeon.

"How is he doing?"

"Lucky to be alive, and he's not through it yet," replied Matthys honestly.

Craven put a hand on Moxy's arm, who was clearly working to show a brave face through the pain.

"You keep it together, you hear? That bastard Mardel is going to pay, and I'll need a good shot to get it done, you got that?"

"I'll be there," insisted Moxy.

The night soon wound down as the wounded tried to get what rest they could. Despite the celebration of what many saw as a victory, having survived the deadly ambush, there was a solemn tone through the camp for those they had lost and the many more who had been wounded.

Craven lay awake on his blanket for many hours. The events of the day and all which had led up to it would not fade from his mind. Finally, he fell asleep from sheer exhaustion, as he could no longer keep his eyes open. They seemed to shoot back open as quickly as they had closed to find it was daytime once more. He'd gotten little rest, but his troubled and busy mind was like a shot of adrenaline or a strong coffee to get him to his feet.

Timmerman and his Bandidos were already long gone, but few amongst those who remained were not eager to do anything beyond see to the wounded and rest and recuperate. Paget was busy grooming his much-loved horse Augustus who had found his way back to the camp, but most were numbed from the previous day's experience; not just from their losses but the realisation of how close they had all come to death. They had been told nobody would come to save them, and Timmerman's aid had been a one-off and a stroke of luck he had even been in the area. Ferreira and his riflemen seemed out of sorts, not knowing how to act or talk to the rest, having missed the action altogether. Birback scraped his sword blade along a stone as he sharpened it, and the sound drew Craven's attention, though he first went to Matthys.

"Everything okay?"

"Birback, you had eyes on him all the time I was gone?"

Matthys looked confused.

"What's this about?"

"Has he been with you all this time?"

"Yes, I..." stuttered Matthys, "There was one day he was out hunting and came back empty handed, why?"

Craven said nothing as he went to leave, but Matthys felt compelled to stand up for the man who'd saved him.

"You know he stood up to Timmerman?"

Craven didn't get his meaning.

"Birback. When Paget went for him and I got between them, Timmerman put me down. He could have killed me, but it was Birback who stepped up to him. Clocked him hard, and he could have been hanged for that."

Craven sighed as he took in this new information to an already troubled mind. He strolled over to Birback, leaving Matthys wondering what it was all about, but he soon had his hands full as he went back to Moxy's dressing. Craven loomed over Birback for a moment until he looked up to acknowledge the Captain.

"With me, we're scouting to the East. I want to know if that bastard Mardel is going to come for us."

"Sure, Boss."

Birback sheathed his sabre, and the two went for their horses. They mounted up and rode out of camp without a word, for nobody needed nor wanted orders as they rested for the day. Craven led them out a little over a mile to a tall vantage point he much liked for its view over all the rolling hills and valleys beyond. On part of the Eastern edge was a rocky outcrop leading to a sheer drop a hundred yards to the valley below. He galloped right up to the edge for the best viewing point, a location they were all familiar with. As they drew near, he stopped his horse and dismounted so as to not spook the horse at the edge, walking the last few paces. Birback did the same as they stepped up within a yard of the drop. It was a magnificent sight, though they were all growing weary of seeing it. The rolling hills of Southern Portugal and Spain seemed to have no end.

"That was a hell of a thing yesterday, wasn't it?" Craven asked, thinking back to the near disastrous events.

"It sure was," agreed Birback.

"You know we'd all be finished if it were not for Timmerman, the one man who shouldn't have been there. The most unlikely of rescuers."

Birback shook his head in amazement before agreeing.

"You know what bothers me most about it? Nobody could have predicted Timmerman having been in the area, let alone coming to our aid. And so Mardel chose the best moment he could hope for. When we were at our weakest, and with the safety of Lady Sarmento hanging over us."

"He is a clever one."

They looked out across the vast expanses before them and looming mountains that would surely mark the road they would soon take. Birback crossed his arms as he took in the morning air and basked in the sunlight. Yet seemingly out of nowhere he was struck in the temple with a solid blow. The robust and tough fighter staggered a little closer to the edge as he tried to recover. Craven grabbed him by the collar and drove him right up to the cliff edge and dangled him over. Birback tried to resist, but he soon found Craven's dirk blade pressed against his throat. He could not move as he hung precariously over a drop he knew he could not survive. He tried to push forward but felt the tip of the blade cut into his flesh, and he could get no leverage as he was held firmly in place.

"What are you doing!"

Craven stared into his eyes as he waited, as if expecting an explanation. A rock under Birback's feet came away from the edge as he tried to find his footing, and he slipped a little, only saved from falling by Craven's hold.

"What did I do? What is it?" he panicked.

"You led us to Mardel," Craven scowled.

"I saw him. I saw him that's all, and I came to tell you!"

"You skipped out on Matthys, missing for most of a day,

and you came back empty handed?"

"It's tough out there," pleaded Birback.

"And when we got in a fight, you were nowhere to be seen. You never miss a fight. You knew what was going down yesterday, and you saved your own skin."

"I swear I didn't!"

"And that ring? Where did that come from?"

Birback's expression turned from fear for his life to terror that he had been found out. The look was all over his face as his eyes rolled, and he stopped resisting. He'd been found out and he knew it. Craven said nothing, waiting for an explanation, or at least an attempt at an excuse.

"Look, I'm sorry. You brought us out here to make us rich, and all I got so far is shot, beaten, and stabbed. I didn't come out here to die a nobody. I was promised gold, more than you can imagine. And revenge," admitted Birback.

Craven looked furious, and yet part of him understood. For he, too, had come to foreign lands to make his fortune, and this life was a far cry from the one he had been hoping for.

"You gave us up to that traitorous dog?"

"Not to Mardel, I had no idea he was part of the deal until it happened."

"Then who, who did you take money from?"

"Claveria."

Craven relaxed slightly as it was not as nefarious as he had first thought, though he looked no less angry.

"I only did it for the gold."

"And you traded our lives for it?"

"You have to understand. You know this life. We don't have forever. I saw a chance, and I took it."

Craven was still furious but also conflicted.

"Don't tell them, not any of them," Birback begged.

Craven was surprised to hear him plead for his reputation and not his life. The anger on his face seemed to melt away as he pulled Birback away from the edge, but he kept a firm grasp on his collar and the blade of his dirk at his throat.

"I'm sorry, okay," insisted Birback.

"There won't be a second chance, do you understand me? You cross any of us again, and you'll be buried, do you understand?"

"Yes, yes I do."

"And Moxy. If he dies, you better be a thousand miles from my blade. Do I make myself clear?"

Birback nodded in agreement. Craven finally removed his blade and sheathed it.

"I am going to be rich before this war is over, and every man who is still standing with me at the end will be, too. I need to know I can trust everyone who rides with me. Nothing you can say now will earn that trust, so don't ask for it, and don't expect it. You've got a lot to make up for, you hear me?"

"Yes," Birback simpered.

The hulking man was reduced to a begging schoolboy.

"Don't ever cross me again," scowled Craven as he shoved Birback away.

He stumbled a few paces almost to the edge once more, but the fight in him was gone as he crumpled down to his knees full of regret and shame. Craven's hand reached for his sword as the anger in him was still boiling over, but he thought of Matthys' words and stayed his hand before returning to his horse. As he turned to leave, he spotted Major Thornhill trotting up the hill, appearing seemingly out of nowhere as he so often did. Thorny rode up beside him and marvelled at the view for a moment as he took in a deep breath.

"What is it?"

"Wellesley is in Spain," he smiled.

"What?" Craven asked in amazement.

"Your efforts here have worked. The leading brigades crossed into Spain on the 3rd of July, and the enemy has no idea of their number or intention. Above all they have no inclination Wellesley is leading them, for all the enemy knows he is still in the North. As I said, communication is everything. What you and the rest of the guerrillas have done in Portugal and Spain has given us a chance to do what no large army could dream of. Now Wellesley is well into Spain and preparing to do battle."

"And General Cuesta?"

"He's eager to fight, but still far from cooperative. He marched North in pursuit of the French thinking he faced twenty thousand demoralised men, and when he discovered he faced almost fifty thousand hardened soldiers, and that King Joseph had left Madrid at the head of further reserves, well, he understandably realised his folly. Cuesta has never been a cautious man, but I think many bitter lessons have finally got through that thick skull of his."

"So, the Spanish are in in retreat?"

"Yes. They foolishly believed they could take Madrid without us, something Cuesta, Venegas, nor Wellesley could manage without the support of one another. The last weeks have been no end of arguments over movement and support. Venegas may threaten Madrid if he can just time it right, but Cuesta is now falling back to support Wellesley. It is nothing but luck his army was not lost as it withdrew slowly to the River Alberche. Had the French known this, Marshal Victor might have crushed Cuesta there. Yet they are still blind much of the time. Information is everything."

"Why are you telling me this now?"

"The work you have done here is admirable, but the time for skirmishes and manoeuvres is over. We face a battle the likes of which will shape this war. The battle that will mould Wellesley and show England and France what kind of General he is, and what kind of men he commands. This is our chance. The Bandidos will continue their work here, but you and Ferreira are to move now to join the army."

"Where, Sir?"

"Talavera."

CHAPTER 16

27th July 1809.

Craven's eyes widened in astonishment as he led his small party to the crest of a hill that looked down over the town and surroundings of Talavera. British soldiers were encamped all around them, including a large artillery battery; defending the vantage point which looked out across the town and far to the East, though it was not the tallest elevation in the area, which lay a little to the North.

"That's one hell of a sight," declared Moxy.

His left arm was held in a sling, although his rifle was still carried across his back, for he would never wilfully let go of it. Birback nodded in agreement as he looked upon the pale Welshman, knowing he had almost caused his death, and in turn his own. Craven could see the mix of remorse and fear in his eyes, which meant a lot for a man who was always fearless.

"I've never seen the likes of such an army," marvelled

Paget.

To the South was the town of Talavera on the Tagus River, which provided a natural defence to that flank.

"Come to see a real battle!" a friendly voice cried out.

Captain Harcourt Doyle of the Royal Artillery approached on horseback.

"Those are our orders," replied Craven.

"Orders?" Doyle laughed, knowing how much of a rebel he was.

The eccentric artillery officer came up between them to take his place between Craven and Paget. His vast mutton chops had grown further still, and his long curly hair could not be contained by the forage cap he wore so casually. He looked weary and yet still enthusiastic as he drew out a small map.

"We are on the Pajar de Vergara, an artillery position on this small mound. We divide the British Army spread far to the North and Cuesta's Spanish troops positioned in the city of Talavera, and these vast olive groves which stretch out all around it," he declared as they looked at the old medieval walls, "They wouldn't stand up to a siege, but in open battle they might as well be a fortress. The stone walls of the olive groves being themselves many defensive lines for which the Spanish may use."

"The Spanish get the walls and we get open country?" Paget asked.

"The way Thorny spoke I don't think Wellesley has much faith in our Spanish allies, or at least not in the officers who lead them," replied Craven.

"So, they are put behind walls so they might feel safe?"

Craven smiled for the young Ensign had a keen eye. Doyle

pointed up to the tallest hill directly to the North.

"That is Cerro de Medellin. Whoever controls that hill controls everything."

"I don't understand. This is a defensive line, but are we not on the attack?" Paget asked as he looked at the vast defensive line covering four miles from North to South.

"I know who is where, but not Wellesley's mind," replied Doyle.

"And there?" Craven pointed to allied troops on the Eastern side of the Alberche River, seemingly far ahead of the defensive lines.

"Mackenzie's division under Wellesley is seeing the last of Cuesta's troops across."

"What is taking them so damn long?"

"The Spanish seem to work at whatever pace they desire," laughed Doyle.

"I am sure that pains Wellesley greatly," replied Paget.

"Indeed," replied Craven as he marvelled at their own lines.

"More than fifty thousand men they say," declared Doyle.

"Will it be enough, do you think?"

"How can it not?" Paget questioned.

"The size of an army is only impressive in relation to those it opposes; do you know how many Frenchmen march on us?" Craven asked him.

"No, Sir."

"And neither do I," sighed Craven, who as a gambling man didn't like to be in the dark when so much was at stake.

"Do you think we can win, Sir?" Paget asked the artilleryman.

"We didn't come here to lose!"

"Let us be on. Wellesley called us back to the army. It is for him from which we must gather our orders."

Craven spurred his horse on down East from the knoll and out from the protection of the allied lines. As he began the shallow descent, he realised just how complex a battlefield it was. For the hills North of Talavera were far from even. There were dips, troughs, and undulations all over; many tiers to each hill, which may conceal troops both in defence and attack. The position of the allied army was strong, but the battlefield before them was challenging and would be no easy contest.

"Is this really it, are we finally going to meet the French in open battle?" Paget asked enthusiastically.

Matthys could barely believe his tone after all they had been through. They had battled with the French in skirmishes that had cost so many lives, including his good friend Nickle, and yet he was glad to see him in good spirits.

"Perhaps, but I cannot see how we can wait here too long. Time is not on our side."

"How so, Sir?"

"You remember what Thorny told us. Keeping Wellesley's position a secret from the enemy was quite a feat, but the moment they know his location and that of this army, they will be on the move."

"Is that not the idea?"

"To bring Marshal Victor and General Sebastiani to battle, yes, but what of Soult? Soult who waited in the North after his humiliation at Porto. He waits for news of Wellesley, and he surely has had it now. He will come for us."

"Sir Arthur must know this. He must have planned for it,"

insisted Paget.

"I surely hope so," replied Craven as he led them on through an olive grove and finally into more open country. They reached the Alberche to find Spanish troops wading through at a shallow section just twenty yards wide. The water still reached their thighs, and scores of troops were queued on the far side to follow them.

Craven led his horse on into the water, causing the Spaniards to separate and create a path for his troop to pass through. He led them on until he found the familiar sight of redcoats, and eventually, Wellesley. He was waiting at the roadside with several of his staff, overseeing the withdrawal of the last remnants of Cuesta's force amongst the ruins of a grand old stone house, Casa de Salinas. It appeared more as a small castle with its square towers. Craven gestured for the others to stop whilst he and Paget continued on.

"Captain Craven," he declared with a friendly smile.

"Sir Arthur," Paget saluted as they came to a stop.

"Your orders, Sir?" Craven asked.

"Craven, do you know what strikes me when I see a man such as yourself?"

"No, Sir?"

"That one does not realise there is such a need for an officer such as yourself until the moment arises."

"Yes, Sir," he agreed, just thankful he was not the target of Wellesley's fury any longer.

"I am going to win this war for one simple reason, Captain. Meticulous planning. I would know everything I have at my disposal, and everything which I do not. The location and strength of every resource of myself, my allies, and my enemies."

"Yes, Sir."

"But not you, Craven. You are the sum that does not add up on paper. Unpredictable, and yet somehow invaluable."

"Thank you, Sir."

"These are not qualities I would wish for in any officer, and yet your value cannot be underestimated."

"What are your orders, Sir?"

Wellesley sighed as he took out a small map from his jacket and tried to find some place for Craven amongst his perfectly formed plan. Yet he struggled to find the answer, and before he could discover it, they were all disturbed by the sound of musket fire. Wellesley's horse was shaken as cries of panic rang out amongst the British troops posted to defend the area around the ruins. Wellesley himself was appalled to see Frenchmen advancing from the North. It was a surprise attack of which nobody had seen coming, and it clearly rattled the British General.

Large volleys rang out, and within moments there were two British battalions broken and fleeing for their lives. Few could believe what was happening as General Mackenzie himself galloped up to their position, the commander of the division responsible for covering the rearguard action Wellesley was overseeing.

"Sir, an enemy division has crossed in the North and threatens our position. You must withdraw immediately!"

Wellesley looked furious to have been caught off guard so easily, but he was also rattled by the experience even though he did his utmost to conceal it.

"We cannot afford to lose the troops we have here. Continue to repulse the enemy as you withdraw in good order,

Sir!" he roared furiously as he looked around for anything else that might have gone unnoticed.

"How did a whole division advance on us unopposed and unknown?" Paget asked.

"Only by incompetence," Wellesley growled.

It was a bad start and perhaps even a bad omen, and they all felt it as redcoats rushed to plug the gaps as others fled, broken by the ruthless and unexpected assault. It was a trap nobody has seen coming.

"That damn Cuesta. We should have been away from here before dawn of yesterday!" Wellesley scowled.

"Withdraw!" the cry came as officers relayed the commands. It felt like a defeat, and everyone knew it.

"Sir, we should get you to safety," insisted Craven.

Wellesley looked infuriated, and yet he knew it was for the best. He had only a small number of his staff with him, not expecting to be anywhere close to a battle. Yet more British infantrymen ran past in horror at the brutal assault that had struck them. The French were advancing like a flood, enveloping all before them. Three British battalions were in retreat, and a hole had been punched in the line. The 45th Line and 60th Rifles held firm, but the General himself was at risk of being encircled.

"This way, Sir!"

Wellesley raced Westward with Craven's troop screening him from the North. They got only a hundred yards when they found themselves intersecting French infantry who pursued fleeing redcoats with bayonets fixed. Ferreira's riflemen fired from horseback as they closed, and Craven himself drew out his sword, his right arm finally strong enough to wield it once more.

Amid the chaos of French and British infantry they were forced to slow. Wellesley's horse came to a stop at the backs of redcoats who were bunched up amongst the trees and shrubs and began to bottleneck. One Frenchman aimed a bayonet at Craven who parried it away with his sword. He grabbed hold of the muzzle and wrenched it forward, pulling the man onto the tip of his sword. Yet as he turned back to Wellesley, he could see a Frenchman grab at his reins. Craven cut down with all his force at the man's extended arm just as it got purchase and removed the hand at the wrist.

Birback urged his horse into two more of the French infantrymen as they tried to close with the General. His horse smashed them both to the ground before he swung his sabre down and cut into the neck of a third. Paget shot another and drew out his sword as his musket clashed against cold steel. Yet Wellesley look more angry than worried now, furious that the enemy had gotten the better of them. He spotted a clearing and rushed through and along the lines of broken infantry who fled for their lives. Drawing his own sword, he cried out to them as he galloped amongst them, "Rally! Stand against them! Do not show them your backs!"

Some took heed as they realised who was calling to them, and soon enough lines began to reform, but as Craven reached them, he could see there were no officers in sight, not even a Sergeant as thirty men gathered together to reload and take a stand in a thin red line.

"Load!" he cried out as he turned his horse about and took position beside them. Ferreira's mounted riflemen formed beside them as they followed suit. Wellesley watched proudly as Craven took charge of the remnants that had gathered from three different battalions, and the sight of it caused more to rally and join the line.

"Aim! Fire!" Craven ordered.

The blistering volley from the ragtag punch that had rallied together had a devastating effect on the Frenchmen advancing on them who were just fifty yards away.

"Load!"

"Sir, we must withdraw," insisted one of Wellesley's staff, but the General would not be moved, as he was fascinated as he watched the Captain take charge. Then the French cried out as they charged and had gotten within twenty yards when Craven's command echoed once more.

"Aim! Fire!"

The volley was even more devastating than the rest and encouraged more of the fleeing British troops to rally to their side as they saw Wellesley himself take a stand.

"Load!"

The Frenchmen were rocked and began to withdraw in the face of hundreds more redcoats flocking to Wellesley's side. Some paused to take shots as they fell back.

"Fire at will!" Craven shouted.

Cheers rang out at their victory as upon finishing loading, the British troops raised their shakos into the air triumphantly, celebrating their small victory. Yet more columns of French infantry advanced on them.

"Withdraw in good order!" Wellesley yelled as two infantry officers rushed to take charge.

"With me," Wellesley said to Craven,

The newly arrived officers barked their commands as Craven followed on after the General; his troops and those of the Caçadores operating as his personal guard for the moment, which was the last thing any of them would have expected that day. They were soon back in open country and closing the distance back to the battle lines Wellesley had so carefully drawn up. Gunfire continued at their backs as a fighting withdrawal took place.

"Much obliged to you, Captain," declared Wellesley.

"Sir," he replied in acknowledgement.

"How is it that you manage to be the man one needs when one least sees it?" smiled Wellesley.

"I try to make the most of things, Sir. What would you have me do? What are your orders, Sir?"

"By all accounts you should have your own battalion, and yet I do not believe that would suit your talents, Captain. I would have all things as I intend them, but you have shown yourself to be useful in the most chaotic of times. I leave your position and your orders to yourself. Do as you must and be where you need to be, for I fear you are a force of nature which one should dare not attempt to tame."

"Yes, Sir," he replied, taking it as a compliment.

"The enemy caught us with our trousers down this morning, but they are not ready to do battle. We should not see any more of them till tomorrow, I imagine. As I said, much obliged to you, Captain," replied Wellesley as they rode into the British lines once more.

Sporadic fire continued across the rolling hills as Mackenzie's division withdrew in good order, and by the afternoon all was quiet. Craven and the others gathered around two small fires within full view of the battlefield. The troops around them were resting easy as nobody expected to see more action that day. Discussion about the fire was rife as they relived the day's events, but it was Paget who was silent and deep in thought.

"What is it?" Charlie asked him as she sat down beside him.

"Just how close Sir Arthur came to disaster today."

"But there was no disaster."

"But there could have been. I have never known a man be so meticulous in his planning. So precise and with such a grasp of all things a military man must know, and yet even he was caught by surprise."

"Because mistakes happen, and we cannot control everything in our lives. We must rely on others, and not one of us perfect," replied Craven.

A warm meal did wonders to calm Paget's nerves, but at seven o'clock they were shaken once again as cries rang out from the pickets on duty. He shot to his feet to look East in time to see French troops coming into sight.

"Already?" Matthys asked in surprise.

"It can only be advance units, not enough to launch an attack," insisted Craven.

Yet they watched in horror as artillery batteries were brought up, and it became clear the French intended to begin the fighting this day and not the next. It was not long before the guns began their bombardment, but of far more concern to them all was the light cavalry advancing towards Spanish positions. Craven took out his spyglass for a better look and sighed, realising it was no small threat as hundreds of French cavalrymen advanced on Cuesta's troops, who everyone worried would not stand.

"What do we do, Sir?" Paget asked.

"We do nothing. It is not our job to."

"They're scouting, that's all," Matthys added.

But Paget was not consoled, for a vast mass of well-armed cavalrymen was an intimidating sight. All of the British line watched with anticipation. This was the big moment they had all been waiting for, the first major encounter with a French army in open battle. They knew whatever happened next could be a major indicator as to what to expect, as well as have a significant effect on morale. The Spanish troops lay ready for the cavalry, and it seemed they had the strongest position any soldier could hope for, amongst the walls of the olive groves and with the French cavalry in plain sight. Four battalions totalling two thousand men awaited the enemy, yet long before the French had come into range, they were ordered to take aim.

"What the hell are they doing?" Ferreira asked in horror.

A grand volley rang out as all two thousand muskets fired. Yet not a single Frenchman went down for the balls fell short, and the Frenchmen were only spurred on as if the incident had made them feel immortal. They waved their sabres about their heads as they increased their pace and soared towards the olive groves. Cries of panic rang out from the Spaniards, and they began to flee in a panic. The rest of the army watching on felt their stomachs turn as they realised how easily their right flank could fold. Cuesta's cavalry quickly moved to recover the broken troops and drive them back towards their positions, but the damage to morale was already done. The French cavalry celebrated victory without a single drop of blood spilled on either side, cheering and waving their sabres around, as they circled about in the olive gardens so recently abandoned.

It was no great loss, but a symbolic loss, and the Frenchmen knew it. Before long they withdrew back to their own lines, clearly knowing they could not maintain the position as allied troops regrouped, and British artillery began to rain down upon them. Yet it was a heavy blow to the whole of the allied army who had been witness to the humiliating events.

"Amateurs," Ferreira scowled and shook his head in disgust at the Spanish troops.

"Now they know. Now the French know our right flank will not stand," gasped Paget.

"Wellesley saw it, too," said Matthys.

"This country will never be rid of Napoleon if its men run at the sound of their own volley," declared Ferreira.

Craven sat back down at the fire with a sigh, and the others soon joined him as they realised the excitement was over.

"Tomorrow will be a long day," said Ferreira.

"What are we to do, Sir? Where should we be?" Paget asked, as if increasingly feeling the weight of being helpless and without purpose.

"We will be where we need to be. This battle will be a bloody mess. Of that you can be sure."

CHAPTER 17

The sun had gone down without incident, and that was a great relief for the whole army as they reeled from the ambush at the Alberche River and the shameful breaking of the Spanish infantry in the evening. Everyone was anxious, yet nobody expected to see any more trouble until morning, which is why a distant volley lighting up the sky surprised them all. The thunderous echo of fire soon reached them whilst they were huddled about a fire and not long for bed. Craven shot up to see lines of muzzle flashes from muskets up on the Cerro de Medellin, the best vantage point in the area and the strongest point on the British lines.

"They've gone and done it. They've come right for us," declared Matthys in horror.

The rest of the British troops around them watched on with concern, but there was nothing they could do, for defending their posts was as important as defending the Cerro de Medellin.

"What do we do?" Paget asked.

"Nothing we can do," replied Matthys.

"The hell there is." Craven snatched up his sword and rushed to the horses. The others eagerly joined him, for excitement was building that they may finally face the French for real.

"We shouldn't leave our position."

"It's not our position, Matthys. There are more than enough troops to hold here. Like Wellesley said, we go where we are needed, and right now, we are needed right there," he replied, looking at the dark hill looming in the distance as flashes of light sparked over it whilst the French made their assault.

"We have no idea what we're going into," warned Matthys.

"I'll tell you what we're going into. That hill is the key to it all. If we lose it tonight, then the hole army is compromised."

"I am sure Wellesley knows that, too."

"We shall see, and if it is under control, we shall have a pretty sight as the French run," replied Craven as he urged his horse on, expecting the others to catch up.

"Does he want to get himself killed?" Paget asked.

"I don't even know anymore. A few months ago, you would not find that man anywhere near these horrors, and now he rides towards them like a man possessed."

Matthys charged on after the Captain. Craven soon recognised Major Thornhill galloping past, and when he called out to him, the Major came to a stop beside them. He was breathing heavy and clearly concerned.

"What is it?"

"A full assault on the hill, the French have smashed through Low's brigade on the Eastern slope."

"And the second line?"

"There is no second line. It seems as though the two brigades responsible for it made camp farther West."

Craven shook his head in disbelief.

"If the French can hold that hill, we may have to withdraw entirely and this battle is already lost," Thorny panted before digging in his heels and continuing on as he spread the news.

"What do you want to do?" Matthys asked as Ferreira and his sharpshooters joined them, all mounted, and ready for action.

Craven took another look at the silhouette of the hill, lit up by the flashes of muskets. It was the sort of fight he went out of his way to avoid, and yet he now remembered Wellesley's words earlier that day.

"What happens if we lose this battle?" asked Paget.

"Likely we will be driven back to the sea and back out of the Peninsula once again," replied Matthys.

"And it was all for nothing," added Ferreira.

"That won't do. I haven't got what I came for yet," Craven shouted and soared forwards towards the hill.

They passed countless British troops watching the lights of the fight from afar whilst on alert and ready for face a similar fate. Soldiers leapt out of the way as Craven galloped recklessly through the camp, even causing one Major to fall to the ground as he leapt out of the path of the charging horsemen. He called out something furiously, but from the speed at which Craven went, and the thunderous roar of the hooves of their horses, the Major's cries were entirely drowned out, but Birback still got a kick out of seeing him sprawled out in the dirt.

"What do you think we can do up there?" Paget yelled as he soon caught up to the Captain. His beautiful horse Augustus far quicker than any other amongst them.

"Whatever we can!" Craven he panted.

At the gallop it didn't take them long to reach the South-Western edge of Cerro de Medellin. The French had already taken the crest and were cheering as they waved their flags ahoy and cried out to insult the British troops below. The remnants of some of those who had been driven off the top were scattered about and tending to their wounded.

"The King's German Legion?" Matthys asked in surprise as he looked at the iconic black uniforms of the men who had fled from the ridge.

"Has to have been a hell of a fight to move those boys," replied Craven.

Shots rang out as a smattering of troops part way up the hill exchanged shots with the French light infantry who had taken it. It was half hearted at best, but from the base of the hill came a cry from an enthusiastic young officer.

"Worcestershires! Advance!"

The 1st Battalion of the Worcestershire Regiment began a climb of the hill, determined to dislodge the enemy, and do the work of the two battalions who should have been stationed there.

"On the right flank, now!" Craven leapt down from his horse and drew his sword before rushing on to join the advancing redcoats. He soon came up beside a Fusilier officer on the right flank of the Worcestershires who didn't know what to make of Craven and his peculiar mix of soldiers.

"What are we dealing with?" Craven demanded.

"The 7th Light Infantry smashed the KGL like they were nothing. We are going to take this hill back," replied the officer proudly.

"And we are happy to help."

"You are, Sir?"

"Captain Craven,"

"James Craven?"

Craven nodded in agreement.

"Then we are sure to succeed!" The officer looked over to his men.

"Listen up, lads. Crazy Craven is with us!"

A cheer rang out down the lines, and Craven looked shocked.

"You've made quite a name for yourself, Captain. Not all of it good, but I'd not take any other man into battle over you," he smiled.

Paget laughed.

"You knew about this?" Craven asked him.

"Of course, who doesn't want to hear about your exploits, Sir? They are a mighty source of entertainment on long and laborious days."

"You did this?"

"Not just me."

Craven shook his head.

"Isn't fame what you always wanted?"

"Riches, riches are what I always wanted, Matthys," protested the Captain.

"What's your name?" he asked the Fusilier officer.

"Captain Hawker."

Craven couldn't help but marvel at the huge sabre he had resting on his shoulder. It was of the 1803 regulation with its brass slot hilt in gilt, an elaborate but effective design. Yet its blade was not that of the size commonly carried by an infantry officer. In fact, it looked longer and larger than a cavalry sabre, being two inches wide and with little taper. He was certainly a man worthy of carrying such a monstrous weapon as he was of impressive stature. The Fusilier spotted Craven eyeing up his beastly blade and felt compelled to explain why, for it was clearly the subject of much pride.

"I would have a sword I would only need to strike once with, and be sure the enemy knows it," he smiled.

"And that?" Craven gestured towards a peculiar pistol he carried in his other hand. He tilted it forward to give Craven a better view. It was a pistol the size of the Land Pattern carried by the cavalry, yet it had two barrels side-by-side, with two firelocks and two triggers.

"If you're going to get close to the enemy, you better be sure you have the tools to get the job done right. And you, you are without pistol, Sir?"

Craven nodded in agreement as he drew out his dirk into his left so as to not feel quite so naked.

"That won't do at all," Hawker insisted as the troops continued to march steadily up the slope. Sporadic fire came back their way, but fire from the base of the hill kept many of their heads down. The drums beat as they advanced forward not knowing what they may face, yet as they came to the crest above, they received a single volley and only sustained a few casualties before drawing up in one long line. The French rushed to reload in full view on the narrow crest as the orders were passed down the lines. Muskets and rifles took aim as the whole line prepared to fire. The first order rang out, and it was repeated, but all other commands were drowned out by the devastating salvo, tearing through the French Light Infantry who had only just so bravely taken the hill for themselves. The volley had them wobbled, but they continued to load as a command echoed across the British line, "Advance!"

The line went forward as one. A smattering of shots came out from the French, but they covered the distance quickly, and soon another order they had all been eagerly awaiting for. For their blood was up now, and they were ready for what came next.

"Charge!"

Craven could feel the pain in his leg once again as he got to a jogging pace. Bayonets came forward, and a roar of excitement rang out amongst the troops before they surged forward. The French 7th Light Infantry were clearly not expecting such a robust counterattack or were at least expecting to have more of their own number, for the Worcestershires swarmed them.

As they closed the distance, Hawker fired his first shot and struck one down, whilst he closed with a French officer who held up a short and light sabre to defend himself. Hawker's blade smashed it down and cleaved into his head in the most visceral display of forcing Craven could hope to show the young Paget. A French sergeant tried to avenge his fallen officer as he directed a bayonet at Hawker, but he merely shot him down with the second barrel of his pistol. The powder smoke was soon dispersed up on the hilltop as the clash of musket furniture and bayonets rang out.

One Frenchman made a concerted effort to thrust in at

Craven, deceiving his sabre with a quick feint before plunging his attack home. The feint had worked, but Craven scooped up the musket and bayonet with his dirk and pushed it high, delivering a brutal rise cut up under the musket before striking his man in the face with his ward iron.

Caffy was ahead of them all as he leapt in amongst several infantrymen, ignoring all Craven had taught him and fighting like a whirlwind, cutting from one side to another. He had taken on too much, and yet gained a lot of respect from them all for his fearless nature. Charlie and Birback went forward to help him.

Another came at Craven with his small infantryman's sword, his briquet. It was now Craven's turn to launch deceiving thrusts as he quickly outmanoeuvred the short sword with a few flicks of his wrist before plunging his thrust home into his chest. As the man dropped before him, he realised Captain Hawker had got well ahead of him now and was engaged with two infantrymen. He parried from one side to another. His hulking blade was nothing as quick as Craven's, but it had such mass it beat them easily aside until finally he was too slow to one parry, and only partially defended himself. The musket drove through his guard, and the bayonet thrust into his abdomen. He let go of his treasured double-barrelled pistol, took hold of the bayonet, and brought down his sabre with such power it cleaved the man down to the chin, yet the other thrust his bayonet towards his chest.

Craven launched his dirk at the man, embedding it in his chest and causing him to stagger back in horror. Yet he recovered to fight as Craven closed the distance, but the Captain did not stop as he dropped his blade over the bayonet in a circular action, dropping the tip of his blade over to his left. He circled it around to move the bayonet aside before pivoting around it as if it were a smallsword, and driving a thrust up from below. He pushed his vanquished opponent off his blade as he dropped to the ground and turned back to Hawker to see him pull out the bayonet from his side.

"Look at that, it barely scratched me."

He smiled as he showed where it had gone in and out at his flank and just skimming a few layers of flesh. Cheers rang out from the troops beside them as the French turned tail and ran. Yet as the redcoats pushed them back over the rest to the Eastern edge, they could see another battalion of the French 7th Light Infantry advancing up the slope to take their place.

"Load!" the cry came.

Moxy rushed up beside Craven, his sling hung loose where he had taken his arm from it and stayed in the fight, just out of any close quarter actions. His rifle was loaded and ready, and he took his shot whilst everyone else was still loading. One of the French sergeants went down, and a cheer rang out along the line of redcoats. Once again Craven was left to watch as those with firearms did the work. Captain Hawker felt just as helpless now, nodded in acknowledgement of the fact, and further supporting his claim Craven needed a pistol.

"Fire!" the order rang out once more as the whole line of the 29th blasted the advancing French reserve, who backed away as so many of their comrades fell. Their officers cried out to try and rally them, but another volley followed, and the luckless French reserves were sent into utter disarray to the cheers of the Worcestershires and the Northamptonshires, who had come up on their right flank. Hawker breathed a sigh of relief.

No sooner had the muskets fallen silent was Sir Arthur Wellesley cantering up the hill to the scene of the fight. General Stewart went to greet him as he looked at the carnage laid out of the hilltop. The troops could barely see much in the darkness, but they'd recognise Wellesley's figure anywhere.

"Sir, we have control of the area. The French have been repulsed," declared Stewart.

"This ground is yours, as those who took it from the enemy. You will remain here and strengthen this position, and I shall stay here beside you to coordinate any further efforts should the French make another go. Congratulations to you all. Your quick response and fearless bravery has secured the battlefield, I commend you," declared the General. He spotted Craven and his troop, and at first he looked a little surprised, and then not surprised at all.

"As you were, secure your foothold on his hill, General. We may be in for a rough night," ordered Wellesley.

Stewart was quick to go about his business as Craven withdrew the dirk he had thrown.

"I was right about you Craven, wasn't I?" Wellesley asked.

"It would seem so, Sir," he replied as Wellesley went on to inspect the ridge overlooking the enemy positions.

"Here," declared a voice from behind Craven.

He turned about to find Hawker offering him his prized pistol. Craven took it and marvelled at the weapon. Hawker had dark black hair that was unkempt, though his long sideburns were in a far better shape. He carried himself with a supreme confidence.

"How will you manage?"

"It is one of a pair. I shall have the other brought up. An

238

officer should never be so naked as to not have a pistol when standing in the face of the enemy."

"Thank you," replied Craven as the grenadier handed him a small cartridge bag.

"It was an honour to march into battle with you, Captain. I wish you every luck tomorrow."

"And you." Craven lifted his sword up to his face and saluted. Hawker did the same before returning to his duties.

Craven turned back to his comrades to find them gathered together and awaiting news.

"Get comfortable. We're in for a long night. Ellis, Caffy, get back down to our camp and retrieve anything we left behind. This is where we're staying until we know otherwise." Ferreira relayed much the same orders in his own language to two of his own riflemen.

"That was a close call, wasn't it, Sir?" Paget asked as Craven stepped up to the Southern edge of the ridge to look out across what was set to be the battlefield for the next day.

"More than close. If the French had committed a serious effort to this hill, they would have taken it."

"So why did they not do that, Sir?"

"How can you know the enemy's mind?"

"Sir Arthur seems to."

"And yet he did not envisage such an invigorated effort on this day," mused Craven.

"Then the enemy doesn't know our numbers, and they wait on us to attack," replied Ferreira as he joined them.

"Attack?" Paget asked.

"Of course. This is our advance into French held territory, and they expect us to be the attacking force."

"Then why are we not? I don't understand."

"Because we can't risk it," replied Craven.

"But we would surely succeed, would we not? We have fifty thousand troops!" Paget cried out enthusiastically.

"Yes, and what do they have? The same? More? We have a large army, but the Spanish troops are levies for the most part, and the British troops aren't much better. Inexperienced with hurried training. The French Army down there is one that has waged war for years. They have conquered near enough every capitol of Europe. Battle hardened veterans up against this, a mess," he said and looked at their own army.

"Can they really be that good? The French? We didn't seem so terrible when we stormed this hill."

"That wasn't a battle. That was nothing more than a skirmish. Soon enough you will see the vast columns of Frenchmen marching under their eagles. What happens on this field could certainly make or break this army of Wellesley's."

It was a lot to think about, and Paget was clearly scared now, despite the seemingly unwavering faith he had in their own troops and especially their commanders. Craven sat down and took out the small cartridge bag he had been given. He began to reload his pistol, which is when Paget noticed it and his eyes lit up.

"Sir, where did you find such a piece?" he cried.

"It was a gift."

He had only just finished loading it when a shot rang out from one of the pickets up on the hill. He leapt to his feet and was alert once again as he looked around for any sound of trouble.

"Stand down!" an officer called, signalling it was nothing

of note.

As the camp settled down, they could hear the clatter of heavy gun carriages in the distance. It was the French bringing up their artillery for the next day. It was a most unwelcome sound, as if they were great fiery beasts of antiquity. Everyone was restless that night, and shots rang out regularly as pickets on both sides took shots in the dark, yet never hitting anything. None of them got more than an hour of sleep at a time, and several times Craven awoke he could see Wellesley was up and checking the hour with his staff. For he, too, slept on the ground that night, with little more than a rough bivouac to share between himself and his staff. His anxious pacing and questioning of the time betrayed his anxiety for the coming dawn. Nobody would blame him for it. They were in for a long night.

CHAPTER 18

29th July 1809.

"How did we find ourselves here?" Moxy asked. He was sitting on a verge beside Craven that overlooked the rolling hills to the East. The army was awake, though you'd barely know it for the troops had not moved from the positions they had held all night. The thousands of troops in their bright tunics for as far as the eye could see painted a pretty picture on what was a bleak landscape of scrub and dry olive fields. It was first light, and the morning rays of sunshine cast long foreboding shadows over what were peaceful lands, soon to erupt into complete chaos. The French Army was in full view from their high vantage point. Thirty thousand French troops opposed the sixteen thousand of their own. The Spanish evened out the odds, but few felt that way after what they had seen before. There was a mass of activity amongst the French cavalry to the South, opposing the walled city of Talavera, "What are we, showmen, hunters, gamblers?

And here we are at the front of the biggest battle one could imagine. How did that happen?"

"We flew too close to the sun," replied Craven, as he was deep in thought, too.

"The one thing we aren't, is soldiers."

"Are you so sure about that, Moxy? Maybe we never set out to be, but what is it we are doing now, if not soldiering?"

"And you are okay dying for the flag and the King's shilling?"

"Absolutely not. I didn't come here to die."

"Neither did any other poor bugger, but it happens," replied Moxy as he looked down at his bloody arm sling.

Craven was well aware how close they had both come to death, and it left a bitter taste in the back of his mouth.

"You shouldn't have come with us last night, and you certainly shouldn't have been firing that rifle." Craven pointed at the weapon resting in the Welshman's lap.

"If I can't use this, of what use am I?"

"You're not healed yet, and one rifle isn't going to make the difference, is it?"

"I beg to differ about that."

"I'm sure you do. Why did you even come with me? After the Manchester and Salfords ended, why come with me?"

"When we were just prizefighters, before we were recruited to the Regiment, we had nothing. We put on our shows and we made merry, but we lived like peasants, and the way our lives changed didn't really become clear until I went home after disbanding. What life for me was there? Farming? Work at the iron works? The life we were offered in Manchester elevated us to something most of could never have dreamed of, and I guess we're now chasing after it once more."

"Had we been born into money we could have raised our own regiment, or even a yeomanry," smiled Craven.

"If we could make our fortune out here, maybe we still can do that?"

"Do you think there would still be a need for them once this war is over?"

"If this war ever ends. Napoleon will have the world if he can. So, we're either stuck fighting it till we die, or he wins, and then what? We go home to that same life we used to lead all those years ago?"

"No, when this is over, things will never be the same again. All we can do is stick together, and when all is said and done, we will make our own future."

"Is that a promise?" Moxy asked him sincerely.

Craven pointed to Caffy who was standing at the edge, admiring the view as a free man.

"You see that? That is a man who has known what it is like to have nothing. A slave, beaten down and treated as though he were nothing, and look where he is now."

"On the eve of battle and maybe the end of his days?"

"No, Moxy, he's carving his own path. Nobody forced him to come with us. In fact, he practically begged to come. He could have gone to live a simple life with his father and a good living at the Lady Sarmento's residence. We aren't that different to him, you know. We just had a luckier start in life."

"What are you getting at?"

"Look at him. He is alive, more than he has ever been. We all are. I said we came here to make our riches, but maybe we already have? For there is more to wealth than gold and coin, we have each other," he replied solemnly as he came to the revelation himself as he spoke the words. For the first time in his life he felt as though he had purpose rather than just a hunger for the things he did not have.

"You're still going to make us rich though, right?" Moxy joked.

Craven smiled, for he could see the Welshman appreciated the sentiment. Yet as they fell silent, they could hear the thunderous beat of the French drums in the distance. It was an imposing sound, for so many across Europe had come to fear it, as if it signalled the coming of the Four Horsemen of the Apocalypse. For Napoleon's columns often marked the end of whatever they approached.

Cries rang out across the lines as the troops prepared themselves. Moments later a cannon shell struck the ground nearby and ploughed through several redcoats of the Northamptonshires. The crack of cannons firing in the distance soon caught up to them as the bombardment began. Nobody was under any illusion as to why. The French wanted the position they had so briefly held the night before. It was the key to the battle, and everyone knew it, which is why Wellesley was right there amongst them. He was standing in defiance of the bombardment as he surveyed the French movements ahead.

"Down, lie down on the ground!" Wellesley cried, his orders being quickly roared by every officer on the rest of the much-valued Cerro de Medellin.

"Stay put," Craven said as they hunkered down, and he rushed forward towards Wellesley's position to see for himself, as even those who stayed down at the front watched with anticipation for the enemy. Yet they advanced under the protection of the rolling hills and verges. The beat of their drums was growing louder, and finally they came into view as they marched relentlessly towards the British positions. Five thousand soldiers came at them in three columns, the preferred method of the French. The British marched in columns, but they preferred to fight in lines. The French relied on their massed column to manoeuvre with pinpoint precision, smashing through all who stood before them by sheer weight of numbers and brute force. Unfortunately, it was a strategy the British could not afford to employ, for they so rarely had such numbers as to amass. And so they preferred their thin red lines where they could amass such great firepower as to overcome any deficiency in numbers.

Even so, the French column was a fearful and awe-inspiring sight to behold as they marched unwaveringly forward with absolute confidence in their ability to triumph, no matter the circumstances. No wonder so many levy troops fled so quickly in the face of such a terrifying formation, for it even turned the stomach of many a professional soldier. The French cannons continued to roar, though they inflicted little damage, for Wellesley had set up his forces on the reverse slopes of every hill and undulation. This was a strategy that flew in the face of the long-established doctrine of defending the top of an elevated position. Wellesley had his troops on the slope opposite from the attacking force, lying down near the top so they may be ready to fight for the high ground, but hidden from enemy guns. French cannonballs ricocheted off of the tops of the hills and whizzing dangerously close to the men, but inflicting little damage for the natural cover they were afforded. Craven looked South where he could see thousands of troops down on the ground. He wondered how it might look to the enemy, who without a vantage point would see little but open terrain. The British and Spanish troops were concealed and lying in weight as if to spring a trap.

"Only one assault?" Craven asked.

"They test us," insisted Paget.

Craven turned in surprise to see the young officer had followed him to the front.

"What did I say?"

"But, Sir, I had to see it with my own eyes. French columns, are they not a sight to behold?" he asked excitedly, marvelling at the gleaming white-fronted uniforms as the three masses of Frenchmen marched in a determined fashion towards them. The sun glistened from the Imperial Eagles they carried with such pride as their tricolour flags fluttered in the wind. The three columns advanced along the whole Eastern edge of the Cerro de Medellin and a little to the South of it.

"But, Sir, they only attack here?"

"They still hope we will become the attacking force, but are testing our strength to see if we'll stand."

"Why, Sir?"

"Because advantage is in the hands of the defender who chooses the terrain he fights on; who rests whilst the enemy marches and has no risk of becoming disorderly in an advance."

"That really happens?"

"Of course. An army might parade with perfect order when going before the King in open field, but in mixed terrain and in the face of the enemy? That is a far harder task, believe me."

Paget looked disappointed.

"Don't be too eager to get into battle with the enemy, for this is just one army. Should we win here, we have more to face. We must not just win here. We must win decisively, or we will gain nothing."

"How do you know this, Sir?" asked Paget curiously.

"Think of everything Major Thornhill told us and the work he had us doing in the mountains. Our work was vital because if the French armies can come together as one, we would be crushed underfoot. Soult waits in the North expecting Wellesley to cross over. The secrecy of Wellesley's movements has kept him in the dark, but how long do you think that illusion can last now? They know where Wellesley is and the whole British Army, and they will come for us with everything they've got."

Fear overcame Paget at the realisation they were in such a precarious situation.

"I had thought being on the attack we had the advantage, and that it meant we were stronger," he gulped.

"Don't be under any illusions. Wellesley gambles with a weak hand. He plays tricks and games and stays one step ahead, but he plays many a dangerous game."

"I thought it a rather more even affair, this war I mean," replied Paget naively.

"That is what you will hear back home. For since the threat of England being invaded has passed, few now know the dangers abroad. If we were half as strong as you would believe, would we not have crossed the English Channel, just as William the Conqueror did? The Pas-de-Calais is what, fifty miles? And yet we came all the way here to Southern Europe to wage war? We are hanging on barely in this war, for Napoleon's dominance of Europe is all but complete."

"And if we lose here?"

"Then we would have to seek a truce, one which Napoleon would never keep; for if we leave Europe, he would only bide his time until he could invade, and he would have all the ports and ship builders of Europe at his disposal to make it happen. It would be the beginning of the end for England."

Paget's face turned pale at the prospect, for never before had he realised how much was at stake.

"You know this to be true?" he questioned.

"Yes, a gambling man always considers the risks even when he watches a game from afar."

General Hill paced back and forth along the lines dismounted, as they all were so as to not present a target for the French artillery. He was a robust looking officer who Craven recognised from Porto, for his division had crossed the Douro to secure the victory Craven himself had been witness to.

"Wait for it!" Hill roared.

The French artillery soon came to a halt, and everyone knew what that meant. The assault was about to begin, and now the drumbeats rang in everyone's ears.

"Come on." Craven led Paget back to their own unit who were squeezed in between two British regiments. They seemed to be nothing more than a modest spec on the vast battlefield.

"Steady, lads!" an officer called out nearby.

The anticipation was almost unbearable as Craven had to consciously think to breathe. He had faced the enemy in battle before, but nothing on the scale of what they were now facing, and certainly not Napoleon's finest in an open battle.

"This is what we came for." Paget was trying to recover

some of his confidence in the face of such a danger he never could have imagined.

"Now is your time!" a voice roared.

Officers all along the line cried out as they brought their men up from the ground. The entirety of General Hill's division rose up at the crest of the Cerro de Medellin. Four thousand troops taking aim at the French columns as one, just two ranks deep. The enemy was just one hundred yards from the skyline and still advancing en masse. Their regiments were eighteen ranks deep but not more than a hundred in the front rank. They were compressed together as one large mass, as if a battering ram being hauled towards the armoured gates of a fortress.

"Fire!" the command rang out.

A deafening salvo erupted in near perfect symphony. The fire smashed the French columns, several ranks being completely obliterated. The British troops all along the battle line to the South cried out in support as a cloud of smoke billowed out from the Cerro de Medellin. It was as though a volcano had roared to life after so many dormant years. The French colours of one of the columns fell, but it was soon picked up without hesitation. The columns came to a standstill as they took aim at the British lines silhouetted along the rise above. A duel began between the lines as they each hurried to reload. Craven could only watch as those around him went about their work. For as fine a piece his pistol was, it would do no good at the distances that the two sides slugged it out. A small calibre pistol would struggle to put a man down beyond fifty yards. For several minutes the two sides exchanged fire, yet the thin red line was raining down significantly more fire onto the Frenchmen who were standing out in the open. After several volleys they began to waver.

"Advance!" the roar came from the South side of the Cerro de Medellin as General Sherbrooke's forces there saw their opportunity and advanced on the left flank of the enemy. A volley rang out from the newly arrived troops before another from the thousands along the hilltop when the French finally accepted defeat and began to withdraw in good order.

Wellesley was standing beside the fluttering colours of the 29th when he gave the order, "Charge!"

"On to them, boys!" Captain Hawker cried out as he swung his massive blade about his head, his spare pistol in his other hand just as he said it would be. The redcoats stormed downed the hill with fixed bayonets as those advancing from the South rushed on to not lose out on the moment. Yet as they advanced, sporadic fire still rang out from the French, and General Hill was struck on the head as he went over the crest. His sword fell as he collapsed to the ground. His officers gathered around him, but he shrugged at them as blood trickled down his head.

"Go on, go at them!" he cried out.

It was enough to incense all around him. Several of his staff drew out their swords and leapt on after the troops to take their revenge.

"You wouldn't want to miss a fight, would you?" Craven asked his posse, who already had their swords in hand in expectation.

Birback was the first to leap over the edge and storm on after the enemy, though it wasn't clear if he was trying to prove his loyalty, for he was always spoiling for a fight. Craven took one last look at the others to see Ferreira seemingly had no intentions to join them as he reloaded and kept his feet firmly planted on the ground.

"We're riflemen, not common brawlers."

Craven laughed at how stubborn his Portuguese friend could be. He then leapt out over the edge, leading his small band on after the infantry who charged at the enemy like lions. Craven's leg hurt for every step he took, but he could bear it so long as he kept it safe.

The French columns had suffered badly, but they still had significant strength and numbers, and those numbers were now a detriment as the columns were forced down into the valley of the Portiña. Craven stormed past several redcoats as they tussled with Frenchmen and found his own opponents. A staggered line readied their weapons to fire ahead, and Craven took aim, shooting two of them down before they could lower their weapons into a firing position. Paget fired at another, although five began to take aim before they could close the distance. Yet before they could fire they were riddled with shot and three were killed. The other two went down wounded as shots whistled over Craven's head. He looked back up to the crest of the Cerro de Medellin and could see Ferreira and his men amongst a cloud of smoke. The Portuguese officer waved as if to prove his point.

"It is good to have friends," declared Paget.

"Yes, it is," growled Craven, having to admit he was a fool to rush in.

He thrust his pistol into his scarlet officer's sash and drew out his dirk as he went on after the rest of the enemy. Redcoats swarmed down the hillside like a sea of red as they cried out enthusiastically. They watched the enemy run and clashed with any who dared stand their ground against them. Craven went forward at one of them, a stubborn looking veteran with a large grey moustache. He took the man's bayonet with his dirk as he closed and plunged his sword into his chest, crashing into him and knocking him to the ground.

As he withdrew his blade, he could see the charge was coming to a stop. The French were now scattered and running back to their lines at a fast pace. That was when his eye was drawn to several officers in the distance. He would recognise one of them from a mile away, yet he was within a half a mile, and it was Major Claveria himself. The butchering of Maria and the entire townsfolk was still fresh on Craven's mind, and the ambush he and Mardel had concocted only poisoned his mind further. He spat on the ground before him, knowing Claveria could see as they glared at one another. Craven heard the cock of a rifle lock into place and looked to his side to see Moxy taking aim.

"Once shot, Sir, it's all it would take. Let me do it."

"No, that bastard is mine. I will find him on the field soon enough."

Moxy pulled the trigger anyway. Flint struck frizzen and sparks flew, but there was no powder to ignite, for there was neither primer in the pan nor charge in the barrel. The Welshman was merely having some fun, and Craven laughed before taking a moment to catch his breath. He then noticed Paget beside him with a huge smile.

"That was really something," he declared as he watched as two men of the 29th swing French standards, trophies of their glorious counter charge.

"Yes, it was," replied Craven.

"They will be back before long," Matthys said as he

encouraged them to get back to their positions. It was a weary climb back up the hill after such an enthusiastic descent, but it had done wonders for morale, as those on the top and the lines to the South cried out enthusiastically in support. Soon enough they reached Ferreira's position, and the cocky Captain had an expression upon his face of 'I told you so.'

"Thanks for that." Craven patted him on the shoulder.

"You were riflemen once. It is a wonder you do not spend more time with those rifles and a little less time with swords, perhaps then you would live longer."

"Truth be told we were never riflemen. We were brought in to help riflemen learn the use of the sword, and we did it rather well. Cold steel has gotten me this far in life."

"Or you could say that perhaps it has gotten you into this much trouble?"

Craven laughed, for he knew there was a lot of truth to what his Portuguese friend was saying, but he valued his swords too much to ever admit it. The rest of the troops were soon back at their positions, and the ring of ramrods rang out as they reloaded in readiness for whatever came next.

The defence of Cerro de Medellin had been nothing short of a total success, although there were still hundreds of wounded hobbling back to the rear and many being carried, the dead awaiting movement. It was this sight of which Paget became focused, for he had never seen so much death, or at least not of his own comrades. For at Porto they had inflicted such heavy losses on the French, but at far less a loss themselves.

"I knew men died in war, but I never imagined it to be so many in so short a time," he mused.

"The trick is to not be amongst them," declared Craven.

Paget looked upset by his brash sentiment, and yet the Captain stood by it.

"Many more will die before this is over. All you can do is look out for the man beside you and fight your best fight," he reassured Paget.

CHAPTER 19

The battlefield had long fallen silent as each side awaited the other's move. Each wanted the other to commit to a dangerous assault as the French had learned that morning. A costly venture that no General would risk lightly. A single rider broke the silence as Major Thornhill stormed up the hill and onto the crest. He still wore his civilian jacket and clearly came with urgent news. A dust cloud kicked up around him as he brought his horse to an abrupt halt and leapt from the saddle like a spry young man.

"This is either very good or very bad news," declared Ferreira.

Nobody dared speculate as they watched him rush up to Wellesley. He had remained with the division on Cerro de Medellin. The lines of troops were silent as everyone was eager to hear news and prayed it was for the best.

"Well?" Wellesley demanded, seeing the smile on

Thorny's face, and realising he brought good news.

"Sir, two items of news, both of which have already reached the French."

"Well, what news?" Wellesley asked impatiently.

"General Venegas has finally moved North and threatens Madrid."

Wellesley could barely hold back a cheeky smile as he realised what they meant.

"And the second item? Go on, man!"

"General Soult's march South is delayed and significantly slower than he would have hoped."

A gasp of relief rang out from an officer beside Wellesley. Not all the troops knew quite what that news meant, but Wellesley's face spoke a thousand words, for their typically stoic leader could not contain his joy at hearing the news.

"What does this mean?"

Wellesley heard Paget even from twenty paces.

"It means the enemy before us has no choice but to attack, for they must defeat us if their King Joseph is to save his capitol. They can delay no further. They must come to us."

Cheers rang out, as everyone knew that is what Wellesley wanted. They had made their defences, and now the enemy had no choice but to come at them as they waited, ready and able to fend off the storm.

"Let them come," remarked Wellesley.

It was mid afternoon when they once again heard the beat of the French drums, and French troops began their next advance. But this time it was not against the Cerro de Medellin, but spread across the Spanish left flank of the city of Talavera and the Pajar de Vergara where Doyle and his gunners had already begun to pound the incoming French. British infantry to Doyle's left flank eagerly awaited their shot at the French after having celebrated the successes of the morning.

"Now we will know if their courage is as bold as their uniforms," declared Ferreira as he watched the Spanish troops.

Those on Cerro de Medellin watched with intrigue and concern as the French moved through the dense olive groves. The mixed terrain slowed them down, and the columns became staggered and disorganised as they made they advance. The British artillery roared as they cut down the centre of the advance, and the redcoats to the North soon opened fire on the enemy. Soon enough it was the Spaniards turn to fight. All eyes were on them as they prepared their first volley, and those depending on them waited to see whether they would throw down their muskets as before or stand and fight as their allies had done. The anticipation was unbearable, for they held their fire as to not risk a repeat of their ineffectual fire the last time the French advanced on them.

Finally, their muskets rang out, and the French columns took heavy casualties. The Spaniards did not run at the sound of their own guns this time, and spurred on by the success of the first volley, they eagerly loaded for the next as skirmishers continued to pepper the enemy. Craven smiled at Ferreira, for he had been wrong.

"No one is happier about that than me," he sighed.

Though Craven laughed, for the Portuguese Captain had the look of a gambler who could afford the loss he had just suffered, and yet felt insulted having lost to such a player as he did. Just as soon as the French had engaged in the South, more drums were heard as a massive force advanced on the British centre at the South edge of the Cerro de Medellin. The troops atop it could only spectate as they held the vital vantage point from which Wellesley himself oversaw the battle. It was a terrifying sight to behold. Twenty-four French battalions were advancing towards eight British battalions spread thinly, stretching from North to South. It was the thin red line that Wellesley could not afford to lose. The anticipation was killing all who watched, for none but those on the Cerro de Medellin had a full insight into the whole battlefield and the progress of either side as they watched the battle unfold around them.

The French advance appeared to be relentless, and it seemed impossible it could be stopped. Everyone was anxious, none more so than Wellesley who had now done all the planning he could do, and committed all the troops he could afford to. For he knew there were yet more French troops waiting to exploit any opening as troops were pulled from their posts to reinforce existing actions. The eight battalions waited on the reverse slope of the shallow hills, just as those on Cerro de Medellin had. Concern was growing for the enemy was within one hundred and fifty yards now, and the British had not risen up to meet them.

"Come on, give them hell," whispered Craven.

The vast horde of French infantry got to within one hundred yards, and still the British had not formed up.

"Come on, what are you waiting for?"

Finally, there was movement as the four divisions got to their feet all as one. The enemy were just fifty yards away when the redcoats took aim and opened fire, all eight battalions firing as one in a grand salvo that caused a cloud of fog to rise up. Powder smoke rolled over the hills, much of it passing over the

Cerro de Medellin. Paget coughed as it filled his lungs. He watched opened mouth as the battle unfolded, though they were blinded for a few moments before the fog lifted. Another salvo rang out before they could get another clear view, further adding to the haze that swept the battlefield. The cloud of musket smoke was at least a momentary rest from the dazzling rays of sunlight, for the entire area was now bone dry and baked by an unrelenting sun. Sweat dripped from the faces of even those who merely watched the battle unfold.

"To the North!" a voice cried.

Wellesley hurried over to the crest where he could see onto the other side, and Craven rushed on after him. Not falling under any direct command, he went as he pleased, and was too curious to stay away from the General. Wellesley, having already been saved once by Craven, did not protest. The French were widening the front of their attack as they advanced North of the Cerro de Medellin toward a broad flat valley. He looked to Major Spring.

"Send word to General Cuesta. We need his support to the North, and despatch the cavalry to hold. We cannot lose the left flank, no matter what!"

Major Spring quickly despatched riders, and it was not long before royal blue jacketed Hussars of the King's German Legion and the 23rd Light Dragoons began to swarm into the valley. It was a grand sight, and yet also a terrifying one. For the infantry atop the Cerro de Medellin knew it meant one thing, Wellesley was deploying his reserve as he funnelled any forces he could muster into the valley, no matter whether they were suited to the task or the cost they would endure. Yet the dragoons advanced bravely, fully trusting in the necessity of their advance. The troops atop the Medellin cheered on their comrades on either side, for it was all they could do.

The battle raged on, and the Medellin was soon like an island in the clouds as the fog of war floated all around them, only offering brief glimpses into the events below as the occasional welcome gust of wind created openings. As the fire began to reduce on the South side, they heard an almighty war cry that preceded any bayonet charge. It turned many stomachs; for they feared the French columns were about to smash the outnumbered divisions who had opposed them. The fog began to clear, and to their amazement it was the British infantry charging forward with their bayonets.

An elated cry rung out from the Medellin as the men erupted with excitement, waving their shakos in the air and cheering on their comrades. The British infantry swarmed across the rough plain as they bayoneted any they could catch. The French were in complete disarray, having been badly battered by the disciplined musketry of the British redcoat who had been drilled to use mass musketry to devastating effect. Yet the British infantry's success got the better of them as they stormed onward. Their counterattack did not stop at merely defeating the forces they had opposed, as it pursued the enemy too far. Nothing could be done to stop them as six of the British battalions ploughed into the French second line and were met with massed volleys.

The British formed up to return fire but were fatigued and badly bloodied by the opening fire of the French. They were soon met with more volleys as the French second line had been waiting for them, just as they had been for the initial French charge. It was now the turn of the British to retreat in disorder.

Craven and the others couldn't help but feel powerless as they watched the dreadful sight unfold below them. And as he turned his eyes North, he could see more troubles unfold. The 23rd Dragoons had encountered a hidden stream along the valley floor and had been stalled, and so lost all advantage they might have in speed and surprise. The stragglers now engaged French cavalry, but it was bloody and costly. To the South he was amazed to see the Spanish had held, for supported by the guns of the Royal Artillery they had repulsed several attacks. The battle of Talavera had devolved into a bitter and bloody affair, but it was not over yet.

Wellesley was facing a crisis, and everyone atop the Medellin could see it unfolding. The British centre was fleeing, and those of the infantry further to the South were moving to fill their place. But with not nearly enough men to plug the gap, and the French could see it. Massed columns now advanced on the gap, the hole in the British centre that could drive a huge wedge between Wellesley and Cuesta, and potentially send the entire army into a rout. The battle hung in the balance.

Detachments of Cuesta's Spanish troops stormed into the valley to the North, and Wellesley had to believe they would be enough, but there was nobody left to plug the vital hole in the line. Wellesley only had one resource left at his disposal, the intrepid two regiments who had seized the initiative to retake the Medellin the night before. They were all the General had to defend the most vital part of the British line, and if he did not commit them it, would all be over.

"48th, march down that hill, and you stop the French. You stop them, do you hear!"

The 1st Battalion of the Northamptonshires formed up to cheers from the Worcestershires who had fought alongside them to secure the Medellin. They now spurred on their comrades as they marched down the South bank to face an almighty French force beyond anything they could hope to withstand, and yet still they went. Wellesley nodded towards Craven, for he need not utter a single word.

"On me!" Craven drew his sword and led his squad down the slope after the 48th with Ferreira and his Caçadores by his side.

"We walk into the jaws of death, Sir, do we not?"

Paget sounded half excited and half terrified.

"We do, but we go well armed!" Craven cried out.

CHAPTER 20

Craven's two ragtag squads formed up on the Northamptonshires' right flank, spread out as skirmishers, but also to try and fill the gap left by the six battalions that had fled. Nobody was under any illusions that one battalion and Craven's small posse could do the work of six battalions. However, the two that had restrained themselves and not pursued the enemy were still standing their ground, and all they needed to do was buy time. For Wellesley could look down either side of the Medellin now and see the enemy had been stopped everywhere else along the line. They were being ground down by troops who would not run, not even the Spanish who held Talavera town and had been the target of such contempt and ridicule.

"Is this how you make us rich?" Moxy joked as they marched to face a seemingly unstoppable advance of Frenchmen.

Birback smiled at the sentiment but dared not comment

on it. He was already on thin ice with Craven, and so was just grateful that the Captain had not shared his deceit with the others.

"This is how you get remembered for great deeds," replied Paget.

"Or how you get dead," replied Moxy.

"I didn't come here to die, not before them," seethed Charlie.

Orders rang out from the officers of the Northamptonshires, but Craven needed not say a word, as his friends wheeled about and came into position beside the line of redcoats. The drums of the French thundered, but they could still hear the cheers of the Worcestershires atop the Cerro de Medellin, cheering them on as brothers all under the watchful eye of Wellesley, who knew more than anyone how much the battle now hung in the balance.

"All of England is watching, boys!" cried out an officer of the 48th.

"Aim!" another officer called out.

Craven relayed the command, but he need not have, for his motley crew and the Caçadores were now standing amongst the British line. Their rifles and their training forgotten, redundant as they were relegated to the duties of line infantry as the desperate situation required.

"Fire!"

The volley rang out and struck the first line of the Frenchmen down. It wasn't enough, but the two other battalions who had held the gap with them now opened fire and whittled down the French, who merely continued to advance with the beat of their drums. The British hurried to reload as the French marched stubbornly on towards them. The rifles were slower to load, but they worked as quickly as they could.

"Fire!" the order came, and the line erupted with another volley, soon followed by the two other battalions, and then finally Craven's squads were ready.

They had little firepower between them, but every shot was well chosen. He didn't need to issue the order, for they fired when ready and picked off their targets with ease. They might not have been natural riflemen, but they had enough training to fit the role, except perhaps for Craven himself. Target shooting had never come naturally to him. The French troops began to spread out into broader lines as they prepared to duel with the musketry of the 48th. The French were in far greater number, but not nearly as well trained and disciplined in massed firepower, for which the British had come to rely upon to make up for in numbers.

The first French volley rang out, though only a fraction of their troops was able to fire at once, as despite redeploying they were still many ranks deep. A dozen of the Northamptonshires went down, but they were soon loaded and ready to return fire.

Craven's unit seemed to go unnoticed by the French infantry who took aim at the block mass of redcoats and ignored the seemingly insignificant skirmishers supporting their right flank as they hurried to reload. The rest of the British line continued to pour fire into the French whose momentum had been broken.

They could not make best use of their massed numbers as they had been brought to a standstill by withering fire and now duked it out with a more modest force that was far better suited to the task at hand. The Frenchmen fumbled to fire two shots a minute whilst the British could muster four as their relentless training ensured they were at peak performance under even the worst of conditions.

Burning rays of sun beat down on them, and the massed musketry only added to the inferno. The dried grass all around them began to catch alight, causing smoke to rise all around as the wounded scrabbled to save themselves from the flames. It might as well have been a desert for the men of the 48th. They seemed to forget all reason and regard for their own lives, as they loaded and fired with such speed and discipline as to ignore all that came back at them. More and more of their comrades fell amongst them. One shot clipped Ellis' jacket, and he completely ignored it, as he went on to load his rifle. One shot took Craven's shako from his head whilst another shot clipped Birback's shoulder, causing him to wince with pain. As he reached for the hole in his jacket, he found his hand covered with blood. Moxy laughed at the sight, and even Craven managed to smile for it was a return to normalcy.

"Why does it always have to be me?" Birback protested

A bloody exchange followed as the hills became thick with smoke. The Cerro de Medellin vanished in the fog, and the enemy lines became little more than faint silhouettes. The powder smoke was intoxicating, and they all struggled to breathe as it burnt the backs of their throats and nostrils. The riflemen picked off officers and the standard bearers in an attempt to demoralise the enemy. But it was the line infantry with their Brown Besses who dealt the most devastating blows, as sweaty and bloody hands continued to load and fire like a well-oiled machine. The redcoats would not run, and the French could not outshoot them. They were unable to bring their superior numbers to bear as the chaos descended. Officers fell even before orders could be given, and the French columns became lost in the grey fog that engulfed them, and yet still they fought on. They were fully aware that if they could break through it would mean victory. It was the moment of crisis for Wellesley's army.

Another volley rang out, and Matthys was struck in the leg. He collapsed to the ground whilst a ball struck Caffy's neck, and he dropped to one knee. Craven rushed over to the Sergeant's side.

"Keep firing!" he cried as he looked at the wound. It had passed through the thigh, but the bleeding was light.

"I'll be okay," insisted Matthys.

Caffy was holding his bloody neck and pulled his hand away to see a bloodstained palm. Dozens of the Northamptonshires lay dead and wounded whilst the Caçadores had suffered four casualties, too. The thin red line was now little more than a thread holding the weight of the entire army. They would not run, but even so they faced the prospect of complete destruction. Craven spotted movement to their rear, and he could see scattered troops who had been broken returning to the fight. They were rushing into position to bolster the 48th. Even Ned Clinton, the Commisarie's Clerk rallied to them. He looked exhausted and bloodied, but was up for one last push.

"Come on! Do what you were born to do!" Matthys picked up his rifle and thrust it into Craven's hands, "Or will you be beat by a Frenchman?" Matthys could see Craven needed no further motivation.

"Never," replied Craven as he took the rifle and cartridge box, throwing it over his shoulder. He began to load the weapon as he gazed out at the enemy who looked on in disbelief, as the thin red line seemed to grow stronger with every volley they fired upon it. The French were beginning to waver, and they could all see it. Caffy was spurred on to do the same, and he wiped the blood from his palm onto his trousers. He then went about loading his musket to rejoin the fight.

"They're gonna go, boys, give them lead!" cried one of the Northamptonshires.

Craven loaded just in time to take aim as the redcoats levelled their muskets one more time, their numbers now bolstered by the many troops who had rallied to fight once more.

"Fire!"

A bristling volley ran along the line and smashed into the French as they desperately fumbled to load their muskets. Much of the front two ranks collapsed under the weight of fire, and those behind looked pale with fear at the brick wall they seemed to have run into. For the British centre would not fold.

"Advance!" the order rang out from the 48th.

The prospect seemed unfathomable for many of the French. They had supposed they were on the offensive against a weakened enemy, and yet the British line now came forward, and did so with complete confidence. For even those who had so recently broken now went towards the enemy, invigorated. Everyone could feel it. They had assembled a desperate defence, but now they imagined what nobody had dared imagine just ten minutes before.

Craven looked to Moxy, not wanting him to go forward for he was still weak.

"I've got him," he said as he went to Matthys' aid.

Ferreira had already had his riflemen fix bayonets. They didn't need to share any words as they were of one mind. The desperate defence was over, and now the troops advanced and demanded victory, and they were willing to take it. Craven threw down Matthys' rifle and drew out his sword and pistol, as he led his small band forward. And Ferreira ordered his Caçadores on. There was only a small divide between the two battle lines. The French had marched into close range thinking they might bullishly smashed their way through.

"Charge bayonets!" the 48th Major roared.

A line of glistening steel descended as the troops presented their weapons forward in readiness for the attack.

"Charge!" came the cry.

A ferocious roar erupted along the lines as the steadfast troops were vindicated and rushed forward, certain of their victory now. All thoughts of fatigue faded away as the infantrymen rushed at the enemy, who held their ground but were clearly appalled to see their opponents come at them. Many of the British troops were bloodied and filthy and appeared invincible, like an army of the dead who could not be killed. Bayonets clashed as the British front rank smashed their way through into the column. Musket butts crashed into faces and knees as bayonets were plunged into bodies, and an all-out melee ensued.

Craven crossed his sword and pistol as he ran into one bayonet. Driving them both high as he closed the distance. He placed one foot behind his opponent's heels and shoved him forward, causing him to fall back. He thrust his sword into his chest as he fell to the ground. Another swung at him with the stock of his musket, but he quickly slipped back, narrowly avoiding the blow as it clumsily sailed past. He lunged forward in riposte, thrusting straight into the man's heart.

Caffy smashed one in the face with the stock of his musket, and as he fell back, delivered a devastating slash with his prized French sabre.

Paget shot one as he parried another bayonet, though the force pushed down against him caused him to drop down to one knee as he struggled to keep his sword up to protect himself. Craven looked concerned for a moment, but the young officer needed no help. For he dropped his pistol, grabbed hold of the furniture of the musket, and cut under to his attacker's legs. He returned to his feet and plunged his sword into the man's chest. Charlie ran at another and pushed his bayonet down with her sword. She slashed across his throat as if a cavalryman passing their target, moving onto her next victim as she took the revenge she so desperately sought.

Ellis was struggling with one of the infantrymen who had grabbed hold of him as he closed, but Birback swung a heavy punch into his attacker as he passed him. It was a thunderous blow that sent the Frenchman reeling and barely able to stand on his own feet. Ellis quickly seized his opportunity and followed up with a quick cut of his sabre.

The French began to break and calls to retreat rang out across the lines. Yet in the disarray, Craven saw several officers press forward on horseback, and once more he spotted the man he had been seeking.

"Claveria!" Craven cried out.

The Frenchman would not hear him because of the volleys of musket fire that still rang out on their flanks, but those around the Captain did.

Claveria was swinging his sabre about in the air and shouting at the fleeing infantry as he tried to rally them, of which he was having some success. Craven stormed towards him. They all remembered the atrocities they had witnessed just weeks before, and they all knew it was Claveria who was responsible. He also had almost been the death of Moxy. Craven ran forward like a man possessed. There were still French infantrymen between him and the Major, and many still fought on as the melee descended into a sprawling brawl.

One French sergeant looked determined to block his path, and he simply raised his pistol and shot the man down. Another levelled a thrust of his bayonet at him, but Craven cut down at the muzzle, knocking it down before slashing him across the face. He continued on without breaking stride. His comrades could see him going after Claveria as he cut a path through the enemy, and with no hesitation they hurried to join him. The Frenchmen had been reinvigorated by Claveria's presence and fought hard for every step.

"Claveria!"

This time he noticed as the redcoat officer stormed towards him. He urged on the two cavalrymen by his side to rush forward to attack him. This only served to infuriate Craven further, that the Major would not face him personally. He raised his pistol and shot one out of the saddle with his second shot. As the other approached, he reversed the pistol in his left hand so that the barrels ran down the length of his forearm. The cavalryman rushed up to him and cut down with a mighty blow, but Craven raised his left arm with the pistol braced against it as a shield. The sabre was stopped dead against the hardened steel barrels, and in doing so Craven's own sword had remained free to do as he pleased. He thrust it up into his chest. He let go of his prized pistol and pulled the dead rider down before climbing onto the animal himself. He pulled the reins around until he faced the French Major.

They both pressed their horses on as they rushed toward one another. Claveria swung for his head, but Craven quickly parried it and returned a cut for his face. The Major parried it and returned a thrust at his chest. Craven brushed it aside and made a quick snapping cut to Claveria's forearm, but the large protective bars of his sabre guard stopped the blow, and Craven's blade glanced off. The Major snapped a quick cut at Craven's face. He took it on a hanging parry and tried to thrust under in riposte, but Claveria set that aside, too, before cutting towards his ribs. Craven parried, but as he did so, Claveria lifted one foot out of his stirrups and kicked his heel into the spot where he had cut Craven on their last encounter, knowing it would still be weak. Yet the Major had no idea how weak, for the collapsing of Craven's horse onto the wound had opened it up since.

Craven cried out in pain as he reeled forward, knowing he must act before Claveria's sabre came down on him once more. Doubled over, he was within reach of the Major and grabbed hold of him. He pulled him in closer, causing them both to be pulled from their saddles, and they crashed down to the dry ground below. It hurt Craven more than it did his opponent, and the Frenchman swung for him even from the ground. He rolled over, and the blade struck the earth where he had lain, though he now found himself without a sword, as he got to his feet and struggled to put weight on his aching leg. Claveria grinned at his pain as he could see just how much he suffered with it.

Craven drew out his dirk to continue the fight and held it out in a guard position, causing the Major to laugh at him, but for more reasons than one, as a passing French infantryman smashed his musket over the back of his head. Craven's legs buckled under the blow, and he momentarily lost consciousness as he crumpled to the ground, regaining it as he landed sitting on his one good leg.

Paget spotted Craven, and his face turned to horror at the danger his Captain was in.

"Charlie!" he yelled out as she struggled with one of the Frenchmen. Yet she followed his gaze as he pointed frantically and could see the cause for his concern. She grabbed the blade of her sword with her left hand, wrapping it tightly so she could get leverage on her own blade, and pushed her opponent's musket down with the sword held between both hands. She drove the point of her sabre into his body.

She and Paget rushed forward to help the Captain, but there was still so many of the enemy between them, as Craven had got well ahead of them all when he ruthlessly pursued Claveria. A French officer with a sabre in hand and two infantrymen came straight for them.

Paget ducked as a bayonet was thrust at him. It pierced his cocked hat right through, taking it from his head as he traversed out from under the weapon and cutting at the man's left hand. He struck the wrist, and it was enough to deaden the arm as he opened a deep cut. The musket fell from the man's hands, yet he was quick to rip the briquet from its sheath and fight on.

Paget was unable to take advantage whilst he was unarmed for the officer swung a cut at him. He parried it aside and returned one of his own, but the Frenchman was quick to parry before backing away to stand with the other two.

"We have to get to the Captain," pressed Paget.

"Easier said than done," warned Charlie.

Craven watched as the musket was dropped down over his head and placed around his throat. The Frenchman put his knee into his back as he began to choke him. He was already weak but fumbled around in the dirt as he felt the energy sap from his body.

"No!" Paget cried out furiously as he saw the life draining from Craven. He rushed on at the enemy blocking their path. He scooped up both bayonets with one big sweep of his sword and crashed into one of the infantrymen, collapsing to the ground on top of one of them. The French officer thrust towards him, but his blade was beaten down by Charlie's sabre. She slashed across his lead arm and caused him to drop his sword. He collapsed to the ground, as he held up his left hand for mercy. She would not give it, but a cry from Paget as he was punched in the face caused her to leave the officer be. She rushed to her friend's side and hacked down at his attacker, hauling him to his feet as the last one came for them both, thrusting towards Paget. He caught the bayonet by locking his sword into the elbow and grasped the barrel with his left, allowing Charlie to cut down against the Frenchman with all her fury. But as he dropped, more came forward to take his place.

Craven's hands scrambled about in the dirt and finally he found his dirk. He took a firm grasp and swung it past his shoulder, plunging it into the body of his attacker. He collapsed down with the blade still embedded in his body. Craven picked up the musket and bayonet the Frenchman had dropped and faced off against Claveria once again. He aimed the bayonet for the Major and thrust home, yet with half the speed he was capable of. For he was weak and slow on his injured leg, and Claveria parried it off before sadistically kicking his wounded leg once more. It was too much to bear, and Craven dropped down to one knee. He barely looked conscious as the Major raised his sabre to finish the job.

Before the blade descended, a clenched fist smashed into Claveria, knocking him back as Birback flashed past. Claveria staggered back and lifted his sword to parry, but Birback redirected his cut and slashed open the Major's thigh, mimicking the wound he had inflicted on Craven. Adrenaline allowed the Major to fight for it, and he swung back at Birback, who took the parry and closed in on the Major. Claveria managed to bring his blade up to Birback's face and draw a quick cut down his cheek to his chin as he pushed him away. He fell back a few paces as he felt for the blood trickling down his face and over his uniform. He looked furious and rushed in again with a powerful downward blow which Claveria was forced to parry, yet it only concealed the big man's real intent as he closed in and took Claveria by the throat. He lifted him off his feet and smashed him down onto his back. The wind was taken from the Frenchman, but from the ground he kicked Birback to the face and sent him reeling.

Claveria rolled over and back onto his feet, but he found himself looking down the blade of Craven's Ferrara blade, and it was in the Captain's hand. Birback stopped as he acknowledged Craven's intent to take over, and Craven nodded appreciatively toward him.

"You can never win this war. You will never beat

Napoleon. You are a nation of shop keepers, drunks, and fools," spouted Claveria angrily.

"Yes we are, and you will have to suffer the humiliation of losing to us," growled Craven.

Claveria cried out as he ran forward and launched a strong thrust. Craven parried and stepped forward beyond the point. His left hand pushed against Claveria's sword arm for control, and his own weapon rotated around behind his lower back. The tip penetrated into the Major's flank. A strike he never saw coming. His body went bolt upright and rigid. Craven drew out the blade as he ripped the Frenchman's sabre from his hands and stepped away from him. Blood poured from the wound at a significant rate, just as Paget and Charlie reached them in time to see the French Major collapse dead to the dirt.

Gunfire still rang out as the French withdrew, but the massed musketry had come to an end, and a welcome breeze carried away the haze, allowing Wellesley and the Worcestershires to see the French columns in retreat. An elated cheer rang out, and it was infectious, for the entire battle line could see what had happened. French forces on both sides of the battle could see their centre collapsing, and it was enough to break the spirit of the whole army as they turned and fled from the field of battle.

Men threw their hats up into the air as the celebrations ignited to an even greater level. Victory had been snatched out from under the enemy at what had seemed the most critical of moments. Many could hardly believe their eyes, for all doubts that they could defeat the most feared of French armies were washed away. It was a new dawn, and they could all feel it. It was the trial they had all feared for so long. Craven turned to Birback and saluted him, for the bloodied man had vindicated himself. He had saved Craven's life, and he would never forget it. Yet no words were spoken, as they understood one another.

"Did we really do it, Sir? Did we do it?" Paget asked, as he could barely believe his eyes when he reached them. Matthys staggered up to join them, using his rifle as a crutch in one hand and resting on Moxy's shoulder.

"You okay?" Craven asked him.

"Better than him," declared Matthys as he looked down at the body of Claveria.

"What does this mean?" Paget asked.

"It means the armies of Napoleon are no longer invincible," replied Craven.

"There is hope for us yet," sighed Ferreira, who clearly had never imagined they could win such a significant battle.

Flames licked the battlefield as the dried grass caught ablaze. Bodies littered the ground for as far as the eye could see, as many British as there were French, and yet it was the redcoats who remained triumphant.

The Spanish cries of excitement at the walls of Talavera could be heard for miles, for they too had shared in the victory after so many bitter losses against the invading armies. Craven could see it meant just as much to Ferreira and his countrymen, as the fate of their country and Spain were intertwined. The only one amongst them who didn't look relieved was Ned Clinton. He looked severely pained but without any sign of significant injury.

"Are you hurt?" Paget asked him.

"No, Sir, but I lost the books," he confessed.

Craven began to laugh, but Paget clearly had no concept

of what was happening.

"You took treasury books into battle?"

"It was the only way to keep them safe."

"Safe, ey? And where are they now?"

Ned looked out towards the fleeing enemy, for he had lost them to the French.

"I suppose I no longer owe a debt," joked Craven.

"I fear many a man will say the same," grumbled Clinton.

Craven slapped him on the back.

"Worry about tomorrow when it comes. The day is ours, and may there be many more like it!"

"Said the man who didn't come to fight," joked Matthys.

Craven smiled as he watched the last of the French soldiers flee from the field of battle. It was a delightful sight after such a hard won victory, and yet he lost himself as he imagined what the future had in store for them all. He ached all over, and he could barely walk. Sweat, blood, and dirt mixed together with the wine he had just consumed. The bitter taste of gunpowder clung to his nostrils, and the unrelenting sun still beat down on them as smoke from grass fires swept over them. And then he smiled, for he was still standing.

"Whatever becomes of us, we shall face it together."

THE END

Printed in Great Britain
by Amazon

78306195R00161